THE FIFTH SUN

Wendy Lozano

Long Beach, California

Wendy Lozano / Citrine Press
3360 East 7th Street, #221
Long Beach, California 90804
www.wendylozano.com

Publisher's Note: This is a work of historical fiction. Apart from
the well-known actual people, events, and locales that figure in
the narrative, all names, characters, and incidents are products
of the author's imagination or are used fictitiously. Any resemblance to current events or living people is entirely coincidental.

Cover illustration and design © 2018 Doug Cox
Book interior template © 2014 BookDesignTemplates.com
The Fifth Sun / Wendy Lozano. -- 1st ed.
ISBN 978-1-7324179-0-8

Acknowledgments

Writing is a lonely occupation at best. Of course there are stimulating and even happy associations with friends and colleagues, but during the actual work of creation the writer cuts himself off from all others and confronts his subject alone.

–Rachel Carson

While the work of writing can be lonely, publishing is not a solitary enterprise. Several people have been tremendously helpful in bringing *The Fifth Sun* to print. First, I want to thank Abby Saul of the Lark Group, who read two early versions of the manuscript. Although the early work was not a good fit for her, she steered me in the right direction, and her patience and encouragement were very helpful.

I am grateful to Monica Stel, whose discussion of the need for safe, non-judgemental spaces where one can be listened to led to "speaking secrets."

My editor Ann Creel was wonderful. Her comments and suggestions helped to make this a much better book than it was before reaching her. In fact, working with her was almost like taking a graduate course in fiction writing. I did not follow all her advice, however, so any failures are mine alone.

Amy Riseborough, my talented niece, created the maps of the Mexica Empire and of the route taken by Cortés from where he landed to the city of Tenochtitlan. She also did the one of the causeways that led over the lakes into the city. The story of the battles would have been hard to follow without her work.

My sister, Gay Riseborough, has always supported my writing. She knows that spelling is not my strongest talent, and so checks everything very carefully. She proofed every draft of this novel, and there were several of them. She also buys my books, which is always appreciated.

Finally, I want to thank my husband Doug Cox. When I vacillated between hybrid self-publishing and the more traditional type that is increasingly more difficult and seems to take forever, he encouraged me to consider publishing it myself. He even attended self-publishing workshops with me. He proofed and formatted the book, designed the cover, built my author's website, researched marketing strategies, and fully supported my every keyboard stroke.

ALSO BY WENDY LOZANO

Sweet Abandon
She Who Was King

Nahuatl Words

Amoxtli (*a MOSH tl*) elder priestess of Xochiquetzal, trainer of young priestesses and temple dancers

Atlatzin (*at la TSIN*) counselor and warlord to Moctezuma, member of the nobility and leader of the Jaguar Warriors

auianime (*ow ia NI meh*) courtesans, skilled prostitutes for young warriors, who were not supposed to marry before the age of 20

Cacamatzin (*ca ca MA tzin*) Prince of the city-state of Texcoco, the second-most important city in the Mexica Empire

calmecac (*cal MEH cac*) school, primarily for noble children; education was basic priestly training, military skills, the arts, etiquette, and leadership

Chamali (*ka MAIL ay*) Atlatzin's older brother, deceased

Cuauhtémoc (*kwau TE moc*) nephew to Moctezuma; elected Great Speaker in 1520 after Cuitlahuac's death. The last Aztec Emperor.

Cuicatl (*QUEE catl*) young priestess of Xochiquetzal

Cuitlahuac (*queet LA wac*) younger brother to Moctezuma; succeeded him as Great Speaker

Hueyi Tlatoani (*huey TLAY toe annie*) Great Speaker (sometimes simply *Tlatoani*)

huipil (*WE pil*) loose-fitting tunic, often heavily embroidered

Huitzilopochtli (*wheat zi lo POACH tli*) Hummingbird, God of War and the Sun, patron god of the Mexica

Iztapalapa (*EES ta pa LA pa*) causeway town

Mexica (*meh SHE ka*) today we use the word Aztec

Mictlan (*MIC lan*) Land of the Dead

Moctezuma (*mock tey TSU ma*) Great Speaker, Emperor of the Mexica

Nahuatl (*NA watl*) language of the Mexica

Papalopil (*pa pa lo PEEL*) slave, temple dancer and young auianime

pipiltin (*pi pil TIN*) Mexica nobility

pulque (*PULL kay*) fermented beverage made from the sap of the maguey cactus

Quetzalcoatl (*KETS a qua tl*) Feathered Serpent, God of Creation, the wind, and the eastern star

Quetzali (*ket ZAL lee*) Atlatzin's sister

telpochcalli (*tel poch CAL li*) school for sons of commoners, education in military and economic matters appropriate to their station

Tenochtitlan (*ten och TEET lan*) capital city of the Mexica

Tepin (*TAY peen*) young warrior-in-training in service to Atlatzin

Texcoco (*tesh CO co*) a causeway town, member of the Triple Alliance

tlachtli (*ta LACH tle*) a popular ball game where a hard rubber ball is thrown through a metal ring without the use of hands

Tlacopan (*tla co PAN*) member of the Triple Alliance

Tlaloc (*tla LOCK*) God of Rain

Tlaxcala (*tlash CA la*) tribe never conquered by the Mexica; Enemies of the House

Xipil (*SHE peel*) priest of Quetzalcoatl; Atlatzin's teacher as a child

Xochiquetzal (*sho chi KET sal*) Goddess of Flowers, Love, Pleasure, Beauty and the Arts

zócalo (*ZO ca lo*) main ceremonial center in Tenochtitlan, in front of the Great Temple.

Author's note: As Nahuatl was not a written language, names were originally written in Spanish after the Conquest, and thus had Spanish pronunciation. Today, online "experts" pronounce the same word in different ways. I have tried to provide the most common pronunciations.

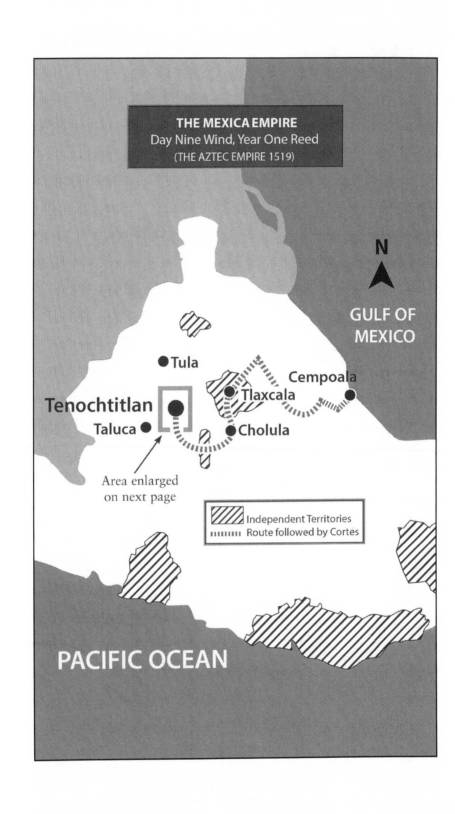

THE MEXICA EMPIRE
Day Nine Wind, Year One Reed
(THE AZTEC EMPIRE 1519)

N

GULF OF MEXICO

Tula

Tenochtitlan
Taluca

Tlaxcala

Cempoala

Cholula

Area enlarged
on next page

Independent Territories
Route followed by Cortés

PACIFIC OCEAN

THE FIVE LAKES REGION

Tenayuca

Tepeyacao

Texcoco

Tlacopan

Tenochtitlan

Coyoacann

Iztapalaca

Chalco

The Earth was a naked body of rock, without water, without air. Within its iron core were buried atoms of radioactive elements, debris of stellar explosions that had occurred when the universe was young. Over the eons, some of the atoms disintegrated and, in the process, produced small nuclear explosions that heated the stones in the planet's interior. The temperature climbed until, after 700 million years, its stone core began to melt.

Fiery magma welled up from the depths and broke through weak spots in the Earth's crust. The lava that spewed out carried with it gasses trapped within the planet when it was formed. Clouds of steam condensed over the mouths of the growing volcanoes, warm rains fell, moisture collected, and the oceans were formed. Storms tore across the planet. Lightning ripped open the sky. The lava cooled and, as it cooled, it shrank and cracked, leaving fissures that were quickly filled with the still fluid magma.

In a spot rich with silica and potash, a rift opened inside the rock. Lava poured in from the Earth's fiery heart and turned the rift into a dike. Hot gasses formed pockets as the slow cooling process began, and small quantities of water developed which coated the walls with mineral deposits before seeping back and becoming one with the magma again. The dike bent and swelled along its length, reaching red fingers upward toward the surface of the young planet. The boiling waters worked outward into crevices, creating mineral-lined cavities. At a particular place in the planet's western hemisphere, in a dark hollow in the rock, a huge quartz crystal began to form.

Although without life, the crystal grew. Its creation was a dynamic union of fire and water and stone. At some point, for some unfathomable reason, the crystal twinned and grew to twin again. Its planes converged about a common line, producing a circular grouping of identical parts. It grew as the magma around it hardened, until it reached the limits set for it by stone.

Far above on the planet's surface, the forces of destruction tore away at the exposed rock. Erosion ate away at the crust. Caves formed. The Earth slowly shifted and the jewel was brought closer to the surface. Vegetation crept across the land. Small living things fed and sought shelter there when it trembled from the footfall of giant reptiles. The crystal lay in darkness while above it the ice came and went again and again, and mammals entered the realms of forest, ocean, and air. Time was still fluid when, on a far distant savannah, an ape first stood erect.

It would not be long now. The crystal waited to be born.

CHAPTER ONE

"There has been a new omen," the rootseller said in a low voice to the old woman examining the dried herbs spread out on his reed mat.

She did not look up, but the young woman with her heard a note of surprise in her voice as she asked, "What is it this time?"

"No one knows for sure, but everyone in the market is talking about it," the rootseller told them. "A runner came racing across the causeway from Iztapalaca straight to the Palace."

"And how do you know he brought news of an omen?" the old woman demanded, finally looking directly at him.

"Because everyone is saying so. Something about a bird. The runner was carrying a cage tied on his back and people heard squawking. That is all anyone knows so far, but we will find out the details soon enough. Here in the market, we always do." The man saw that the old woman had been fingering the soaproot he had on display. "Until we know, all we can do is be obedient to the gods and keep ourselves and their temples clean. I see by your dress that you are a priestess, so

I will reduce my prices some. As a small offering to the gods, of course."

"I may be old," the priestess scolded the merchant as she poked her walking stick at the mat where his wares were laid out on display, "but my eyes can still see that plant is older than I am, and I am three times your age! Your soaproot will crumble to dust before it makes decent soap!" She straightened up to her full height, although she only reached the shoulder of the young woman with her. "Come, Papalopil," she said addressing her, "we will look elsewhere."

"They are fresh enough to make soap suds to clean the temple floor," the vendor rushed to assure the priestess. "And, since there has been a new omen, I will charge you only half of what I usually charge. Perhaps that will bring favor from the gods."

The old priestess feigned reluctance, but turned back to the mat. Papalopil smiled. The walking stick fooled people, who always assumed the priestess was so old she could be taken advantage of easily. Old as she was, Mama Amoxtli always managed to get a good price for temple supplies. Papalopil assumed it was one of the reasons that she was the elder priestess at the temple of Xochiquetzal. Tucked next to the main temple of the war god, Huitzilopochtli, the small temple of the goddess of flowers, pleasure and beauty was the official home for both women. They spent their days there doing temple work, although they slept in a building on the Street of Perfumed Nights.

The large basket on her arm now full of dried roots, Papalopil started to ask Mama Amoxtli about the omen, but the priestess quickly wove her way in and out of the mass of people filling the huge market of Tenochtitlan. The young woman had no choice but to follow. The place was crowded today. Vendors from every corner of the Mexica Empire were there, hawking shell necklaces from the south, blue and green turquoise from the far north, bright feathers from birds Papalopil had never seen, and everywhere she looked there were flowers. The women passed by the vendors who sold meat, the turkeys, geese, rabbits and venison laid out on mats alongside the bodies of the small hairless dogs that were such a delicacy. There would be a feast today and the vendors were kept busy. The display of jaguar and fox skins caught Papalopil's eye. Next to them lay small cakes of dried powder that was used to dye the clothing of the nobility a blood red. She absently smoothed the skirt of the woven maguey fiber dress the temple dancers wore. Although she tried to keep it clean, it was no longer new. The painted design around the bottom of the skirt had faded and the fabric itself was beginning to fray. The dress would have to last, for the temple was unlikely to supply her with a new one this season.

It was surprising how quickly Mama Amoxtli could move through the crowd, thought Papalopil, as she hurried after the elder priestess. Of course, she did wave her cane about a bit. Papalopil had to smile at the sight of people moving out of the way of the tiny woman.

"Hurry, Child," the old woman called over her shoulder. "We cannot waste all day here."

Papalopil rushed to catch up. Although called a courtesan, an *auianime*, and wearing the dab of yellow paint on her cheeks signifying her availability, she was still young and little more than a Temple Girl. She had been raised to dance before Tlaloc, God of Fertile Rain, to clean the temple of Xochiquetzal, to cook, weave cloth, and serve the young warriors before and after battle. Like the young priestesses-in-training, she spent most of her time doing whatever needed to be done on the temple grounds. Unlike them, she was a slave, and so this morning in the open market helping Mama Amoxtli was precious. There was so much to look at! And rumors of an omen as well. What was it all about?

The women walked quickly past the section in the market where desperate people sold themselves as servants. Papalopil tried not to hear the cries of the children being sold as slaves. She herself had been sold there when she was very young and was bought by a priest from the Great Temple. The gods had smiled on her, though. Mama Amoxtli had spotted the small scar on her side that showed she had been dedicated to the life of a priestess at the age of three. Her parents must have fallen on hard times, as they sold her before she reached five years when she would have entered religious life. Even though she had been sold as a slave, the life she ended up with was not a bad one, and she could not resent her parents. It was just the way things were. She had enough to eat, shelter, and, although the girls in training to be priestesses kept their distance from the slaves, the other temple dancers were friendly enough. Mama Amoxtli, who looked after all the temple's young priestesses and *auianime*-in-training, had taken the child under her wing and seemed to be fond of her. But Papalopil was still a slave and seeing the sobbing children reminded her of what she preferred to forget.

They paused by the long stairway to the Great Temple, where the huge disk of the dismembered goddess lay. Mama Amoxtli stopped to catch her breath and sat on the lowest step in the shadow of the large carved stone serpent that crept down the temple steps. Her bald head, the mark of an elder priestess, glistened with sweat and Papalopil watched as drips ran down the side of her neck and wet the front of her cotton tunic. She offered to run to the public aqueduct and fetch water, but the woman refused. Concerned, the young *auianime* tried to cool her off with a fan of woven reeds she carried in her skirt for that purpose.

"What do you think the omen means?" she took the opportunity to ask. "The way the rootseller said it made it sound like there have been other omens. How many? Why don't we learn about these things at the temple?"

"There have always been omens, especially the last ten turns of the wheel. The priests decide what they mean; sometimes they tell us. Usually they tell the Emperor and then keep it to themselves. The marketplace may learn what they were, but not what they mean. It matters little, Papalopil. The omens have never affected your life so you do not need to learn about them." It was clear Mama Amoxtli would say nothing more about omens. As a slave, even a much-favored one, Papalopil knew better than to press with questions.

As they rested on the steps of the Great Temple, a commoner and her two children drew near. The mother pointed to the enormous disk that lay in the dirt and told the story of the goddess who plotted war against her mother and was killed by her brother for her treason. It was a story every mother told her children, a story about duty and family and honoring the gods. Papalopil had heard it many times, although she had no memory of her own mother telling it.

"Was the brother never sorry he killed his sister?" asked one of the children.

"He was sorry she had plotted against their own mother," the child's mother replied. "It is one thing for the gods to have an argument. That happens in families. It is quite another for the gods to wage war against one another. That caused the forth sun to die and every living thing to perish. Before that could happen to our sun, the brother-god cut his sister into pieces and threw them down these steps of his Great Temple." She gestured up the large stairway where Mama Amoxtli sat. "Afterwards, he was sorry she was dead and threw her head into the sky where it became the moon," she continued. "But it was his duty to protect his mother, the Lady of the Serpent Skirt, and to prevent a war between gods. And it is our duty to honor him, for he is our protector and the warrior god of the Mexica."

"It was Huitzilopochtli, Lord Hummingbird!" cried the children in unison. Their mother nodded in approval, and Mama Amoxtli smiled at Papalopil.

"And so another generation learns to honor their mothers and protect the family. Come," she said. "We need a few new spindle whorls. One of the younger girls broke the last spare one."

Papalopil had broken one of the clay whorls herself when she was learning to spin and knew how important they were. Every city, temple, business, and family paid taxes to the Great Speaker Moctezuma, who ruled over the Mexica Empire. The most common form of payment was in woven cloth, and the most valuable cloth was cotton. Every female in the Empire was expected to spin and weave, even Mama Amoxtli. But, unlike the young priestesses-in-training under her care who were from noble families, Papalopil was only given maguey fiber to spin, not cotton. As they moved through the market looking for the potters where spindle whorls could be found, Papalopil decided to ask for something she had been thinking about for some time.

"Mama Amoxtli, you know I am one of the best spinners in the temple. My thread is smooth and even you, yourself, have praised my speed. I spin the longest thread without breakage."

The old woman stopped and looked appraisingly at Papalopil. "And?" she asked.

"I know it is forbidden for commoners to wear cotton. I would not suggest anything specifically forbidden. Most commoners make no cotton cloth because they cannot afford the raw fiber. But the temple has baskets of cotton bolls waiting to be cleaned and spun. If you would give me cotton to spin and weave, the temple would be ahead in the taxes it has to pay."

"And you would want a very small token for each bolt of cloth you weave," the old woman said, knowing the answer.

"You already do this when I weave more than my quota of maguey cloth. Since cotton is so much more valuable, the small token could be a little more as well," she suggested. "That way, everyone would be happy."

"Is this about you wanting to buy your freedom, Papalopil?"

she asked, searching the temple dancer's face. "Remember that, since you are a slave, I should not be giving you anything at all. I only do it because your weave is so fine and my heart is soft with age. You have yet to become comfortable with being an *auianime* and serving the warriors. I know. But it has only been a year, and you will become accustomed to it soon, I promise. It was make you into a courtesan or send you to the priests at the Great Temple to be their slave. At least this way your life is a little easier."

"I am grateful that you chose this for me instead."

"You mentioned buying your freedom a year ago. But you have seen the temple's record books. It will take years to pay your debt. You are worth more now than you were as a child. I suspect your price would be almost twenty cotton blankets now."

Papalopil swallowed. "I knew my debt was high, I did not think it was that high. Still, I must think about my future. You have been very good to me. But, much as we might wish, you will not be here forever. What will happen to me when you are gone? I need to start earning my freedom now."

"And just what would you do with it? You will never marry, you know. You have no trade except as an *auianime*, and not a great deal of experience as that. How will you live?"

"I do not expect to marry. I know priestesses serve in the temple for a year or two and then leave and marry, but not an *auianime*. No man would ever consider me for marriage." Papalopil also knew that, although Mama Amoxtli's spirit might be young, her body was old. The elder priestess had joked about her age, but she and Papalopil both knew that she could no longer make out the smaller details in the Temple's ledgers. Fortunately, Papalopil, like every child in the Mexica Empire, had been sent to school. Unlike many girls, she could read the picture-writing, for Mama Amoxtli had taught her. It was a secret they kept between them and made their relationship even more unique. It also meant that Papalopil knew exactly what the temple paid for cotton fiber and how much it was worth once spun and woven into cloth.

"I have not really thought about it much, Mama Amoxtli. But perhaps I should be some kind of healer. You have already taught me which herbs to use to bring on a woman's monthly flow and how to prevent illnesses common to *auianimes*. Of course, an apprenticeship would take many years, even if I could find a healer who would accept me." The elder priestess nodded in agreement and Papalopil continued thinking out loud. "I think I would like a job like yours, helping to take care of the children who are brought to the Temple to be trained. I am good with children and they seem to like me."

Mama Amoxtli frowned. "The priests would never permit that. They would point out you were never really a priestess, just a temple dancer and courtesan."

"Maybe I could be a teacher of girls at the school for commoners. They might not care that I had been an *auianime*. I know they would not care that I had been a slave. At any rate, what is important is my freedom. Once I have that, I will figure out what to do."

"You best start thinking about it now, no matter how improbable paying off your debt may be. I fear you will find that freedom is not enough. I was born free, but being a priestess gave meaning to my life. Now you are a slave and you do a slave's work. What you do shapes who you will become. You should be thinking about who you want to be."

"Of course, Mama Amoxtli," the girl responded automatically. "But first I must earn my freedom. That is the most important thing to think about now."

"The impatience of youth." The elder priestess smiled fondly. "You are practical by nature, my child. But if freedom is what you want, you will have to be even more practical. Even if I were to give you cotton to spin, you will be an old woman before you finish paying your debt." Papalopil could see the pity in Mama Amoxtli's eyes, but the young Mexica was determined.

"I will do whatever needs to be done."

The priestess studied her face briefly and then nodded. "Do you remember what I told you about beauty when you first became an *auianime*?"

"You said that the key to beauty was to be clean. That I was to wash every single part of me at least once a day, make sure my flesh and breath always smelled sweet and my hair shone in the sun."

"True. I also told you that you were pretty, but you were not beautiful, Papalopil. That has not changed. That means, as an *auianime* and a slave, you need to be very smart. You are naturally intelligent enough, but you need to be smarter. It is a harsh world, and you need to be able to learn how to best survive it. You need to study the warriors you serve so that you know them better than they know themselves, so you know their weaknesses as well as their strengths. You need to watch and listen, so you know what they want and need before they know it themselves. If you please them enough, they will give you small gifts. These you must use to make them believe you are beautiful."

"But you said I am not."

"Beauty is a fantasy, Papalopil, a dream of flowers and feathers, butterflies dancing on the breeze like your name, a dance of joy and grace done by our goddess Xochiquetzal. Use the gifts the young warriors give you to buy yellow pollen to illuminate the clearness of your skin, not the cheap yellow paint the temple gives you. Buy the heavy, dark cream that gives hair a purple sheen in the sun and the bright red to stain your lips. Your eyes are a bit large for your face, but some men like that. Since you cannot make them smaller, line them with black so they seem even bigger. Wearing cotton is forbidden to you, so wear good, clean maguey skirts and tunics with brightly colored designs. Make sure your tunic is folded so that it always covers your breasts in public, unlike the commoners. Let the warriors wonder what they look like. Let them dream of you."

Papalopil almost snorted. "I would have to spin a lot of cotton to afford any of those things. How could I ever buy my freedom then?" she asked plaintively.

"You start small and invest your resources in yourself. When you start getting more gifts, you split your resources between yourself and paying for your freedom. Eventually, you might catch the eye of a nobleman. You have to look as if you have been given many gifts, as though you are accustomed to wealthy men in order to attract one in the first place. Once you do, your freedom will be closer.

"Or you might decide instead to be a wealthy man's concubine," Mama Amoxtli added with a wink. "It would be easier on you than becoming a teacher of young girls." Papalopil had to laugh. The elder priestess frequently pointed out to her charges how hard it was to teach the young priestesses and the *auianimes*. But, in spite of the fact that she was demanding, the girls she supervised knew she was fond of them. There was a reason they added the affectionate word "Mama" to her name.

"I am getting tired. I should return to Xochiquetzal's temple. Go and buy the spindle whorls and meet me back there. If you bargain well enough so there is a small bit of change, use it to buy yourself something," she said, handing Papalopil a small pouch. "I will think about your request for cotton."

The young *auianime* smiled happily as Mama Amoxtli headed off. Spotting the place where the potters displayed their wares, she saw a mat full of clay whorls and small bowls. She was not as skilled as Mama Amoxtli at bargaining, but had learned a few techniques by watching the priestess. Soon two whorls lay in the basket tucked in safely against the dried herbs. They were pretty, with flowers carved into the clay, but not expensive, so Papalopil moved to the market street where the *auianime* bought their goods. Soon a small packet of yellow powder was nestled in the basket between the whorls.

On her way back to the temple, she cut past the reed mats filled with dyes for making writing ink and the decorations on cloth, when the crowd swept her to the corner of the market where the Emperor's appointed judges sat. This was no normal dispute between merchants. A counterfeiter had been caught with hollowed out *cacao* beans filled with worthless clay. Papalopil managed to wiggle her way out of the crowd, knowing that the judgment would be swift and unforgiving.

Fool, she thought, did he honestly think no one would notice? Cocoa beans were the standard medium of trade in Tenochtitlan. And Tenochtitlan was no backwards town. It was the capital of the Mexica Empire, a city built on five adjoining salt lakes, chosen by the god Huitzilopochtli to be the very center of the world. The counterfeiter must be from one of the conquered tribes along the coast, she decided. No one local would be that foolish. She paused by the section where the merchants sold jewels. Rows of jade bracelets and amber earplugs lay on the reed mats next to silver earrings shaped like two-headed snakes and goose quills filled with gold dust.

"Not for you, *auianime*," laughed the vendor. "Find yourself a rich nobleman and come back with him."

She smiled as though in agreement and moved away. If only things were that simple, but the life of a temple dancer was far more complicated than most people knew. Papalopil had always known that the time came in some dancers lives when the god Tlaloc would claim his sacrifice. A priest would move silently behind the woman as she danced and, with one blow of an obsidian club, her life would be ended. The dancers called it the god's kiss when the priests were not there to hear them talk. They even joked about it and made flippant comments. What else could they do? They knew the god's kiss did not end of the life of every dancer. Some died of disease; some even died of old age. Exactly to whom and when the kiss would come was a mystery. That it would come during the dance for those chosen was not. It was considered a great honor to be selected and sacrificed that way, as it was to be chosen to be a temple dancer as a child.

But Papalopil saw more than the priests suspected and had noticed that only children from poor families were chosen to be dancers. Girls from the nobility were never given that "honor." And the god tended not to be in a hurry to kiss the dancers who had wealthy sponsors. The third thing that Papalopil had observed was that the very best dancers and the very worst tended to be those sacrificed. So her challenge was to dance well enough but not too well. It wasn't that she was defying her fate, if that was to be her fate, but she was in no hurry to be given that particular honor. She once hinted at this to Mama Amoxtli, who had hushed her quickly, telling her never to speak of such things.

The vendor's laughing comment combined with Mama Amoxtli's advice set her thinking. Since she had no choice but had been made an *auianime*, she decided she needed to embrace the role. It offered the possibility of both protection by a wealthy patron and a way to earn her freedom. She would listen and learn everything she could and be a very good *auianime* indeed. Hopefully, she would have time to do so before Mama Amoxtli passed on. Papalopil had reached the age when many young Mexica women married, and one of Tlaloc's priests had been eyeing her recently. She had to be careful. All but the high priests were chaste, so she suspected he was not looking at her with desire on his mind.

So lost in her thoughts was she that she almost bumped into a tall man in a green cloak as he swept past. She murmured an apology, but the man hadn't even noticed her. Papalopil shook out her should-length hair and bit her lips to make them red. There was to be a ball game tomorrow. Perhaps it would be lucky for her. She set cheerfully off for the Temple with her purchases. Any thoughts of omens were forgotten.

CHAPTER TWO

As the sun reached its height, the black-clad priests in the temple of the god of war announced with drum and conch shell the arrival of Huitzilopochtli, Lord Hummingbird, on his high throne in the sky. The plaintive sound drifted down into the great square, carrying the message that the god was pleased with the daily sacrifice. Among the thousands of people who crowded the *zócalo*, few paused to think about the scene they knew had just been enacted on Huitzilopochtli's behalf. One man did slow his stride as he looked up past the lime-washed walls toward the two wooden temples, one red, one blue, atop the great step pyramid. Although the structure was designed so that the details at the top could not be seen from its base, the man knew that at this moment the high priest held in his outstretched hands the symbol of life and power. He offered to the sun a black obsidian knife and a bleeding human heart that had not yet ceased to beat. It was the daily sacrifice of this sacred fruit that gave the sun the strength to move in the heavens and the Mexica to rule under them.

The man, Lord Atlatzin, head of the Jaguar Warriors and

advisor to *Hueyi Tlatoani* Moctezuma II, quickly smoothed the frown from his proud face. This was not the time to ponder the ways of the gods. Moctezuma had sent for him and, from the fear on the messenger's face, Atlatzin knew it was something serious. As the crowd respectfully parted at the sight of the dazzling fan of feather and reeds in the headdress and long green cloak that marked his rank, the young nobleman wondered at the urgency of the summons.

Atlatzin could remember when the Emperor was elected, back when his own father was still alive and was the new Emperor's shield carrier. Even though the nobleman was still a child then, he remembered that Moctezuma surrounded himself with strong warriors and beautiful women from the *pipiltin*, and still found moments free to speak with the common people in the *zócalo*. Time had changed that.

Little by little during the seventeen years of his reign, the Emperor had surrounded himself with the trappings of divinity and become a living god.

Atlatzin passed by the giant stone snakes that guarded the steps to Huitzilopochtli's temple. Moctezuma's withdrawal into sacred isolation had made the Emperor vulnerable to this god and his blood-thirsty priests. Having been raised to be the high priest until his brother who held the throne died, Moctezuma had a tendency to look first to the gods for answers. It did not make things easy for those men who were his advisors.

Atlatzin shook his head to clear his thoughts. Whatever had upset the Emperor, he was willing to bet it had to do with the gods.

The sun beat down on the palace as the young nobleman arrived. He entered one of the many gateways that spanned both footpath and canal and passed quickly by the public treasuries holding food and clothing and the cotton blankets paid as taxes. A craftsman looked up from his bench where he sat carving precious stones into birds and flowers, but Lord Atlatzin was a common sight, and he went back to his work. Musicians practicing for the evening's entertainment fell silent upon seeing the tall aristocrat. Servants darted out of his path as he swept through gardens that held every herb and flower in the Empire and past the gleaming pools. Winged jewels in the wicker-domed House of Birds sang out to him, jaguars roared from their wooden cages, and deadly snakes hissed as he passed their feather-lined jars. He reached the stairway leading to the upper floors and ascended to the Emperor's private apartments. Groups of judicial officers and military commanders waiting for an audience with Moctezuma bowed respectfully and servants leapt to pull back the hangings covering the entrance to the throne room.

Silence greeted Atlatzin. Tapestries depicting the life of the feathered serpent god Quetzalcoatl surrounded an empty turquoise throne. At the far end of the room, behind a jade and obsidian screen, he heard a soft murmuring. He slipped off his sandals as custom required and approached. Before he could give the gentle cough that would announce his presence, his sister Quetzali appeared from behind the screen. The concern in her dark eyes was touched with relief when she saw him and she crossed quickly to his side.

"There has been another omen," she said so softly that Atlatzin had to bend close to hear. "Take care what you say to him, Brother. He has spoken with the gods and his mind is not yet free of the sacred mushrooms."

Atlatzin nodded. It was always important to weigh one's words when speaking with the Emperor, but the strangeness that held him as he recovered from the holy drug made such caution doubly necessary. Atlatzin touched his sister's arm in gratitude for her warning before following her beyond the screen.

"My Lord Moctezuma," he said, quickly dropping to a crouch and touching his fingers first to the floor and then to his mouth in obeisance. Even though he was a member of the *pipiltin* nobility and a distant blood relative of the Emperor, Atlatzin was forbidden to look directly at Moctezuma. Instead, he allowed his eyes to sweep past the Emperor in a practiced glance that missed very little, and what he saw was like a cold breath on the back of his neck.

The monarch's short black hair was plastered against his head with sweat from trance, and the bronze feathers in his hair were crushed and broken. The great crystal that hung from his nose and proclaimed him Great Speaker shone dully as Moctezuma turned his head and caught sight of his advisor. For a moment, Atlatzin almost forgot himself when he glimpsed the tightness around his lord's eyes. This was not how he usually appeared after the sacred mushrooms. He almost looked afraid. Was that possible? Was the Emperor afraid of an omen?

"A runner brought the news first. He was followed by a fisherman who found and brought the bird to me," began Moctezuma without preamble. "In my royal aviaries there is none like it, and I have two of every bird in my Empire. Its color was that of pale ashes when the fire is dead, but its crest was black and speckled like the deadly nighttime sky. I looked at it in curiosity, Atlatzin, simple curiosity, nothing more. And as I looked, the black feathers became the heavens and the speckles angry stars. Suddenly the heavens parted and became the eastern sea. I could tell it was the East for the sun rose there and burned my eyes."

Moctezuma's long delicate fingers toyed absently with the blue fish and shells embroidered on his cloak. His voice came out in a harsh whisper as he continued. "From the sea came monstrous creatures, grotesquely shaped, and yet strangely beautiful in their own way. From the waist up they appeared to be men. But their hair was thick and curled like an animal's." He reached up and touched his own thin beard in horrified wonder. "They wore strange clothing that shone like the sun, and they seemed to laugh and converse with one another in some ugly, barbaric tongue.

"And from the waist down they were not men at all! Where there should have been two legs, these creatures possessed four! Huge, muscled things they were, like the haunches of great deer. The sight so unnerved me that I found myself wrenched out of my trance and back here in Tenochtitlan. I ordered the bird sacrificed and consulted with Hummingbird's priests. I sent for you and my other advisors, but I fear I understand the meaning of my vision." Moctezuma peered around nervously before leaning back on his jaguar skins and sighing heavily. When he spoke again, the fear in his voice was hidden. Had Atlatzin not known better, he would have doubted it had ever existed.

"I suspect the god Quetzalcoatl has decided the time is right to return and claim his kingdom from the Mexica," said Moctezuma.

Atlatzin fixed his stare on the intricately carved cedar beam above his head in order to hide his surprise. The prophecies foretelling the rise of the Mexica Empire had also predicted its fall. Every Mexica child knew that. The end was supposed to coincide with the return of Quetzalcoatl, god and king of the ancient Toltecs, founder of the *pipiltin*. Atlatzin also knew this was due to occur when the great calendar wheel within the wheel turned to bring together a Nine Wind day in a One Reed year. That only happened every fifty-two years.

With a start, Atlatzin realized that this was a One Reed year and Nine Wind would come this year. Of course Moctezuma's thoughts would turn in this direction. But the wheel had turned before, and the fated day had come and gone several times in the centuries since Quetzalcoatl was forced into exile, he thought quickly. There was no reason to think that the coming Nine Wind day would be *the* day. The wheel would turn and the day named would come and go again.

"You pause long before addressing me, Counselor," said the Emperor sharply. "What are your thoughts?"

"My Lord, I confess I find your vision confusing. Such strange creatures are indeed a puzzlement, but I fail to understand their bearing on Quetzalcoatl," Atlatzin said slowly. "Perhaps some strange things, like your creatures, will come to pass, but they need not mean the god's return."

"What about the other omens then?" demanded Moctezuma. "Can you explain the strange light that blazed in the eastern sky for forty nights or the fact that one of Huitzilopochtli's temples mysteriously caught fire and burned to the ground? Can you tell me why the lake suddenly began to boil though the earth did not tremble and the wind did not blow, or who sent the fiery comet to circle above Tenochtitlan? Explain away the ghost woman if you can, the invisible one who cries out in the night. And when you have finished, Counselor, talk to me of the two-headed child. I myself took it to Huitzilopochtli's main temple, but even his high priest could not give me answers.

"Atlatzin, come closer," Moctezuma beckoned and leaned forward. "You are one of the few men alive privy to the fact that the history of the Mexica was rewritten by one of the ancestors you and I have in common," he whispered. "Our ancestor was so powerful he refused the throne of Great Speaker three times! You know that he created a glorious past for us and laid the structure for our future by rewriting the sacred scrolls. I understand his tampering with history. The Mexica needed a sense of pride and purpose then, and he gave them to us." Moctezuma shook his head slowly and leaned back. "But what our ancestor did resulted in no little confusion in interpreting the omens. We struggle today to know what is true and what is not. The only men alive who are skilled in that art are a few of the magicians and high priests. And now, even they fail me."

"My Lord, I am no magician," said Atlatzin. "I am a warrior

and a teacher of warriors. But it would appear to me that the signs of which you speak have been scattered over the past ten-year cycle. They have not all happened recently. Of course, it has not been given to me to understand such things. My skills lie in fighting the wars and taking prisoners for Huitzilopochtli. Ask me about political alliances and matters of diplomacy. That is why you have named me one of your counselors. Ask me where your enemies will strike next; my spies will even tell you what they had for dinner. But do not ask me to interpret sacred visions or prophecies. My value to you lies elsewhere."

"And you prefer that it remain so." Moctezuma allowed himself a smile that was as brief as it was unexpected. "No doubt you heard that I ordered the execution of a few magicians. The gods may force prophecies of doom upon me, but it is not easy to accept some of the prophets who voice them. Besides, they were fools and annoyed me. But you, Atlatzin, have my word. No harm will greet your answer today. Tell me the truth. Do you believe Quetzalcoatl will return?"

"Some day, my Lord," Atlatzin replied slowly. "I see no reason to believe it will happen during your reign."

"Then why do I hear the hissing of the Feathered Serpent in my dreams?" Atlatzin stole a careful glance and saw the tortured expression on the Emperor's face. It pained him to see it there and he struggled for the words that might help.

"Perhaps it is because your family sprang from his loins and his sacred day is in your blood," he suggested gently.

Moctezuma seized on this. "But your grandmother was one of my father's sisters. Although diluted, you carry the god's blood as well. You do not hear the hissing or feel his presence drawing near?"

"No, my Lord."

"I remember that you were pledged to him as a child. Like me, you were expected to enter the priesthood."

"True, my Lord. As a younger son, I was intended for the

temple and dedicated to Quetzalcoatl. My brother was to be the warrior who would bring our family honor. But when he died, my father had me rededicated to Huitzilopochtli. As you know, he wanted me to be a warrior, and that seemed to suit my temperament better," Atlatzin confessed.

"But you do not feel the god coming closer? You feel no threat? You have no lingering doubts?"

"None, Lord Moctezuma," was the firm reply.

"Perhaps you are right then. Perhaps I simply grow obsessed with Quetzalcoatl as his day nears. There is no real reason to suspect the end of my Empire. Perhaps they were my own concerns I saw in the strange bird's crest. Nothing more." The monarch clapped his hands and a servant appeared bearing a cup of foaming chocolate. Atlatzin could smell the chilies Moctezuma used to season it as the Emperor studied him thoughtfully.

"You are young to be my counselor, Atlatzin. I will admit your counsel has always been valuable. I hear the men you lead into battle call you the Jaguar for your fighting skills. Your father would be proud."

Atlatzin knelt in surprise. The Emperor was not free with his compliments, so this was indeed an honor. "Thank you," he mumbled with a touch of embarrassment. "I try to be a model warrior for my men."

"That does not mean you are right about the omens not signaling the god's return this cycle, however. Feathered Serpent's return is foretold and he will come. And when he does, he will not be happy with the Mexica. If there is a chance he might return during this cycle of the wheel and the Empire might fall, I need to be prepared.

"Pick out one of your very best warriors and send him to the sun," the Emperor ordered abruptly.

Taken by surprise, Atlatzin started to voice a protest but Moctezuma cut him off.

"Send him to the sun, Counselor. Tomorrow is a ball game. Let it be then. Remember, it is the sacrifice, the sacred fruit that keeps Huitzilopochtli strong. And it is the god who keeps the Mexica strong. One of your finest, Atlatzin. After tomorrow's game."

Knowing it was useless to object further, Atlatzin bowed and was dismissed.

As he went to retrieve his sandals, his sight fell upon the tapestry of Quetzalcoatl. Thousands of tiny feathers were woven into a large wall hanging depicting the god's life. At the far end of the weaving, Quetzalcoatl's mother was shown conceiving him by swallowing a piece of precious jade. At the other end, the god was forced into exile on a raft made of the intertwined bodies of living rattlesnakes. Atlatzin frowned and slowly shook his head. He silently resolved to increase the network of spies and runners he had posted along the eastern coast. Although he had been quick to try to dispel Moctezuma's fears and honest in denying his own, he hated to see Moctezuma so upset. Besides, there was something about the Emperor's vision that disturbed him more than he cared to admit.

CHAPTER THREE

Atlatzin deftly popped a crayfish out of its shell and scooped it into the warm tortilla, along with the beans in roasted chili sauce. It wasn't often that he and his mother and sister Quetzali were together at the dawn meal. Usually, he would already be at the palace or the university, but the previous night had been a late one, and both he and Quetzali had slept in.

He watched as his mother poured honey into her cup of *atole* and toyed with a cake of amaranth seeds. She loved the syrupy corn drink and he suspected she was trying to figure out how to broach something with him. Otherwise her cup would be half empty by now. He knew he was correct when she loudly cleared her throat and gave him a stern look.

"I am getting older," she announced, and Atlatzin smiled. Quetzali looked up at the announcement.

"Yes, Mother." He took care to say it agreeably.

"I am getting older and I have no grandchildren."

There it was. Was she reproaching his celibacy again? he wondered. But, no. Her next sentence clarified the direction of her thoughts.

"When I was Quetzali's age, I was married to your father."

"Mother!" protested the girl.

"You may have only seen 15 turns of the wheel, but you are old enough for a husband, a home of your own, and a belly swollen with child!" her mother proclaimed. "Your brother will not give me grandsons and I refuse to take my journey to Mictlan where the dead dwell without seeing the faces of my children's children."

"Then I should never take a husband and you will live forever," said Quetzali teasingly, making Atlatzin smile again.

"Do not smile at her foolishness, Atlatzin!" His mother admonished him. "If you will not marry, she must. I fail to understand why you took that stupid oath of chastity anyway. You were far too young to understand what you were doing."

"He is the perfect warrior!" announced Quetzali, and Atlatzin looked at her quickly to see if she were now teasing him and decided she was not.

"If he were truly perfect, he would be finding you a husband. If your father were still alive, he would have found you a prince by now. A prince!"

"Because we have royal blood," said Quetzali with a wink at her brother. "We are descended from the ancient Toltecs, you know, back to the fourth sun. The blood of the gods runs in our veins."

"Laugh if you must, Quetzali, but everything I am saying is the truth. Our family is among the best, the most noble in the Empire. You deserve a prince and I deserve grandchildren! Have I not raised you both to honor the gods and serve the Emperor? Have I not kept a good home for you, even after losing my husband and first-born son? Is our line to end now because you choose for some ridiculous reason to be celibate, Atlatzin, and you to be unwed, Daughter? Is this to be my fate? My shame?"

Atlatzin and his sister exchanged warning looks. When their

mother worked herself up like this, it could last for quite a while. It did not happen often, and but neither of them wanted to be around when she was like this, so he rushed to reassure her.

"Quetzali will be wed soon enough, Mother. Girls tend not to marry as young as you did now."

"I will not wait until she finds someone by chance the way commoners do. You must speak to the Emperor about this, Atlatzin. He has known you both since you were children and will do it for your father's sake. The two of them were warriors together and back when..."

Atlatzin interrupted before she could get started on one of her long stories that they had heard a million times before. "I shall speak to him, Mother."

"Good," the woman nodded her head with satisfaction. "I am sure he will suggest a man worthy of Quetzali, of our family lineage." She patted Atlatzin awkwardly on the arm as he rose to leave. He kissed her lightly on the forehead and his sister followed him out of the room.

"When she says 'first-born son,' you know you are in trouble. She almost never mentions Chimali."

"It is best not to name the dead. You know that."

"I know. I was so young when he died, but I remember him. He used to tickle me, and sometimes he would tell me stories. I miss him sometimes. Do you?"

"You were so young when he died. You could not remember much to miss," he retorted sharply.

"Well, I do. And if Chimali were alive, he would find me a good husband, a prince, like a good older brother!" And suddenly she was laughing.

"I will speak to Moctezuma as soon as an opportunity presents itself," he promised.

"Do not marry me off to Lord Moctezuma himself, Brother. He has one hundred and forty-nine minor wives and concubines already. If I must marry, let it be to a man who will honor me as our father did our mother, a man who will have time for me."

"A prince, Quetzali, a prince," he promised fondly.

"I do not think there will be one at the ball game today."

"Probably not, Sister. But I will be sure and look." He laughed and she smiled back.

The crowd in the ball court roared its approval as the hard rubber ball was thrown into the air and the game of *tlachtli* began. The smack of rubber against the masonry sounded loud as the players tried to ricochet the large ball around the court and through the stone rings set vertically in the walls. Spectators called out to encourage their favorites. At one end of the court crowded men and women obsessed with gambling. Here great quantities of cloth changed hands, along with feathers, cacao, and beaded sandals. It was not uncommon to see a woman wager her earrings of beaten gold, and more than one man lost his cornfields and sold himself as a slave because of the toss of a ball.

The priests stood by the rack of skulls of those who had been sacrificed at Hummingbird's temple and watched the game proceed. It was only fitting. The game symbolized one of the mysteries of the cosmos, for the sky itself was a sacred *tlachtli* in which divine star beings fought to keep the sun from reaching its daily goal. Today's game was a special event; there was to be a sacrifice when it was done. The High Priest lazily waved a small whip at the flies that buzzed around his blood-matted hair as he waited patiently for Hummingbird's sacred fruit.

At the foot of the nobles' platform, a small group of courtesans laughed and whispered among themselves. Although they appeared to be watching the game, in reality they scanned the crowd for warriors and merchants whose rich mantles and headdresses signaled they could afford the price of pleasure. The young women stepped out of the way as Atlatzin approached, but one young *auianime* was not quite quick enough to avoid brushing against the man's cape. She gave a light laugh of invitation as she smiled up at the imposing figure, but he ignored her and continued up the steps to the nobles' platform, leaving her feeling as though she were invisible, as though she did not even exist.

Papalopil knew who he was, of course. Who did not know Lord Atlatzin, War Chief of the Jaguar Warriors and advisor to the *Tlatoani* Moctezuma? Her dark eyes studied him and unconsciously she reached up and touched the yellow powder she used to highlight the beauty of her skin.

He had the high cheekbones of royalty, she thought. She admired his headdress of bronze-green feathers of the quetzal bird and the soft cotton cloak tied across his powerful shoulders that was magnificent with color. Huge embroidered butterflies flew across a field of woven green and smaller ones seemed to dance across his loincloth as he moved. The young woman smiled to see them there, as her name meant Little Butterfly. She wondered idly if that could be an omen. Her eye was caught by the jade bracelets the man wore and the large earrings that hung just below his thick hair. From the golden sandals that laced up strong calves to the top of his proud head, he carried himself with an arrogance that only the powerful possess.

It was no secret that the nobleman was chaste. As a symbol of the perfect warrior dedicated to his art, Lord Atlatzin had foresworn the company of both women and boys. When he was ready to retire from the Emperor's armies and no longer a living example for the Jaguar Warriors to follow, he would take a noblewoman for a wife. Until then, he held himself aloof from physical delights.

Every man must find pleasure in something, thought Papalopil. That was what Mama Amoxtli had taught them. If he denied himself physical delights, where did he find his pleasure? She was brought back to her surroundings by a hard pinch on the arm and realized her friends were laughing at her.

"Do you see yourself as Xochiquetzal tempting Quetzalcoatl?" they teased, pointing in the direction she had been staring. "Will you simply show him your beautiful vulva as she did and expect him to surrender to you?" A chorus of giggles accompanied the words.

"Forget Lord Atlatzin," advised an older *auianime*. "He is far beyond the likes of us."

Papalopil laughed, but she blushed at being caught in her silly fantasy. She flipped her hair and shrugged her shoulders to show she did not care.

Atlatzin was completely oblivious of the women who stood below the nobles' platform. His eyes were riveted on the ball players, though his thoughts were not on the game itself. He watched as the athletes threw themselves into the air to get at the ball and took the full impact of the hard rubber with their bodies. They were allowed to use their hands only to help break their fall and were forced to use leather gloves to protect themselves against the continual scraping against the ground. Sometime the gloves and padding failed to save them and, after being hit hard in the belly, there were some players who never rose to continue the game.

Atlatzin centered his attention on one man who seemed to play with a ferocity unmatched by the others. The ball hurled through the air down the court when suddenly, with a magnificent leap and twist of the hip, the man sent it spinning through the stone ring. The crowd screamed its approval as the man fell back to earth rubbing his hip. Atlatzin knew that, had this been an ordinary game, the man would have had to let physicians make incisions in his buttocks to let out the blood brought to the surface by the blow. But today this would not occur.

The player who strove so valiantly to win had been chosen for Huitzilopochtli.

A breeze sprang up and set the feathers in the nobles' head-dresses to dancing. Atlatzin's glance rose and passed over the cheering crowd, coming to rest on a large group of warriors who stood on the platform across from him. As he scrutinized their faces, he wondered if their cries were inspired by the sacrifice soon to come or by the fact that the heart to be offered would not be their own. The Emperor's counselor repressed a sigh. It seemed an enormous price to pay. Huitzilopochtli demanded the very best, the most beautiful, the most brave. In truth, he some-times feared it was the Empire itself that lay on the god's altar and was slowly bleeding to death. It was not a thought he ever voiced.

Now Moctezuma demanded a special sacrifice as well. Although Atlatzin thought he had managed to calm his lord's fears of Quetzalcoatl, he knew Moctezuma would take no chances. It was Hummingbird who had tricked Feathered Serpent and driven him into exile. It was Huitzilopochtli who had then claimed the Mexica as his own people and made himself the greatest of all the gods. When the calendar wheel turned and Quetzalcoatl again stood on Mexica soil, it would be Huitzilopochtli who would face him. Moctezuma had no desire to be caught between two warring gods, and Atlatzin had to admit that the *Tlatoani* was clever in ordering special sacrifices to them both. Huitzilopochtli had his sacred fruit and Quetzalcoatl, who forbade human sacri-fice, was given butterflies and flowers. Although he understood the absolute necessity of the human sacrifice, Atlatzin could not help but regret that his was the appointed hand to select Huitzilopochtli's chosen that day.

The counselor's eyes rested upon a particularly beautiful young man among the spectators who proudly wore the insignia of the Emperor's Guard, and he recognized one of his favorite pupils. He wore the leather bracelets of a warrior who had taken captives in the Flower Wars and brought them back alive to Tenochtitlan. His cloak was fringed with eagle feathers dyed red and he wore the feathered helmet of a soldier of the sun. With something akin to anger, Atlatzin signaled the waiting priests to inform the young warrior of the great honor he would be accorded at sunset. With cold discipline, he turned his attention back to the game.

The crowd rushed onto the ball court when the play was done. The skilled player who was to be sacrificed stood proudly as temple dancers clothed him in the robe made of flowers and white down that would speed his path to the sun. He drank greedily from the cup they handed him. Atlatzin could see the flush in his skin as the drug in the drink began to spread through his body. The crowd cheered as the man threw back his head and laughed, and, in a moment, he was swept up on shoulders and carried to the great temple's eastern steps. He ascended them alone; a smile of triumph played across his lips as he slowly climbed three hundred and sixty steps. There was silence then. Although no one could see the blue temple high above the pyramid, everyone knew what was being done. The honored victim had entered Huitzilopochtli's secret chambers and bowed deeply before the god's image. He came outside again and held his arms up to the sun. With joyous calm, he lay himself on the sacrificial stone. Four priests held his limbs down while the high priest sank his black knife into the man's breast. In that heart's beat of time, the man became the god, and the miracle of life and death and resurrection was enacted. His bloodied heart twitched rhythmically in the high priest's hands as it was laid on the god's altar. The lesser priests pushed the mutilated body down the temple's western steps, where it would later be retrieved for the sacred communion of the god's flesh. Like the sun, the chosen one had risen in the East and descended in the West.

Atlatzin paused as the body tumbled down the blood-caked stairs. For a moment, he turned away, as though the smell of death was overwhelming. Was it all really necessary? he wondered darkly. Would the sun truly be unable to shine without its daily dose of blood? It had taken some twenty years to perfect that athlete's body and art. And when the man was a symbol of all the Mexica admired, the god selected him for destruction. It seemed such an incredible waste! A surge of indignation rose within him and was quickly replaced with anxiety. It was one thing to be angry with the gods. It was quite another to actually doubt their commandments.

He stood lost in thought as the frenzied crowd pressed around him. In his mind's eye, he was seeing the death of the other young man, the one he had chosen for Moctezuma's secret sacrifice. He forgot he was due at the *telpochcalli*, the school for warriors. He forgot he was to lead them in the daily blood-letting that was also needed to help ensure the dawn of the following day. The sacred fruits offered each day were not enough for the thirsty god; he must have the precious red water of life in order to survive. It was always thus, thought the nobleman, blood, death, physical sacrifice at dawn and dusk, twice daily spiritual death. Death was all a warrior could aspire to. Shortly after his mother gave birth to him, his birth cord was buried with a small shield as a token of the death that was to come. Even the clothing he wore as an adult spoke the same message, for a warrior so beautifully dressed would surely die a beautiful death. Blood was the secret of life; a good death was life's supreme goal.

A powerful sensation swept through his loins and Atlatzin was brought abruptly back from his musings. The swirling crowd had pressed a young woman up tightly against him and, for just a moment, the life and warmth of her were overpowering. She tossed back her hair and laughed up at him as she brushed against his loincloth. Still smiling she stepped back and walked away; her glance invited him to follow.

Papalopil flushed as she heard the nobleman behind her. Chance had again brought them together in the crowd, and she had been unable to resist the temptation to try to make him actually notice her. To her surprise, her arm was seized and she was suddenly swung about to face the man she had tempted.

"What are you doing, Woman? Why did you..." he broke off his demand and Papalopil sensed his question was far deeper than it sounded.

"Why not?" she asked, smiling to cover the nervousness she was feeling.

"You know I am foresworn?"

She nodded quickly and struggled to regain her composure. "But I am not, my Lord."

Atlatzin was going to thrust her away but something held him back. He stared into her painted eyes, and his nostrils flared slightly at the scent of deer musk she had rubbed into her thighs. How could she be so full of life and promise when standing in the midst of death? He started to demand her name when he abruptly threw back his head and snorted.

So lost in his own questioning had he been that he had failed to realize the truth. The woman before him was no mere street courtesan, but one belonging to Tlaloc, God of the Fertile Rain. Although she lived the life of an *auianime*, dancing with and sharing pleasure with the unmarried warriors, she too was marked by death. One day while she danced, a priest would likely strike her down from behind. And by the state of her frayed and faded tunic, that day would probably not be so far away. Atlatzin felt an irrational urge to smear the yellow powder that signaled her calling across her face. The young woman who had a moment before seemed so vibrantly alive, was already dead. She simply was not yet aware of the fact. He dropped her arm and turned away.

As Papalopil stared after him, the Emperor's counselor hastened his step toward the *telpochcalli*. He decided to perform an extra penance that evening. He would cut his ear lobes and draw the usual drops of blood. But he vowed to take agave needles and pierce his foreskin to punish himself for his momentary weakness. He was not an ordinary man and his abstinence was his gift to the gods. It was not to be sullied by an *auianime*, no matter how beautiful her eyes.

CHAPTER FOUR

....

.

She saw him again a few days later. Papalopil had taken her turn serving in Xochiquetzal's temple during the night and was heading back to the Street of Perfumed Nights to sleep when she saw Atlatzin crossing the *zócalo*. It was dawn and the markets were not yet crowded, although vendors were beginning to set up. She stepped back into the shadows and watched.

He looked tired. He was coming from Moctezuma's palace, so whether he had been up all night as well or the Emperor had sent for him before dawn, his sleep had been interrupted. He did not turn in the direction that would take him to the *telpochcalli*, so she assumed that, like her, he was going home to rest.

On impulse, she decided to follow him. It was like a game, and she planned to turn her back and pretend to be interested in something, should he pause or turn around. He wouldn't notice her. The *pipiltin* tended not to see commoners or slaves unless they needed something of them. But Atlatzin paused only to drink from the northern aqueduct that carried fresh water into the city, and then moved on.

Mama Amoxtli had told her to study men and learn as much

as she could about them. Papalopil knew part of her job was to service common warriors, not the *pipiltin*. But Lord Atlatzin was a leader of warriors, head of the Jaguar Warriors, and a model for his men. Surely she could learn more about all warriors by studying him.

She wondered again where the man found pleasure. Perhaps it was in the splendid dress and jewelry he wore when visiting the palace. This morning he had five long red feathers in his head-dress that matched the color of the pattern on his yellow cloak. Papalopil caught the glitter of gold in the rising sun and realized he must be wearing gold bracelets among the jade. But was it the beauty of the colors and shape that gave him pleasure or the wealth and status they signified? she questioned.

Perhaps he found pleasure in the small wars they called the Flower Wars. Papalopil had difficulty imagining that, but she knew that some men gloried in the excitement of battle. Men sometimes experienced a special kind of bonding there, according to Mama Amoxtli. She did not want to think that Lord Atlatzin enjoyed the killing, but naturally he would feel pride at bringing home captives to be given to the gods.

As she followed him into the neighborhood where many of the *pipiltin* lived, she was careful to stay deep in the shadows. She would pass for a servant if anyone saw her, but it would be better not to be noticed. She did not pause to question what she was doing.

She turned a corner and stopped abruptly. Atlatzin had entered a large stone building. In fact, Papalopil noticed, it was the largest on the street. It even had what looked like a smaller building attached on the side and a second floor, something forbidden to commoners and infrequent even among the nobility. Peeking through the open doorway of the house, she could see an interior patio and garden with a variety of plants spilling out of brightly colored pots. She heard a woman's voice from within, and quickly turned around and started back.

She had enough to think about for the moment.

The young women and girls sat in the Temple patio preparing cotton for spinning. The day was hot, but the patio was partially shaded by a small jacaranda tree. The girls laughed and talked among themselves as they carefully picked out the seeds and small stems buried within the soft bolls. The women worked with stiff wooden combs, carding the cleaned boll, pulling the fibers apart into a handful of white fluff. They all knew better than to sit with empty hands as though there were no work to do. They had been taught since childhood that idleness opens the way for vice. Besides, if they sat doing nothing, someone would be sure to find something for them to do, probably something a lot less agreeable than spinning.

Papalopil took a small handful of the carded cotton and attached it to the notch at the end of her spindle. With a flick of her hand, she set the whorl at the end of the stick spinning, and the cloud of fluff began to turn into thread. When the stick had grown fat with thread and become unwieldy, she slipped the fiber off the pointed end of the stick, tossed it into the basket at her knee, and started over again. The soft murmur of female voices in the patio was interrupted by Mama Amoxtli's arrival.

"In the *zócalo* they say there will soon be another Flower War. That means you will be called upon to serve," she announced. "All of you will dance, but only the *auianimes* will serve the warriors."

Some of the dancers reacted happily, as they loved being called upon to dance. Serving the warriors was an honor, and some of them found considerable pleasure in the serving. A few dancers looked grim. A Flower War meant that some warriors would die, others would be wounded, and still others taken captive by enemies of the Mexica and offered to the enemy's gods.

The youngest dancer of all looked frightened. It would be her first Flower War. Mama Amoxtli noticed the expression on her face and tried to reassure her.

"Fear not, Little One," she said soothingly. "If a warrior chooses you, Xochiquetzal will be with you. Remember, all of you. What is it we say?"

"Every touch a blessing. Every dance a prayer," the dancers responded in unison. Mama Amoxtli gave a satisfied nod.

"When you service a warrior, what you do is a sacred act. Remember, this is not the same act that you do with your sponsor, if you should have one, or any "friends" you might make. This is different. It is a sacred act among you and the warrior going into battle and Xochiquetzal. From now until the war ends, you will refrain from eating anything that has been cooked with salt or chilies. By giving up these luxuries, you purify yourself and make your body a vessel for the goddess. Never forget that when you lie with a warrior on his way to war, you are offering him her blessings. If you have been righteous in your duties, you will feel Xochiquetzal flow through you and into him."

"And he will return safely?" asked the youngest dancer.

"If the gods will it. But whether he returns or not, he will have been blessed and will fight bravely. If he is killed, he will go directly to the sun, and you will know that he died blessed because of you."

"And then we bless those who return to the city after the war?" the girl asked.

"No, Child, not exactly. We heal them. When the warriors return, they are filled with the blood lust of battle. They have seen terrible things; they may have done terrible things themselves. They are not fit to go home to their families; the blood lust and anger is still too strong in them. It is your job to dance with them in wild celebration when they return, and then drain the horror from their hearts.

"Remember, you can only do this if you understand the secrets of pleasure. You must open all your senses as a flower opens to the sun. Drinking the *poyomatli* I brew will help this. But you must be willing to open. Now, breathe deeply."

"But I am a priestess-in-training, not an *auianime*," protested one of the older girls. "Why do we all have to learn these secrets? It seems a waste of time to me."

Mama Amoxtli frowned. "I have said this before, and I will not waste my time saying it over and over. Xochiquetzal is the goddess of love and pleasure and beauty. When she moves through you, you are transformed for those moments. You bestow her blessings. But she cannot enter you if your body is not fully awake, if you do not know the secrets of the senses. Without that, you are useless to her, whether you are a priestess or an *auianime*. You are all temple dancers.

"Now either sit down and be quiet, or go home to your parents and tell them you are not fit to be a priestess."

The older girl sat quickly and averted her blushing face. Papalopil felt a moment of pity. Mama Amoxtli could be warm and motherly. But she expected discipline and obedience from her charges. The other females were careful not to look at the admonished girl as they put down their spindles and began the familiar exercise.

"Close your eyes and smell the air around you." Mama Amoxtli's voice was gentle as she guided the group in the lesson. "Is it hot? Dry? Is there perfume in the breeze? Do you recognize the scent? Breathe in and feel the air as it moves through your nose, over your throat, and into your chest. Feel how your chest expands and then collapses gently as you let your breath out. Be grateful to the air, it gives us life.

"Now gently touch the inside of your arm and concentrate on the sensation on your skin. Are you touching with one finger or more? Feel that. Switch your attention to your fingertips. What do they feel?"

Mama Amoxtli's voice grew softer and Papalopil's attention

wandered. She had done this exercise many times, but she had never felt the goddess flow into her when she blessed a warrior. Most of the other dancers claimed they had, but she wondered if they really told the truth. She had confessed her failure only to the elder priestess, and made a practice of smiling knowingly when the other girls discussed their experiences with the blessing. Mama Amoxtli had simply said that some day, she would feel the goddess enter her and would know that Xochiquetzal had been there all along. Until then, she was advised to do the exercises and trust.

Since the houses on the Street of Perfumed Nights would soon be busy, the *auianimes* set to cleaning. Each house was made of adobe and consisted of a large room where five to seven girls slept on reed mats covered with cloth. Papalopil took her sleeping mat and blanket into the shared courtyard behind the house for airing and saw that dancers from the other little houses were doing the same. Mama Amoxtli was in the outside communal kitchen, preparing large quantities of the potent *poyomatli* drink used by both the *auianimes* and the warriors during the blessing before battle. She smiled at Papalopil and turned to stir the fragrant juice.

Back inside, a shaft of sunlight that fell on the household altar illuminated the need for dusting. Papalopil grabbed a rag quickly, embarrassed that so little care had been taken of Xochiquetzal's place of honor. As another girl swept the pounded earth floor, she carefully cleaned the offerings made by each girl. There were small feathers, shells, and a few colored stones scattered around the base of the clay statue of Xochiquetzal. Papalopil picked up the figure of the goddess of feathers, flowers, and pleasure and looked at it carefully.

She was portrayed as standing, her arms held out in front of her holding flowers. Her skirt had ornate designs carved into the clay and was painted bright red. Her green and yellow tunic was covered with flowers. The ends of her long hair were doubled underneath at shoulder length, the way that the *auianimes* wore it. But the ends of the goddess' hair had been gathered together and then pulled up along the side of her head, so that it looked like she had two fat horns coming out of the top of her head. As Papalopil turned the statue over in her hands, the girl who was sweeping paused and turned to her.

"Be careful what you ask of Xochiquetzal," she warned.

"I was not asking her for anything," responded Papalopil, dusting off the clay.

"Still, be careful. She might not cut your heart out like Hummingbird, but she can break it just the same."

Mama Amoxtli, who had come inside to get out of the sun, overheard and interrupted. "You say that because you ignored my warning and fell in love with a warrior. It was a foolish thing to do."

"Well, I am not asking Xochiquetzal for a warrior and I would never fall in love with one anyway," said Papalopil, as she gently returned the dusted statue to the altar. "In fact, I do not intend to fall in love at all."

Mama Amoxtli gave a small smile and shook her head. "Sometimes I forget how young you are," she said before returning to her brew.

Papalopil watched her go back into the patio. "I may be young," she said half to herself, "but I know how hopeless it is for a slave to love anyone." She flicked her wrist and the dust cloth snapped in the air, sending little dust motes to dancing in the sunlight.

CHAPTER FIVE

Atlatzin nodded in approval at the young warrior who knelt before him. In honor of the soldier's first Flower War and as a reward for the captive he had brought back alive, Atlatzin cut the thick braid that hung from the side of the young man's head and gave him a small shell bird to hang from his left ear. It caught the light as the warrior swung his head proudly and grinned at his friends, knowing that now he too was entitled to smoke tobacco and drink the delicious cacao. The Emperor's counselor moved on to the next warrior.

From a spectator's box behind a screen heavy with lattice-work and roses came an impatient cough. Hidden from view was Moctezuma with the other two members of the Triple Alliance: his nephews, the Princes of Texcoco and Tlacopan. Atlatzin was one of the very few who knew they were not alone there behind the screen. Besides them in the box that was perfumed with rose petals and sedge root, sat the Enemies of the House, the lords of the defeated cities of Cholula, Huexotzinco and Atlixco. It was against these tribes that the latest Flower War had been waged. The people believed that the war had been started by Cholulan treachery. Only a handful of men knew that the war, like all Flower Wars, had been carefully prearranged by a treaty between the lords and kings of rival states. In this way, the rulers provided a testing ground for aspiring youths, the "flower" of the Mexica, as well as the endless flow of captives for Huitzilopochtli. Of course, those who had arranged the war knew it would never do for the truth to leak out. After the war, the Enemies of the House were spirited across the frontiers at night and brought into Tenochtitlan before daylight to watch the spectacle. There was no need to spread word of a captive's death in his homeland. His ruler watched it from behind the rose screen.

The last heart of the day had been held aloft to Hummingbird and the last Mexica warrior had been rewarded for his bravery. For these men, the Flower Wars were not a sham. Warriors fought and died, or they returned home to seek the privileges and finery they had earned in battle. Thus it had been for almost a century and, as Atlatzin watched Moctezuma appear and signal the ceremony's end, he felt the custom was fitting. There would always be wars, and the Flower Wars assured that there would be a minimum of unnecessary bloodshed. Meanwhile, the Mexica grew strong and fearless. Those who fell on the battlefield or who were taken prisoner to a foreign state were weak or clumsy. Those who returned victorious to Tenochtitlan had proven themselves. Atlatzin knew that this way, the Mexica race was constantly purified and renewed. In special celebration, the captives' flesh, having been made sacred through the sacrifice to Huitzilopochtli, would be carefully cooked with squash and served to Moctezuma's honored guests, so that they too might participate in the divine communion.

Another cough from behind the flowered lattice drew Atlatzin's attention. It was his duty to arrange an escort to take the Enemies of the House back to the palace for the feast that would take place. It had to be done in the greatest of secrecy, so that no one might suspect that Moctezuma and his closest lords feasted with the Empire's enemies at the cost of Mexica lives. He turned to see to the task.

The grand hall had been prepared for feasting. Guests sat on richly carved stools or colored jute mats as soft as moss. Hundreds of servants passed silently through the noisy gathering, bearing delicacies on platters of gold. The guests numbered over two thousand and were seated according to rank. Those farthest away from Moctezuma were the sons of distant lords, brought to Tenochtitlan as living guarantees of their father's loyalties. Next came the priests of lesser gods together with the palace artisans, renowned goldsmiths, lapidaries, and jade workers. Closer still sat the most famous of the Eagle and Jaguar Warriors, and next to them the lords and ambassadors from nearby towns and states, along with the pilpiltin of Tenochtitlan. The high priests of the most powerful gods sat with the Emperor's counselors. The Princes of the Triple Alliance sat together, while the Enemies of the House were disguised and hidden in the shadows. Moctezuma sat alone. As was his custom, he had eaten in privacy before the general feasting began.

Atlatzin hesitated a moment over a platter of young newt cooked with yellow peppers and a dish of white fish in a sauce of crushed calabash seeds. Dining at the palace was a true luxury to the palate. There were seven kinds of maize cake, tamales stuffed with meat, snails, over twenty dishes of wild game in varying sauces, tiny insect eggs, winged ants, and an almost infinite variety of fruits and vegetables, not to mention platters of rabbit, domestic turkey and dog, piled high with golden sweet potatoes. The spicy scent of the newt decided him, and the Emperor's counselor ate with relish.

A movement caught his eye and he looked up to see his sister enter behind Moctezuma's daughters. Having helped to serve the Emperor's food earlier, she was free to sit with the *pipil-*

tin. Quetzali was tall and elegant like their Toltec ancestors, he decided proudly. Small quetzal birds were embroidered on her white blouse and hem; the colors in their brilliant plumage were repeated in the ribbons woven skillfully into the dark braids that circled around her head. The string of jade beads around her neck proclaimed her noble heritage. Her skin gleamed like dark honey in the torchlight. Cleanliness was a mark of beauty for both men and women, but Quetzali's freshly scrubbed face made her look as much a child as a woman.

Atlatzin shifted his weight uncomfortably, suddenly struck by her youth and vulnerability. She needed a protector. If anything happened to him, she would be alone. He wondered if this were the time to speak to Moctezuma, given that two of the Emperor's own daughters were still unwed. Surely the Great Speaker would be seeking royal husbands for them before any request his counselor might make. Quetzali saw Atlatzin and flashed him a smile. He had to smile back. She was so beautiful, Moctezuma might want her for himself. But whether she would be given to a minor prince or the Emperor himself, when that time came, she would accept the choice made for her. She would do what her breeding and rank demanded of her, and she would do it with the grace and bearing she had been taught since birth. In her own way, Quetzali too had been raised a warrior, he admitted.

Moctezuma signaled to Atlatzin who went immediately to his lord's side.

"My guests appear to be pleased. The dishes are to their liking," said the Emperor, pushing aside his feathered cape. "The Mexica have accomplished much since the days when we were sent into exile to the land of rattlesnakes."

Atlatzin smiled in agreement. The humiliating exile had occurred numerous cycles in the past, but the lesson they had learned from it would never be forgotten.

"Our enemies expected that to be the end of the Mexica,"

continued Moctezuma softly. "But we turned our defeat into our victory. Where others would have died, we fed upon the reptiles and grew strong enough to conquer those who sent us to that forsaken place. The snake of death became our symbol of life and victory. Did you mark who sits among the Enemies of the House?" he appeared to change the subject abruptly, but Atlatzin knew him too well to be deceived.

"The Princes of Cholula, Huexotzinco and Atlicxo." He guessed the direction of his Emperor's thoughts.

"Tlaxcala did not take its place behind the rose screen." Moctezuma leaned forward, creating a shimmer of purple iridescence as feathers in his cape rippled.

"The Lords of Tlaxcala were long in replying to the invitation to the Flower War, and when the answer came, it seemed stilted and evasive," commented Atlatzin. "My spies report nothing of particular import, but the unrest in that state grows steadily."

"Perhaps we err in fighting Flower Wars with Tlaxcala. Perhaps they need to be conquered in a real war and totally subdued. What do you advise?"

"Tlaxcala resents paying such a high tribute in sacrifice, *Tlatoani*. As I have said before, the information I receive is that its rulers believe the share to be disproportionate."

"If we did not take the bulk of our sacrifices from our enemies, we would have to take them from the Mexica. The Lords of Tlaxcala know that we have no choice but to feed Huitzilopochtli. How else can life exist? The gods themselves have sacrificed. It was a god who threw himself into the fire and became the fifth sun that shines upon us. Other gods gave their blood as well so that our sun might draw life from their deaths and begin its course across the sky. Can we do any less?" Moctezuma's voice rose and those seated nearby fell silent.

Atlatzin kept his eyes on the floor and wondered why the Emperor felt the need to retell the old stories so often lately. It was not as though anyone had forgotten them. Moctezuma's religious fervor seemed to be increasing. Much as Atlatzin admired him, he had to admit that the Emperor seemed to be developing a tendency to let religious matters gloss over the subtle political realities. It was the fault of those omens – the omens and Hummingbird's priests. They were as hungry for power as the god was for blood.

"We must increase the tax levied on Tlaxcala," decided the Emperor. "Their impudence will not be permitted to turn into sacrilege. This is not the time to be lax or careless in our observances. The great wheel turns, and who knows what lies in wait for us? Sit here and I will think on this," he commanded, pointing to a carved stool at his feet.

Atlatzin heard the edge in Moctezuma's voice and realized he was thinking about the prophecy of Quetzalcoatl's return again. He had hoped the Emperor's concerns had eased some, but saw now he was mistaken. This was not the time to counsel prudence in dealing with the Tlaxcalans; it would only feed the Emperor's forebodings. Nevertheless, as he took his seat, he knew something had to be done before Moctezuma issued orders that might prove imprudent. Fortunately, the arrival of servants bearing bowls of frothy chocolate chilled with mountain snow proved a fortunate diversion. With a royal wave of his hand, the Emperor ordered his guests to be given pipes carved from pure amber and then inhaled deeply on his own. The smoke curled lazily upward and joined that from the resin torches, where it hung like a thick cape above the room.

Musicians began to play. Flutes, trumpets, conches and drums sounded softly in the background, punctuated by the two notes of a wooden gong. First one guest, then another, rose to move with the music. A figure in the shadows stood and began to sway. The servants quickly lowered their torches so its face would not be seen. They were unaware it was an Enemy of the House, but knew they would pay with their lives if they let light fall on the face of anyone in that area.

An actor began to recite, and Atlatzin found himself echoing the man's words as his voice soared above the music.

> *"If only one lived forever*
> *If one could never die*
> *We live with souls torn apart, lightning flashes*
> *We suffer*
> *We seize handfuls of flowers*
> *They wither*
> *Jade cracks, gold breaks*
> *Even quetzal feathers grow tattered*
> *Shall my heart be as the feathers?*
> *Shall my name be as the flowers?*
> *In only one lived forever*
> *If one might never die..."*

A woman's voice rose like the flight of a bird. She swayed slightly as she sang and her long braids tumbled from their pinnings and brushed against her body.

> *I stand on Popocatepetl*
> *I look down upon the Valley of the Mexica*
> *the huge blue-green lake*
> *now quiet, now angry*
> *foams and sings among the rocks*
> *flowery water, green-stone water*
> *where the swan calls*
> *as it swims to and fro*

Our Father the Sun
dressed in rich feathers and turquoise
thrusts himself down into a vase of gems
among many-colored petals
which fall in a perpetual rain.

She turned to the Emperor, who was watching her in growing approval. He threw his cape back over one shoulder and gestured for her to come forward. With a bold smile, the woman drew closer, being careful not to offend by looking directly into his face. That boldness told Atlatzin that she might be an artist, but she was also an *auianime*.

"Atlatzin, allow this precious bird to perch on your stool. I will not need your services more tonight," the Emperor said without taking his eyes off the woman.

Atlatzin stood so quickly the stool tipped over. For a moment he was annoyed at being replaced so easily by a courtesan, and then realized she was exactly the diversion the Emperor needed. But Moctezuma had seen the stool fall and knew his counselor was not usually clumsy.

"Atlatzin, you always serve me well and your counsel is valued. You may ask something of me," he offered, smiling in exaggerated generosity at the woman seated at his feet.

"I ask only to be allowed to continue in your service, my Lord."

"Well spoken," commented the Emperor dryly, turning back to him. "In the mouths of poets and diplomats words are flowers, beautiful to the senses. But they are also like the small nosegays carried in the streets by the *pipiltin* to disguise the smell of the masses. You must have a request of me. Everyone does."

"I do have one, my Lord, but is not so offensive as the smell of the masses," admitted Atlatzin with a small smile.

"Make it then."

"My sister Quetzali serves you here in the palace, great Lord. You knew her as a child. Now, she is one of the maidens whose duty it is to remain hidden while seeing that your table is set, your food delicately prepared, and your cup full before you feel thirst. She is nearing the age where she should have someone to protect her besides her brother. "

"We all may need protection, said the Emperor, the frown reappearing on his face. "You wish me to marry her to a prince among our allies?"

"A royal husband would be ideal," Atlatzin agreed, "Quetzali is of the pilpiltin, with blood that runs back to the ancients. She would be greatly honored with the position of wife to a prince, and would surely bear him royal sons the gods would smile upon."

"Very well, Atlatzin. I'll grant your boon. But this is not the best time for unions. I'll wait until after the great wheel marks Nine Wind, and then make arrangements. Until then, your sister may serve my daughters here in the palace instead of me. That will make her visible to visiting princes, and them to her. Perhaps a suitable match will present itself.

"Now, go enjoy yourself and let me do the same." With an elegant wave of his hand, Moctezuma called for his collection of dwarfs.

As the nobleman returned to his dinner he hoped the evening's entertainment would be enough to distract the Emperor from his growing obsession with Quetzalcoatl. The day Nine Wind was still a little ways off, but Moctezuma was beginning to look a bit haggard. Atlatzin wondered how frequently he was using the sacred mushrooms. They could not be good for his health. He shook himself slightly and took a long puff on his pipe. The newt, although delicious, seemed not to agree with him. Since Moctezuma's attention was focused on the singer, there was no longer any reason for him to stay at the feast. It was obvious that the Emperor intended to retire early. After checking to make sure the Enemies of the House had been escorted out secretly, Atlatzin slipped unnoticed from the hall.

The streets of the silent city were lit by the moon's cold light. Lady Golden Bells, she was called, but her light was pale and gave little comfort. In every temple a fire burned, and the shadows on the buildings seemed to dance to some secret drum. Atlatzin walked quickly through the *zócalo* toward his home in the nobles' quarters. As usual, few people were about. Fear of the night gods provided better policing for the city than even the Jaguar or Eagle Warriors.

A soft slapping of sandals on stone caused Atlatzin to look toward the temple of Huitzilopochtli, where a long line of priests silently climbed past the giant stone serpent heads and up the steep pyramid steps. These men felt no fear of the night gods. Indeed, in the robes blackened with sacrificial blood, they were almost as terrifying as the gods themselves. And Atlatzin sometimes was uneasy at the thought that the power they held was more than any mere mortal had a right to have.

Pulling his cloak tighter, he moved on. There was no question but that Hummingbird was an insatiable god. People said that the completion of his temple in Tenochtitlan was celebrated with the sacrifice of twenty thousand slaves. Four priests had worked simultaneously, and when their arms tired from lifting high the beating hearts, other priests stood in line to take their places. As a child Atlatzin had heard the stories of temple steps so wet with blood that a man could not climb them unaided. But that was long ago, before the Mexica attained their present level of sophistication. Atlatzin believed that such a day could never come again and secretly wondered if indeed it ever really had. He suspected the numbers were gross exaggerations to frighten their enemies.

Still, it was disturbing to see how much power the priests of Huitzilopochtli had gained over the years. Much of this was because of Moctezuma, and Atlatzin wondered again if the Emperor's religious background were a weakness or a strength. Would the hungry god fight on their side if the Tlaxcalans rose up against the new sanctions Moctezuma ordered? They were not the only tribe ripe for revolt. The Triple Alliance was not as strong as it once had been, and among the Mexica themselves, there were those who murmured against the constant Flower Wars. It was fear of the Mexica warriors that kept order in the world, he knew. But the balance of all power rested on Moctezuma's shoulders, and the Emperor seemed to be concerning himself more with legend than fact. Atlatzin reluctantly decided that the obsession with Quetzalcoatl grew as the great wheel turned.

Of course, if Feathered Serpent were to arrive with this turn of the calendar wheel, there were resentful tribes that would rush to fight at the god's side. If that happened, there might be little Huitzilopochtli could do for the Mexica. The rise and fall of the Empire had been foretold. Nothing could change what was pre-ordained; Mexica children learned this at their mothers' breasts. To deny this was to deny rational thought. Atlatzin shook his head. It was useless to think such things.

He glanced up at the Temple of Tlaloc next to that of Hummingbird's on top of the Great Pyramid. The memory of the temple dancer with the lovely eyes came to mind. He tried to recall her face beyond her eyes and failed. He wondered briefly if she were even then sharing the mat of the young warrior he had rewarded that morning. Annoyed at himself for thinking along those lines, he brushed the thought away, and forced himself to focus on the question of predestination. Was it really irrational to question the concept? Did the very fact of knowing the future alter it in some subtle way? Surely a warrior, knowing he was to die, would choose to fight differently from one who had no such knowledge. But did that change his death? Was it, in fact, the reason he would die?

Reaching his home, Atlatzin dismissed the servants who came to greet him without really noticing them; his thoughts were centered on the question he had never before fully considered. It was a paradox. If the gods intended one warrior to know of his death and the other to be ignorant, they both died in the end, as preordained. If the one who knew he was fated to die escaped because of his knowledge, then his knowledge was false all along. It was difficult, this complex question of fate, and Atlatzin turned it over in his mind much like a crystal held to the light.

"Atlatl," his mother called from her room, using his boyhood name. "Have you made the arrangements for your sister?"

"I saw her at the banquet with the Emperor's daughter, Mother. She seemed to be enjoying herself. I spoke to the Emperor and he will find her an appropriate husband. Quetzali will be safe in the palace. You can rest easy."

The old woman nodded happily. "I knew you would fix things and so I have been celebrating." She held up a jug of *pulque*, and Atlatzin could smell the strong liquor from where he stood. It was obvious she had been drinking for some time; her skirt was awry and there was a dark stain on her good *huipil*.

"I can see you have, Mother," he said patiently.

"She is my youngest, you know. Of all the times the midwife came to me, only the three of you lived. Well, just the two of you finally."

"I know," he said gently.

"It is good to know my daughter will be settled. Our family goes back to the ancient ones. Our blood is as pure as the Emperor's."

"Yes, Mother," he murmured as he bent and kissed the top of her head affectionately. "Soon the Emperor will negotiate a royal marriage for her and Quetzali will bear many sons and live in the comfort and security she deserves."

"I want to live to see my grandsons, so I hope it is soon" said his mother somewhat plaintively as she sank down on her pallet. "No, leave me my *pulque*." She reached out and pulled the jug out of Atlatzin's hand as he started to leave the room. "At my age, I deserve it. The law may punish drunkenness with death for young people. But the Emperor knows that those of us who have seen many years need a special reward for living so long. It gives me something to look forward to."

Atlatzin pulled the cotton blankets up around her and signaled to a servant to stay by her side in case she needed something during the night.

"You are a good boy, Atlatl. You bring your mother joy," he heard her say as he turned to go out to his bath.

Joy? It was a strange word, he thought, stretching out on a mat in the small building in the patio that was his steam bath. He saw to it that she was treated with respect and wanted for nothing. Was that what it meant to feel joy? Was there joy without sorrow? Pleasure without pain? He pondered this as the servant giving him a massage dug his fingers into a tense muscle. It was as though one believed life possible without death, he decided, when they were but two facets of the same jewel.

A fire had been laid against the outside wall of the bath hut and the wall itself was now too hot to touch. Finishing his massage, the servant began to throw water on the porous stone and thick steam enveloped the small hut. Atlatzin scrubbed himself with soaproot and lay back, clearing his mind as the steam cleansed his body.

When his nightly ritual was done, he climbed to the upper level of his house and went out for a moment onto his roof garden. The night-blooming jasmine made the breeze heavy with scent and the splattering of water in a small fountain was loud in the quiet of the night. Below him in the moonlight lay Tenochtitlan. It was a study in silver and shadow. Broad avenues of darkness crisscrossed small canals where the moon's reflection danced. The grandeur of the silent scene made him feel insignificantly small and, at the same time, part of something immense. This was the center of the known world, the home of the Mexica, his Tenochtitlan.

A woman's scream cut the night like an obsidian knife. Atlatzin whirled around, but the cry seemed to come from everywhere and nowhere at once.

"We are destroyed! My children, oh my children! Where shall we go? Where shall we run to?" The voice trailed off into sobbing and then slowly into an eerie silence.

At Atlatzin's call, servants ran with torches into the street. From his post on the roof, he could see their lights as they searched for the woman whose cry he had heard. The night turned cold and the sudden wind pierced like agave needles. He suspected what the servants would report. It was no woman of warm flesh and blood crying out. It was the creature they called the Weeping One, and it was said her children were the Mexica.

This was trouble. This was no strange bird or rumor of an omen. Atlatzin had heard the voice of the ghost woman himself and felt the prickling on the back of his neck. He could no longer doubt it; there was trouble ahead. Whether or not this signaled the return of Quetzalcoatl, Atlatzin did not know. But his boyhood training in the priesthood told him the gods were indeed near. If Moctezuma were right, they would see the end of Feathered Serpent's long exile. Would Hummingbird abdicate his position easily? Atlatzin did not think so. If there were to be a war between the two mightiest of gods, Tenochtitlan could be destroyed. The Mexica would be trampled beneath divine sandals.

Deep within him, pain and anger began to coil around each other like waking snakes. Atlatzin could not stand by and watch his world destroyed, his people enslaved. The ghost woman's haunting voice had torn at the fabric of his life, and he was left with the only decision one of his background and training could make.

He was a warrior and a teacher of warriors. If there were to be a war, he, too, would fight. He would side with neither god; his battle would be on the side of the Mexica. If he needed to lie to the Emperor or defy the gods themselves, he would do so. His spies would gather the tiniest pieces of information like hummingbird feathers and he would weave them into a tapestry that would tell him where and when to act. Alliances would be strengthened, sacrifices made. A group of warriors would be sent here, an enemy's temple burned there. By the time the great wheel turned and day Nine Wind One Rain arrived, the Mexica would be ready. They would survive.

He turned to go inside as a thought struck him. Although it might not be possible to change the path of destiny, he was vowing to try. Whether or not that was his own freely made decision or his preordained fate, he had no idea.

CHAPTER SIX

The runner fought to get control of his breathing. Having
been admitted to the house immediately upon his arrival,
the wiry man had had no chance to recover from his journey,
so he paced the floor of the entryway to keep his calf muscles
from cramping and concentrated on steadying his breath. His
Lordship had not gathered the fastest runners in the Empire and
pressed them into his personal service in vain. The men who wore
the insignia of Lord Atlatzin were proud of the fact that they
could relay information from the coast to Tenochtitlan in one
day and night. They knew their speed and organization could
not be matched.

The man dropped to a crouch, touching his fingers to the tiled
floor and then to his mouth as Atlatzin entered. He signaled that
the messenger might continue pacing, knowing how hard his
runners pushed themselves and he had no desire to inflict upon
them any more pain than necessary. But the man was determined
to show no weakness. He planted his feet firmly, ignoring the
muscles that knotted in his legs and, with a steady hand, gave
Atlatzin the scroll he had brought from the coast.

Atlatzin opened the rolled deerskin and studied the small painting on its whitewashed surface. It was usually easy enough to understand what his spies were saying, but this message was so strange it was confusing. There in bright colors was painted a great temple floating on the sea!

"What village is this from?"

"Xicalango, on the coast, Lord Atlatzin."

"Is this all there is to the message?" he asked, puzzled at the image.

"Yes, my Lord. The scene was recorded and sent on its way immediately. A man from Xicalango follows so you may question him personally, but he is an old man and travels slowly."

Atlatzin nodded, dismissed the messenger and went into the courtyard to think. He pulled absently at his jasper earplug as he studied the drawing. A temple that floated was impossible, of course, Building stones would sink, no matter how cleverly they were cut and fit together. But then other impossible things had been reported, he reminded himself, the boiling lake, the fire that consumed Hummingbird's temple. Atlatzin had full faith in his network of spies. The drawing in his hand had to represent something real. Furthermore, it would be interpreted the worst possible way at the palace. There was no way he could keep the news from Moctezuma; to even consider it would be treasonous folly. The day Nine Wind drew closer and, when the Emperor saw the painting on the scroll, he would immediately see another omen heralding Quetzalcoatl's return.

In growing trepidation, Atlatzin called for a cloak befitting a royal audience. Hummingbird's priests had spies as well, and the nobleman knew he had to be the first to give Moctezuma the news if he wanted to have any influence over how it was received. It would be all too easy for the Great Speaker to turn to the priests rather than his counselors to explain the omen, as he was more inclined to do lately. Moctezuma ruled smoothly and effectively when it came to trade and warfare. But where he saw the slightest hint of Quetzalcoatl, it was different. Atlatzin gathered his thoughts for what he suspected might be a struggle with the priests. It was important that the Mexica be governed by cool logic, not religious hysteria, if and when danger were to strike. Moctezuma needed him to be there. Atlatzin tied on his feathered garter, took his cloak, and swept with such hurry from the house that he abruptly cut off his mother, who was just returning from the market. It was unlike him, and left his mother staring after him with a surprised look on her face and her arms full of the white lilies she used to sweeten the air indoors.

Arriving at the palace, Atlatzin was informed that the Emperor was not there, but deep within Huitzilopochtli's Black Room in prayer and could not be disturbed. The nobleman cursed his luck and then positioned himself so that he would have the first audience with Moctezuma when he returned from the Great Temple. Atlatzin paced at first, and then realized his agitation was too visible and squatted near the throne room. Outwardly, he was calm, but as the hours passed, he caught himself grinding his teeth. The Emperor had always been prone to long hours in prayer, but as the sun god moved across the sky, messengers from the coast surely moved toward Tenochtitlan. Atlatzin was losing the advantage his runners had given him.

The hollow cry of the conch announcing midday had long since faded to silence before Moctezuma appeared. One look at his face was enough. It was obvious the news had arrived and been delivered directly to the Black Room. Perhaps the runners had been one of the High Priest's spies. The thought disturbed Atlatzin. Hummingbird's priests might have even more power than he had suspected.

Moctezuma gestured to Atlatzin to follow him into the audience chamber. For the first time, the nobleman could smell the sharp scent of fear in the Emperor's sweat. Moctezuma called impatiently for his magicians and high priests. Atlatzin had no chance to speak and, from the black look on the Emperor's face, knew he had to hold his silence until after the magicians had caught the full blast of Moctezuma's mood. Perhaps he could then put in a quiet word to bring this strange news into perspective.

Hummingbird's priest entered, pushing before him an exhausted runner. The man had a terrified expression on his face, as well he should, thought Atlatzin. Moctezuma had executed men for bringing news less disturbing than the message this poor creature carried. Approaching the throne, the man dropped quickly to the floor and made his obeisance. Moctezuma pulled his heavy cloak closer and ordered the man to repeat his tale.

"Yesterday morning at dawn, the men from Xicalango went to set their fishing nets as usual, great Moctezuma. When they arrived, they saw mountains, huge mountains floating on the sea," he said in a trembling voice.

Mountains! Atlatzin's mind raced. One man saw temples, another mountains, things that could not float but did. The image of a *chinampa* came to him, one of the cleverly woven rafts that held dirt in such a way it was possible to grow food where it normally could not grow, but did. The five lakes surrounding Tenochtitlan were full of floating gardens of vegetables, fruit, and flowers.

"Could your mountains be huge rafts of some kind? Giant *chinampas*?" The thought was voiced before he realized it, and he flushed under Moctezuma's reproving glance. If he spoke without thinking first, his words would go unheeded and he could not help. He vowed to remain silent until it was to his advantage to speak.

"Chinampas, my Lord?" asked the man with a little frightened laugh. "I'm speaking of mountains big enough to vomit fire, mountains like Popocatepetl."

"Continue," ordered Moctezuma in a hollow voice, and he

seemed to shrink some as he huddled further back on his low throne.

"The fishermen sent for a runner, but before he could arrive, something even stranger occurred. From the mountain came huge canoes. Big enough for gods, they were, and full of magic. While we watched, they spread white wings like giant gulls and flew across the water toward the shore!"

Atlatzin realized his own runner must have left immediately after sighting the floating temple, or whatever it was. He was glad now that he had schooled himself to patience, for this part of the tale was new to him. He glanced quickly in the Emperor's direction and looked away, embarrassed. The red scales on the cape Moctezuma had chosen to wear were intended to make him look beautiful and dangerous like a snake. But the Great Speaker had pulled the cloak up to his chin and his eyes were round with fear like a beached redfish. For the first time in his life, the nobleman felt a flash of impatience with his emperor.

"The magic canoes held warriors," the man continued, as though anxious to get the news out and done with. "They were strange creatures, like men, but gray and pale as though suffering from long illness. The men of Xicalango who had not run away hid to watch. The strangers came so close it could be seen that one of them had hair the color of ripe maize!"

There was a murmur of astonishment from those who listened. A priest began to moan and was joined by another, but the runner had not finished.

"Their heads were covered with animal hair and their black clothing covered their whole bodies, fitting close against their skin."

"Warriors!" cried out one of the magicians, and fell down to the floor where he began to thrash in his own foam. The other seers stepped away and looked at each other in horror. It was clear to Atlatzin what they were thinking. The strange men were dressed for war. Why else would they dress in form-fitting clothing? It had been said that Quetzalcoatl would be dressed in black at his return. But his warriors? What kind of warriors dressed in plain black instead of bright colors? Had they no respect for death?

"Quetzalcoatl! He returns!" The cry came from a group of priests, but Atlatzin could not tell which of them had spoken. "He mocks us. And he mocks death."

"He holds us in the palm of his hand. He rolls us about and we spin like pebbles!" cried another.

"We make him laugh. He jeers at us!" The moaning had become a chant of doom and Atlatzin knew he had to speak out now.

"Did these warriors touch the shore?" he demanded of the runner. When the man shook his head, Atlatzin shrugged his shoulders in exaggerated derision. "How quick some cry out the end has come. Is the Mexica Empire a flower to bloom and so quickly fade away? Are we children to be frightened by mere tales?"

"Do you deny the gods, Counselor?" asked Hummingbird's priest in amazement. "Quetzalcoatl's return was foretold many cycles past. If you deny that, you deny our history."

"I deny only fear. I am a warrior and a leader of warriors. These creatures have not touched our soil. It is not Quetzalcoatl's sacred day. If part of the prophecy is true, all must be. The great wheel has turned many times since the god left us, it may turn many more before he returns. My Lord, these strange doings in Xicalango must be investigated, but not feared. The Mexica do not fear. We instill it! We do not cry out doom; we bring it on our enemies!"

Moctezuma rose slowly to his feet and the great crystal hanging from his septum danced wildly as he swung his head from side to side, searching the faces that surrounded him for the one, true answer.

"The magicians will be my guests until they can explain the events in Xicalango." The Eagle Warriors who lined the hall stepped forward, their spears readied. Everyone present knew the magicians had just been made prisoners and might not see the dawn. "Spread the word that all visions are to be reported, from those of children in their mothers' arms to those seen by aged relatives lost in *pulque* dreams. I would know all that transpires in my Empire. Send messengers to the cities of Texcoco and Tlacopan," he ordered Atlatzin, "and contact your spies among the Enemies of the House. I must have more information before making any decision about all this.

"If further news arrives, seek me in the Black Room. Do not disturb me unless you must." Moctezuma waved his arm in dismissal. The Eagle Warriors quickly made a path for him through the crowd and he left the great room, followed by Hummingbird's priests.

Atlatzin watched the reactions after the royal departure in frustration. It was important to know who had succumbed to fear. As he studied the faces of the gathered priests, he saw with some surprise that Xipil, one of Quetzalcoatl's elder priests, was not among them. If this were indeed the return of Quetzalcoatl, the god's priests would surely be there! He wondered briefly if the man were being extremely cautious or if there were a deeper meaning in his absence. Without further reflection, he decided to find out for himself. Like Moctezuma, he felt the need for more information.

His first stop was the *calmecac*, where he had a student pull out all the scrolls they had on the story of Quetzalcoatl's departure and return. The boy rushed to follow Atlatzin's orders, piling rolls of painted deerskins atop sheets of painted agave paper. In his haste, the student also brought scrolls that told how the god had created humans by gathering ancient bones and anointing them with his own sacred blood. Atlatzin impatiently pushed these scrolls back at him. Every child knew how the people of the fifth sun were created. What Atlatzin needed to understand was what the god who created them would do when he returned.

By the time he had finished studying the scrolls, the sky was dark and it was too late to seek out Xipil. He decided to go home for the night and set out to see Quetzalcoatl's priest with the early light. The man had been his teacher when he was a boy, and they had been close enough that Atlatzin knew he could trust whatever Xipil said. The nobleman walked quickly through the empty *zócalo* and over the bridge that led into the noble's neighborhood. Most of the houses were dark, the people inside them asleep and safe from the angry stars.

But when Atlatzin got home, he could tell from the light of the resin torch burning upstairs that his mother was still awake. He climbed the narrow steps and saw he was wrong. She was asleep but propped up against the wall of her room. Clearly she had been waiting for him.

"Mother," he said tiredly as her eyes flew open at the sound of his footsteps, "lie down now. It is late." He arranged the blanket of rabbit fur carefully over her sleeping mat, but his mother was now wide-awake.

"Your sister complained about you today, my son. Apparently, you are stalking the palace corridors and growling at people as though you were a real jaguar and not head of the Jaguar Warriors."

"Quetzali is..." he began, but his mother cut him off.

"Your sister is not the only one to notice your behavior. You have been grinding your teeth so much your jaw must hurt. You always do that when you are upset. Mothers see these things. You have done it since you were a boy, just like your father. He used to do it as well. And you have been abrupt with me and the servants lately as well. I understand the palace is in an uproar. Quetzali says everyone is taking care to make no noise and draw attention to themselves. Lord Moctezuma seems to walk an obsidian edge between hope and despair and no one seems to know exactly what to expect."

"Things are a little tense there. I apologize if I have been short with you, Mother."

"What is it that has the Emperor so upset?"

"Nothing that need trouble you," he responded too quickly. "You should be asleep."

"It was the same when you father was alive," she said calmly, refusing to lie down. "Sometimes nothing bothered him too. Remember, he had the Emperor's ear too, although he never rose to your rank. But he was the Emperor's friend and sometimes he learned things he could not talk about, not to me, at any rate."

In spite of himself, Atlatzin curiosity was piqued. His mother saw this and continued.

"When that happened, he would come home and grind his teeth and growl at me and you children. He did not intend to, but he was frustrated and we were there. I finally decided I had enough. The blood of gods runs in my veins from my mother and her mother, and I will not be growled at!"

"What did you do?" In spite of everything, Atlatzin had to smile.

"I pointed out he was growling because he was frustrated by something and he needed to either fix what was upsetting him, or he had find someone else to growl at."

"If it was the Emperor who left him frustrated, Father could hardly fix what was bothering him," commented Atlatzin, shaking his head absently, thinking of his own predicament.

"I sent him to the temple of Xochiquetzal," his mother announced with a touch of pride.

"To the priestesses of love? How in Huitzilipochtli's name did that help? Did he growl at the priestesses? Frighten the goddess?"

"You know a great deal, Atlatzin, but you do not know everything," she reminded him tartly. "There is an ancient custom, mostly practiced by women now, but available to men. If you go to the temple and announce you want to "speak secrets" to Xochiquetzal, a priestess will tend you and everything you say is heard only by the goddess. Sometimes it is important to be able to say things out loud in safety, knowing that no one will judge or betray you."

"A story for maidens looking for lovers, Mother," he shook his head dismissively. "Warriors would be laughed out of the temple for doing something like that."

"No one ever laughed at your father, Atlatzin. He may not have risen to your rank, but he and the Emperor were warriors together when they were young. They were friends and no one dared to laugh at him ever! If he were here he would tell you himself to stop growling at the world and go to the temple. Think! If I hear rumors that the Emperor is upsetting you, how long do you think it will be before Moctezuma himself hears? What do you think he will do then? He may have been your father's friend, but he is the Great Speaker and you dare not disrespect him.

"Go seek Xochiquetzal. She will help you." She curled up on the rabbit skins. "I have said enough."

"All I need is for the priestess to tell someone what I might say. I assume she would be forbidden to do so," he said quickly, as his mother began to interrupt, "but priestesses are human. If I were fool enough to do as you say and she said something, I could be destroyed."

She heard the dismissal in his voice and decided to ignore it. "If the priestess is not in a trance and somehow overhears what you say and repeats it, she can immediately be put to death. The speaker has the right to kill her on the spot. The priestesses all know this. Trust me, they guard secrets with their lives. They can't even tell anyone you were there, much less what you said.

"You would be a fool not to go and have the Emperor discover you are unhappy with him."

"I will consider it, Mother," Atlatzin assured her, although he had little intention of doing so.

CHAPTER SEVEN

The small temple of Quetzalcoatl was in the northern part of the city. It was not the main temple, which was in the *zócalo*, but the place where Atlatzin had studied as a child. Unlike the temples to other gods, this building was round. One of the first things he had learned as a child was that, as God of the Winds, Quetzalcoatl could not be limited by the four directions and neither could his temple. As Atlatzin passed through the entrance, shaped like the head of a striking snake, he felt the familiar sense of peace he had experienced as a young boy. In those years, the priest Xipil had been a revered teacher. But every turn of the wheel had seen the priest lose power to the priests of Huitzilopochtli. Hummingbird harvested blood and in return made the sun move in the sky and gave life. Feathered Serpent harvested fruits and flowers and promised peace. But without life, what power did peace hold?

Atlatzin inhaled deeply as he recognized the copal incense of his youth. Even in the dim light the altar shimmered with dust from a thousand butterfly wings. A gong sounded softly and the figure of a man shuffled into view. He was dressed in dark green cotton and carried branches of flowers to the main altar, where he began to garland an obsidian statue of the god in his form as Feathered Serpent. Atlatzin coughed softly and then again more loudly until he was heard.

Xipil turned around slowly. When he made out who stood there, his wrinkled face folded into a smile as he recognized his old pupil. "Welcome, Atlatzin. What a joy to see you! Do you seek comfort or knowledge in the House of Quetzalcoatl?"

"Neither," Atlatzin assured him. "I am the Emperor's advisor. I seek information."

"Nevertheless, I suspect the god will give you knowledge." Xipil lowered his head to hide a toothless smile.

"It is you I wish to question, Xipil."

The priest forced his face to blandness and turned back to the branches of flowers on the altar. The scent of jasmine mixed with copal and hung heavy above the obsidian slab. Tiny white flowers fell and lay caught in the statue's black coils. The old man's hands shook as he worked, reminding Atlatzin of his age.

"The wheel has brought us into a One Reed year, and the day Nine Wind is not long in coming," he said, as Xipil did not respond.

A grunt of agreement was his answer.

"That is Quetzalcoatl's sacred day."

"I taught you all that when you were a child, Atlatzin." The priest kept his back to his former student as though he had no idea where this was leading.

"Has the temple been receiving the Emperor's gifts?"

Xipil turned around then and looked into Atlatzin's eyes. "Lately, he has been most generous: ripe fruits, armloads of flowers, and a wicker cage of orange butterflies. Every fifty-two years, the god receives his due. But in between..." He shook his head. "The Emperors always fear the god's return. And you, Atlatzin? Is that why you are here?"

"He returns then?" Atlatzin pounced on the words.

Xipil shrugged his bony shoulders and admitted ruefully. "I cannot be certain. The omens would seem to herald his arrival. But I confess that my inner sight has grown dimmer with the years. There was a time when I could have answered you in one word, yes or no. Now I cannot say. I have spent my entire life waiting for his return and the age of enlightenment he will bring."

"It will be peaceful then?"

"I cannot answer that either. Our people turned to Huitzilopochtli, to war. Your own father took you from Feathered Serpent and gave you to Hummingbird to be his warrior. You may be leader of the Jaguar Warriors now, Atlatzin, but you spent your early years serving Quetzalcoatl. You belong to both gods now. Your father never understood that.

"I imagine at times it has been difficult for you, no?" Xipil peered up into the nobleman's face.

Atlatzin was not about to admit this, not even to his old mentor.

"If you cannot tell me if this is his return, can you tell me what to expect when he does return?"

"Quetzalcoatl has been sorely neglected during his exile. We may expect him to return an angry god because of that. When he comes, his wrath will have to be assuaged before enlightenment is possible. But I cannot say if he is returning now."

"Then I would do better in Huitzilopochtli's temple," said Atlatzin dismissively. "His priests are full of answers."

"They always are. But I did not say there was nothing you could learn here, my impatient son," Xipil chided gently. "The god may choose to give you knowledge, not in your way but in his. But do not expect to receive it for nothing. There will be a price. There always is."

"Fresh flowers will grace his altar every day. I promise fruit in season, butterflies, and whatever else you think will please him."

Xipil shook his head and Atlatzin thought the expression on the old priest's face held a touch of pity. "Life is rarely that simple," he said gently. "The god will choose the price, not you. And whatever it is, you will pay it, like it or no."

The tall man stared at his former teacher for a long moment, then finally nodded. "How do we begin?" he asked softly.

In answer, Xipil leaned over and gently blew on the obsidian snake on the altar, sending up a shower of tiny white petals. Starting at the left tip of the great forked tongue, his fingers carefully counted the feathered scales. First to the side, then down, over one coil, they came to rest on a scale that looked no different from all the others. The old man pressed it. Shaking his head and grumbling something under his breath, he pressed harder. A scraping noise startled Atlatzin and he stepped back in alarm.

An opening appeared in the base of the stone altar. Xipil bent over and reached into the darkness. After a moment, he grunted in satisfaction and knelt in order to get a better grip on the heavy object he was pulling into the light. Atlatzin offered to take the bundle from him, but the old man waved him away and pulled himself erect.

"There are things you must know before we begin," he said, clutching the bundle tightly to his chest, unwilling to hand it over immediately. Although the cloth that covered it was yellowed with age, Atlatzin could see that it was the finest woven cotton, not agave cloth, and had been embroidered long ago with gold thread. Whatever it was that Xipil held had to be of great value.

"What do you know about the history of the ancient Toltecs?" the priest demanded abruptly.

"Quetzalcoatl was their king long before his exile," Atlatzin said slowly. "If I remember my lessons rightly, he ruled them for hundreds of years. He taught them to grow ears of corn as big as a man and cotton plants of many colors so there was no need of dyes. Quetzalcoatl told the people to build Tollan, the ruins we call the Place of the Gods."

Xipil nodded. "What you are about to see was discovered buried in a mountain cave and taken to Tollan in the year of Quetzalcoatl's exile. No one knows its origin, but the priests took this to be a sign that the god would return. They hid it in his temple and it remained there for two hundred years.

"During the collapse of the Toltecs, the temple's treasures were hidden in the mountains of Oaxaca for safety. This piece," he indicated the bundle in his arms, "was entrusted to a family of artisan-priests and almost forgotten in the lawlessness that followed. Many of the children of the Toltecs married into the local tribes, and the Mixtecs were born. Remember what I say now, for one day you will need to tell this story to another.

"As time passed, life in the mountains became peaceful again. Game was plentiful. Villages sprang up like flowers. The children of the artisan-priests built a small temple to Quetzalcoatl and they decided to make this," he gestured with the bundle, "even more pleasing to the god. They tried using small rubbing stones to sculpt it into the desired shape, as was their custom. But even the hard pieces of jade used by the Mixtecs ended scratched and this remained unchanged. Finally, it was decided that this alone had the power to alter itself. Small pieces of it were broken off and made into a rough paste which was rubbed against its surface, and the slow sculpting began." Xipil licked his dry lips and rubbed a hand across his forehead, leaving streaks of dust from the bundle's wrappings on his skin.

"The work was not completed in one man's lifetime," he continued. "The shape grew beneath the hands of several generations and was complete when we, the Mexica, came into this land and built Tenochtitlan. It was ready when Hummingbird demanded the sacrifice of every adult male from the Mixtec tribe. It was waiting for us when our leaders married the Mixtec princesses of Toltec descent and assured that their own children would be born into the line of Quetzalcoatl.

"I have never understood why it was given the shape it wears." Xipil slowly began to unwind the yellowed cotton. "Perhaps it was rounded when it was discovered. Perhaps it somehow guided the artisan's hand itself. It is sacred and has great power. When the Mexica warriors discovered it in the village, they first thought it belonged to Huitzilopochtli. It bears little resemblance to the god of fruits and flowers. I have always wondered at this, but then, there are many things I fail to understand. It was brought to Tenochtitlan along with a Toltec princess who was the one who told the Mexica that it belonged to Quetzalcoatl. They didn't believe her at first, but they were a little afraid of it, and of her because of its power. It has been here ever since she came to Tenochtitlan. It will remain here until Tenochtitlan is no more.

"Your mother came from the family of that princess. That is why she hoped you would become a priest, so that knowledge of what I am going to show you would remain in the family." There was only one layer of cloth left, and Xipil handed the heavy object to Atlatzin.

The cotton fell away and the younger man stared in awe. In his hands lay a jewel of jewels in the shape of a human skull as big as life, carved from a single piece of pure white crystal. The great stone was as cold as ice and the red light from the temple fires seemed frozen in its depths. Atlatzin turned its grinning face away and studied the skilled workmanship that had teased the line of the jaw along the line of the crystal's growth. He saw with wonder the streams of tiny bubbles captured forever in the crystal depths and the planes where the jewel had twinned during its formation, and then grown to twin again. Unable to resist, he ran his hand over the smoothness of the cranium. He was touching something ancient, ageless, perhaps even one created during an earlier sun. That Quetzalcoatl's jewel would wear the shape of a skull surprised him. But then, death was part of life, as life was necessary for death.

"Hold it before you and look into its eyes, Atlatzin," Xipil commanded in a voice grown abruptly powerful.

The nobleman raised the skull and stared into its hollow eyes. He was hardly aware of the soft drums sounding in the back of the temple. The incense was thick and suddenly cloying. A shaft of light from the temple's roof pierced the darkness and seemed to illuminate the crystal from within.

He felt himself physically drawn toward the empty sockets. At first he tried to resist. He stood there with the great glowing jewel in the hands and knew he was afraid. It was this admission that did it. He shuddered deeply and surrendered himself to the god...

And was sucked into the hollow eye sockets, which had become huge crystal tunnels. Atlatzin became two instead of one, and each of him was but a mote in the god's eye. He sank into the crystal and was caught in the natural prism that lay behind its empty eyes. There where the light was reflected and refracted, his vision split into colored fragments and each fragment was a whole unto itself.

He saw Quetzalcoatl come forth in all his glory. Here the god was amethyst, here sapphire. His other self saw a blood-red god, Quetzalcoatl green like young corn. The rising sun parted and the seven-colored god appeared wrapped in a cloak of rainbow feathers. Atlatzin felt his two selves fuse into one and the very center of his vision was bathed in white light. Quetzalcoatl stood there. Was it Quetzalcoatl? Was it simply a man who wore the god's clothes and a headpiece that caught the sun like a burning crown? Atlatzin could not tell. First it was one, then the other. He watched as the seven figures walked to a small pool. In the white center, it was a pool of crimson blood. On either side, figures walked to colored pools, violet, indigo, blue, green, yellow, orange and red. In each vision, the god-man reached down into the pool and brought up a crystal skull in one hand. In the white center, a great golden carving in the shape of crossed sticks was held aloft. Atlatzin watched in shock as colored hands each brought a cross down and violently slammed it into the smoothness of the skulls. Tears of blood, red, green, and blue, poured from crystal sockets.

Abruptly the scene changed and he saw a different figure in white light standing with its back to him on the edge of a precipice. As he drew closer, he could see it was Huitzilopochtli, Lord Hummingbird made flesh. The god's feathered cape shimmered green with the fire of emeralds. Huge purple wings hung from shoulders woven with gold. The god's headdress was incandescent; a mosaic of tiny jeweled feathers glowed green and purple and turquoise in the rising sun. Or was it a setting sun? Before Atlatzin could fully form the question in his mind, the figure turned around toward him; its huge obsidian eyes stared at him, probing him for the answer to a question that had not been asked. Slowly, very slowly, the god pulled back his headdress and mask to reveal himself.

With a gasp of terror, Atlatzin realized he was looking at his own face.

He felt the skull seized and pulled away and knew he was falling to the ground. His eyes darted wildly as he struggled to orient himself. He lay sprawled on the stone floor of Quetzalcoatl's temple with Xipil bending over him. Atlatzin was unaware of the real tears that ran down his cheeks or the concerned look on the old man's face. He was conscious only of the cold skull that grinned at him safely from Xipil's arms. Its colors were faded, its visions gone.

"Is it the god returning?" asked Xipil in a whisper.

But Atlatzin could not answer his question. He simply stared at Xipil vacantly, and the priest knew it would take some time before the colored fragments were again an integrated whole in the nobleman's mind. It had been so long since Xipil had seen the crystal visions. The gods gave them only to those who were strong enough to carry them, and Xipil no longer had that strength.

"You must tell no one what you have seen today," he warned Atlatzin. "The secret of Quetzalcoatl's jewel belongs only to a very few chosen ones every generation. Not even those who are elected to be the Great Speakers know it exists. The god chooses those who will serve him. It is not the other way around. And he has chosen you, Atlatzin. When I am no longer able to serve, you will answer his call. It is why we both were born, why your mother brought you to me as a child, why you returned to me today."

Atlatzin nodded but still could not speak. Xipil searched his face carefully before slowly helping Atlatzin to his feet. Before the nobleman left the temple, the old priest carefully wrapped the cloth back around the sacred jewel and replaced it within the snake's coils.

Outside the huge fanged entrance, Atlatzin was stopped by one of his spies. The words the man whispered finally penetrated the colored thoughts that possessed him.

Moctezuma had ordered gifts worthy of the gods to be readied: a necklace of huge emeralds caught in the claws of golden lobsters, a great calendar wheel of gold and another of silver, a mask worked in a mosaic of turquoise attached to a crown of long green quetzal feathers. The meaning was clear. Moctezuma was ready to welcome the returning god.

Atlatzin fought the dryness in his throat that threatened to choke him. His crystal visions had not been clear enough to know if it were the god or a man who was coming from the east. And he could not understand why Hummingbird wore his face. Was the god asking something of him or warning him? The nobleman only knew one thing for sure. Whoever, or whatever, was arriving would signal momentous change. Whether or not it would bring the Mexica Empire to an end or not, Atlatzin could not say. He only knew that the old ways would be abandoned and Tenochtitlan bathed in a flood of blood.

Night was coming and Atlatzin raised his face to the dying sun. Would Huitzilopochtli not help his people? After all the centuries of worship, the great temples, the countless hearts laid beating on his altars, would Hummingbird abandon the Mexica? If so, it had all been for nothing. The Empire would be destroyed.

CHAPTER EIGHT

"The girls tell me you have been following a man from the *pipiltin*." Mama Amoxtli blotted the ink on the scroll of temple accounts that she and Papalopil had been working on and turned to face her. "What is your purpose?'

"It is not forbidden," the girl said defensively.

"I am not accusing you of doing anything wrong. I am simply asking why you are doing this," the elder priestess said gently but firmly.

"To be honest, I am not sure," Papalopil confessed, "but the man fascinates me. He is counselor to the Emperor, yet lives at home with his mother while his sister lives in the palace."

"Who is it?"

"Lord Atlatzin, leader of the Jaguar Warriors."

Mama Amoxtli let out a soft snort and shook her head. "You could not have picked a young warrior who was just starting out? You had to follow one of the Emperor's favorites?" Papalopil shrugged her shoulders and did not respond. "He lives at home because his mother is a widow, the elder priestess continued. "I had not heard that his sister had moved to the palace; maybe she is to be a new concubine for Moctezuma.

"But I do not think that this is why you follow Lord Atlatzin, just because he lives at home."

"No, I just like to watch him. He walks through the city almost as though he were one of the gods. People just move aside when he passes, like small waves before a canoe. He never notices them, never even looks at them. The filth from the streets seems not to stick to his clothes. He is different from other men somehow. Yet as he is a leader of warriors, I know I will understand the warriors I serve better if I come to understand him," she finished in a rush.

"You know he is chaste, Papalopil. That is one way he is different. He will never lie with a woman, much less an *auianime*. Even if he were not foresworn, he is far above someone like you. Remember your place."

"I know. I promise I am not reaching beyond myself. I only watch him," the girl said.

"I think you are telling yourself a story in the hopes you will believe it yourself." Mama Amoxtli searched her face as well as she could in the dim light in the temple. Finally, she said only, "Be careful, Papalopil."

When they had finished rolling the scrolls and putting them away, Mama Amoxtli sent her to find the young priestess Cuicatl, who was weaving in the temple courtyard. When the two girls returned, the elder priestess nodded.

"It is time, Cuicatl. Papalopil, you will come with us. We have work that must be done."

Papalopil looked from one priestess to the other. They both appeared to know what this was about, but it was clear she was not supposed to ask them. She followed them outside, through the crowded *zócalo*, and down the winding Street of Perfumed Nights until they came to the room adjoining the *auianimes'* common house, where Mama Amoxtli slept. Inside, the old woman knelt on the dirt floor and opened a chest where she kept herbs and ointments.

"Take a jug and fetch clean drinking water from the aqueduct," she told Papalopil. "Speak to no one and come back immediately."

The girl did as instructed, while the young priestess sat down on a mat with a miserable expression on her face. As she hurried back with the water, Papalopil could not help but wonder what secret the priestesses shared. Mama Amoxtli slept here in this neighborhood only because she supervised the temple dancers. The girls who were priestesses slept in the temple house. Why was Cuicatl on the street where the women who served the warriors lived? When she returned, she saw that Cuicatl was crying softly and Mama Amoxtli had begun to cut a plant root into small pieces.

"Here, you finish this; grind it well," the old woman said, handing Papalopil a stone pestle. "Cuicatl, make a small fire. We will need to heat water."

Papalopil dropped to a mat and began grinding the root pieces against a large flat stone. For a time, the only sounds in the house were those of stone grinding on stone and the crack of kindling catching fire. When the fire was well lit, Mama Amoxtli put a pot of water on the wood.

"While the water boils, tell Papalopil why we are here, Cuicatl," she ordered. The young priestess shot her a pleading look, but Mama Amoxtli refused to look at her.

"My monthly blood is late," the girl said softly.

Papalopil looked at her in surprise. That happened sometimes, especially the first few years. Mama Amoxtli taught the young *auianimes* how to make the tea that would bring on their flow. Of course, since they all took a different, more bitter tea before lying with warriors, there were no real concerns if the monthly flow were late.

Suddenly she understood. But Cuicatl was a priestess, not an *auianime*! Priestesses served for two or three years and then left the temple to marry, untouched by any man! Papalopil knew that on rare occasions an *auianime* might find herself with child. On even rarer occasions, that pregnancy might be ended. But having a child was highly valued among the Mexica, even for a courtesan. And mothers who died in childbirth were honored like warriors. They went straight to the sun when they died. Something else was going on. The shock must have shown on her face, because Mama Amoxtli grunted and Cuicatl's sobs became louder.

"Control yourself, Cuicatl!" the elder priestess ordered. "If anyone hears you, we are all lost." Cuicatl took several deep breaths and sat back. The three again sat in silence until the water began to boil. Mama Amoxtli took the pot from the fire and carefully measured out some of the root that had been ground to powder. She added this to dried leaves from a packet she had taken from the herb chest. She carefully crushed the leaves and tossed them into the steaming water.

"Tell Papalopil the story. She is the one who will take care of you until it is over." She tucked the hair that had fallen to cover her face behind her ears and sat back. "I'll rest for a moment and then return to the temple before my absence is noted."

It was then that Papalopil noticed how tired she looked. This was difficult for her as well, difficult and dangerous.

"My blood is late because I fell in love."

"It was not love that put you in this condition," Mama Amoxtli corrected her.

"I fell in love with a man, and he with me. And we lay together, even though that is forbidden," Cuicatl confessed.

"Love is more than stolen moments of pleasure, Child. It is also sacrifice and commitment," the elder priestess chided her. "Your man can only offer you the briefest of moments. And now he cannot even give you that."

"If you love each other, why not marry?" Papalopil could not restrain herself. "Leave the temple early and marry."

"He is married," Cuicatl confessed.

"Then leave the temple and become his concubine. There is no shame in being the formal concubine of an honorable man." Papalopil still did not understand.

"He is a not a rich man. He cannot afford a concubine. The laws are strict that a man may only have one woman unless he can afford to keep more decently."

"Then he should not have…" Papalopil broke off, finally realizing the depth of the problem.

"They will both be stoned to death for adultery," said Mama Amoxtli wearily. "Her pregnancy is their death sentence. And then there will be two people dead, plus his wife a widow without support, and two children without a father. Now tell me, where is the sense in that?" She got to her feet slowly. "Papalopil, stay with her until this is over. She must drink the tea every four hours until her cramps are strong and the bleeding begins. Keep a pot near, as she will start vomiting soon. Make no noise, either of you. It needs to look and sound like no one is here.

"Cuicatl, take your clothes off. You do not want blood on them. Is your belt cotton?" When the girl nodded in the affirmative, she said, "Good. Roll it up and bite down on it if you feel you might scream. When it is all done, everything must be cleaned so there is no trace of what happened here. There will be a great deal of blood and some clots. What has been growing inside of her will be no bigger than half your little fingernail, Papalopil. You may confuse it with a clot, but make sure it is there.

"I am off to the temple now. I will sleep there tonight. When you are finished, Cuicatl, come to the temple. Papalopil, you may go home and sleep. We will never speak of this day again. May Xochiquetzal be with you both."

After she left, the two girls stared at each other for a moment. They were now bound together in a way neither could have imagined that morning. Papalopil poured a cup of tea and handed it to Cuicatl. The first sip made the girl gag, but she managed to drink the whole cup. She removed her clothes, folded them, and laid them carefully on the chest of herbs.

"Why did she pick you to help?" she asked Papalopil. "I am grateful to you, but I am curious."

"You need not be grateful. I may be a temple dancer but I am also a slave. I do whatever Mama Amoxtli tells me to do." She paused for a moment before adding, "I think perhaps she also chose me because she wants to teach me a lesson about love."

"Are you in love too?"

"No. And she does not want me to be."

After several hours, Papalopil heated the tea again. Time passed very slowly for the girls. Cuicatl lay with her back to the door; Papalopil rested against the adobe wall, each lost in her own thoughts. The only light came from the cracks in the wooden door and the small fire for the tea in the middle of the dirt floor.

Finally the cramping began. Papalopil held the young priestess' hair back as she vomited and wiped her face with a wet cloth. She held her hands as the cramps doubled her over and the poor girl's body twisted in pain. She prepared fresh tea and held the cup while Cuicatl drank. She whispered encouraging words as the girl bit into her cotton belt and soothing ones when she collapsed between contractions. She grabbed a few minutes of sleep when Cuicatl did, and tried to ignore the hunger that began to present itself. The night seemed endless.

Just before dawn, it was over. Cuicatl lay on a mat, too exhausted to move. Papalopil had scraped the floor where the pool of blood had seeped into the dirt and put the scrapings into a broken pot she found by the door. In the poor light, it was difficult to see exactly what went into the pot, but she was fairly sure she had everything. She found sage leaves in the chest of herbs and burned a few to rid the place of the smell of fresh blood. The broken pot she slipped into a canal several blocks away, taking care that traders coming to set up in the market did not see her. Then she went to the aqueduct and brought back fresh water to bathe Cuicatl.

"I need to get back to the temple," Cuicatl told her when all was done. "Mama Amoxtli may be able to cover up my absence for one day, but not two. I must be seen doing my regular duties."

"You are a priestess and should not be seen walking alone in public," Papalopil responded thoughtfully. "I will go with you. You must be very careful of your reputation now. We should carry something so it looks as if Mama Amoxtli sent us here on an errand."

The two girls walked through the streets of Tenochtitlan to the temple of Xochiquetzal, carrying a folded blanket and a basket of sage leaves. When they arrived, Cuicatl went out on the patio, where Mama Amoxtli was leading all the priestesses and those in training in a guided meditation. Papalopil paused by a small interior fountain to splash some water on her face and clear her thoughts. The cool water felt refreshing until she felt the yellow powder from the day before caked on her cheeks. She scrubbed at her skin, wanting nothing more than a good bath, but that would have to wait. She was patting her face dry with her skirt when a large form appeared in the Temple's main doorway.

She recognized the man outlined against the sun immediately and let out a small gasp of fear. Had Lord Atlatzin come to complain to the authorities that she had been following him? She had tried to be so careful not to let him notice her. But here he was, in Xochiquetzal's temple! Mama Amoxtli might be understanding, but if the authorities heard what she had been doing, they would not be. Papalopil rushed to intercept Atlatzin before the women on the patio knew he was there.

"My Lord, forgive me," she began. But with a wave if his fan, he dismissed her apology, and she realized with relief that he had not recognized her.

"I have come to speak secrets to the goddess," he announced.

"My Lord?"

"The goddess. I come to speak to her. I was told you provide that service here, no?"

She stared at him in momentary confusion until what he said began to make sense. She knew of the practice, but was surprised to see a man requesting it, especially the leader of the Emperor's Jaguar Warriors. He was one of the most powerful men in the known world. Why would he need to speak secrets to the goddess of love and beauty? She collected her thoughts and responded to his query.

"Of course, my Lord. We do. If you will wait, I will call..." But he interrupted her again.

"I have no time to wait. I am expected at the Palace. I would have preferred a priestess from the *pipiltin*," he said looking at her soiled dress, "but I suppose it does not really make a difference. I am in a hurry and I need to talk to the Goddess now. Is there a problem?" He threw his cloak back over his shoulder and seemed to glare down at her arrogantly in the half-light.

It was that glare that decided her. She was no priestess, although clearly the man mistook her for one. She had no training for being the vehicle through which the goddess would hear his secrets, and had no idea what such a priestess did, other than sit and listen. But this was Lord Atlatzin! If the nobleman wanted to open his heart and share his inner most desires with Xochiquetzal, who was Papalopil to deny him? In fact, she mused to herself, perhaps his mistaking her for a priestess was a gift from the goddess herself. After all, as a child she was intended to be a priestess, not a slave. If her parents had not...

"Do we just stand here?" Atlatzin impatiently broke into her thoughts. "Is there not some place private where we can sit, or am I expected to stand?"

"Of course," she said quickly and led him to a dark corner near the storage rooms where they were unlikely to be seen, much less heard. "We will sit and you can say what brought you to the temple today."

"You know I have the right and even the obligation to kill you if you ever tell anyone anything of what I say, or even that I spoke secrets" he reminded her as he crouched on the stone floor "And I will do so without hesitation, should you betray me."

Papalopil, who had not thought about this aspect of her charade, stiffened, knowing it was too late to confess the deception. Fortunately, the dim light hid her reaction and she was able to swallow and softly reassure him. "Yes, my Lord. Your secrets belong to you and the Goddess alone. I am only a vehicle." She leaned back against the cool stone and silently questioned the wisdom of her impersonation. What Atlatzin said next commanded her full attention, even though the words were whispered.

"I am only here because I can speak to no one about my concerns for the Emperor. He is beginning to grow obsessed with omens and ancient myths. I have difficulty getting through to him and I fear he may do something we will all regret." Atlatzin peered at the small form sitting in the shadows but she made no sign. Apparently satisfied, he continued.

"Word has come from the coast of floating temples and flying canoes of enormous size. The Emperor believes these may be signs of Quetzalcoatl's return."

This time he saw the woman's eyes fly open.

Papalopil was startled. She had expected the man to speak of personal things, as women did on the infrequent occasions when they came with whispers for the goddess's ear. She had almost hoped for confessions of desire. She certainly had not expected to hear things like this!

"Temples cannot float. Nor do canoes fly!" She spoke before thinking and felt him watching her. She hastily dropped her eyes and reproached herself. She was supposed to be an ear for the goddess, not her mouth.

But Atlatzin continued thoughtfully, apparently not taken aback by her outburst. "Of course not, so there has to be a practical explanation for what was seen. That was what I assumed. On the other hand, the priests say when Quetzalcoatl left this land, he floated away on a raft made of living snakes. No one alive has ever seen such a thing, but snakes do swim. I suppose it could be true."

Papalopil kept silent. She had learned these stories too; one could hardly grow up in a temple and not hear them. She had never stopped to think about whether or not they were true.

"My concern is that the canoes, or whatever they were, apparently carried strange men. The Emperor seems to feel this might be Quetzalcoatl's return. If that is true, he believes he must prepare gifts and then prepare to hand the Mexica Empire over to the returned god. But I argue that these strange men could simply be warriors from a tribe new to us. They have not yet landed, but we should be preparing for war, not battling indecision.

"The priests are no help. They moan and add to the Emperor's confusion. I know he was a great warrior when he was young, but that was years ago. Now I see him tremble with fear and he seeks the guidance of sacred mushrooms and omens. I am his war counselor, but he barely listens to me! Yet the priests have his attention."

There was both anger and frustration in his voice and Papalopil felt an irrational urge to touch his hand, as though a touch could drain the tension from his body like removing the plug on a water gourd. She fought the urge, knowing it would be completely inappropriate, and probably misunderstood. Instead of reaching out, she held herself very still.

"They have not yet landed, but they will. Why else would they be here, whoever they are? They should be met with my Jaguar Warriors, courteously, of course, until we know their intentions. But they should be met with strength. If they arrive on the day foretold and we decide it is Quetzalcoatl, the warriors can be there to honor the god. If not, well..." his voice drifted off and he paused.

"But Moctezuma seems incapable of making a decision," he finally concluded. "I have never seen him like this and it pains me."

Papalopil was surprised at the informal way Lord Atlatzin referred to the Emperor. He must be very troubled indeed to speak of him in this manner in front of her.

"I must be very careful. I cannot let him know I am growing impatient with him. With the priests I can show the frustration they cause me, but not Moctezuma. I dare not let him see that I grow frustrated or that I question him. I may question these strange events, I may even question whether it is the god returned. But I cannot, I dare not question my Emperor. And the problem is I know not how to best be of service to him now. What counsel can I give if he cannot hear me because he is afraid? How can I help him?"

Papalopil realized two things immediately. The man crouched next to her was vulnerable in ways she had never imagined. He was of the *pipiltin*, leader of the Jaguar Warriors! No one questioned his courage or his honor. Yet like any commoner, or even like a slave, he could not say what he thought. It was too dangerous. She had never considered that.

At the same time, the man truly cared about the Emperor. She could hear it in his voice. He was frustrated because he could not serve as he thought best, but he also cared. He cared that the Emperor was afraid. He was angry that the priests upset him. He might even be a little jealous that the Emperor sought the advice of his priests over that of his counselors. Atlatzin was clearly seeking help. What would a real priestess say? Before the thought was fully formed, the nobleman stood up, as though their session was ended.

"I cannot greet the strangers with my warriors without the Emperor ordering it. There is nothing I can do but wait, and waiting eats away at me like the wasting disease.

"I know not why I came here. I thought it might help, perhaps clear my mind so that I would know what to do, how to reach Moctezuma through the mushroom cloud that engulfs him. But Xochiquetzal cannot help me. She cannot tell me what to do when those strange men land." He reached in his belt for payment when Papalopil interrupted him.

"Test them," she said hesitantly.

"What?"

"Test them," she repeated more firmly. "If the Emperor wants to give them gifts, give them something that Quetzalcoatl would not possibly accept. That should tell you if they are simply strange men or not."

"Of course!" He pounced on the idea. 'I will suggest it in a way the Emperor believes is his own idea." He threw a small bag in Papalopil's lap. "A gift for the goddess!" he said and whirled around to leave.

She watched him as he passed the main altar and out through the entrance, walking softly and making no sound on the rough stone. He moves like a jungle cat, Papalopil thought. He was handsome and surprisingly vulnerable, but he was still arrogant. And there was something else, something that he was not saying. She had no idea what it was, but it was part of the reason he came to speak secrets that day. She had been a slave almost all her life and one thing that slaves learned was how to read people who had power over them. Papalopil could tell when someone above her station was withholding some important information. There was something else important, some secret that was eating at away at Lord Atlatzin.

She sighed and stretched out her cramped legs, as she wondered what in the goddess's name she had gotten herself into.

CHAPTER NINE

In the great school called the *calmecac*, Atlatzin again studied a painted scroll that told the story of Quetzalcoatl's return. At his feet lay the scrolls that held the legends of the beginnings of the world and prophecies of its destruction. The colorful rolls of bark and leather recounted the deaths of the four preceding suns, suns destroyed by jaguars, by hurricanes, by flood and by fiery rain in turn. This was the age of the fifth sun, the last that would ever be. This age would end in earthquakes that would shake the stars and sun from the sky. It would be the final end. Nothing would survive, for nothing was eternal – not the tired earth, not the gods, not even time itself.

In back of the nobleman stood the tall shelves that held the records of the past *katun*, the last ten-year cycle. Here were the scrolls telling of the decade's Flower Wars, trade agreements, alliances, and the strange omens so disturbing to Moctezuma. Behind these shelves stood still others stacked with scrolls, and behind those, even more. It was easy for Atlatzin to ignore the soft drone of students' voices as they memorized the glorious tales of the Olmec, the Maya, the Toltec, and the Mexica. The sound rose and fell in a rhythm that was familiar and somehow comforting. He had learned all the same chants as a boy and they could not distract him now.

He sat on a low platform in the library and studied the scroll in his hands. It was a painting of Quetzalcoatl that showed his return. The god was depicted in tight-fitting warrior's clothing, but instead of being made of bright feathers as they were usually portrayed, they looked like they were spun of black cotton. The god's small headdress was the color of the sun and there were no long feathers streaming from it to proclaim his identity and rank. Atlatzin puzzled over the strange costume. It was unlike any other worn by the gods. He wondered if this particular scroll had been altered back when history was rewritten.

The nobleman sighed deeply and stretched his cramped back. He had been bent over pouring over the scrolls for hours, trying to find similarities between the drawings and the colored visions in the crystal skull. His eyes darted down the long hall as a figure appeared, but it was only a student exchanging scrolls.

It was the day after the one set for Quetzalcoatl's return. If the night came without the arrival of a runner bearing dreaded news, the Empire would be safe for another fifty-two years, until the great wheel brought that day and year around together again. Atlatzin bent over the painted figure of the god again. He was determined to behave as though this day were like any other, although it was true that he had drawn more than usual of his own blood that morning at sacrifice. He moved his tongue gingerly in his mouth. It was still slightly swollen from the bloodletting. He sighed again and reached for another scroll.

It was then that he saw the runner coming toward him.

On the day Nine Wind in a One Reed year, strange men landed their huge canoes and set foot upon Mexica land. They wore tight black clothing and that part of their faces not covered by thick beards was strangely pale. The first runner in the relay had not paused to see more before setting out for Tenochtitlan. Other runners were on their way at regular intervals. Atlatzin had planned well, but all the planning in the world could not change one inescapable fact. The first part of the prophecy had come true.

"There have been so many Great Speakers!" cried Moctezuma as he paced the floor before his advisors, "Why should the destruction of our empire be my fate? Why does this happen during my reign? My turn of the wheel?" He looked around, as if demanding a response to a question that could not be answered. "Hummingbird's priests have offered to hide me. They promise to show me the way to the sun's golden abode in the East, the realm of the rain god in the South, or the palace of the maize goddess in the West. They even assure me I can reach Mictlan without harm. Shall I do this? Shall I go to this northern land of the dead?"

Atlatzin quickly took in the frightened faces that surrounded him and decided to speak first. "There is nowhere that so famous a lord could hide and not be discovered, *Tlatoani*. Your place is here in Tenochtitlan with your people. They need your strength and wisdom."

"You believe I will escape Quetzalcoatl's wrath, Atlatzin?"

"If it is the god who comes out of the East, he has no reason to destroy you, my Lord. You have offered sacrifices in his temple."

"What do you know of gods?" Moctezuma demanded wildly. He paused to gain control over himself, but Atlatzin could see his hands shake as he stroked the red and yellow feathers in his fan. "Quetzalcoatl has forbidden the act of human sacrifice. Huitzilopochtli demands it. I am caught between two gods. Can you resolve the puzzle?" He shook his head in frustration.

"We are taught the sun cannot shine without the sacred fruit, yet this is what Feathered Serpent will not permit. How can we tell which god's commandment to follow? Were the Flower

Wars, the sacrifices wrong? Is it all a lie or will the god destroy the sun?" He slapped his fan hard against his thigh breaking it. "My laws are respected throughout the world. The Mexica have neither theft nor murder. But if there is no need for sacrifices, then we are all murderers. The priests tell me this is blasphemy! But will Quetzalcoatl forgive those he sees as murderers and blasphemers?"

Atlatzin was silent then. Moctezuma had given voice to some of his own hidden thoughts. The counselor kept his eyes on the broken fan and knew there was no need to respond.

"I have no choice but to abdicate and turn the Empire over to its rightful ruler. The Great Speakers have always been caretakers for the Mexica. Quetzalcoatl is the rightful ruler. I shall give to him what is his."

"But we are not yet certain it is Quetzalcoatl who has arrived," Hummingbird's High Priest put in quickly.

"The god or his emissary. It was all foreseen." Moctezuma shook his head and his crystal lip plug caught and bent the light, scattering small rainbows across the Great Speaker's face. Atlatzin gave a small start, as the colors brought back the memory of the crystal he had recently held.

"The priest speaks wisely, my Lord," he said, gathering his wandering thoughts back to focus. "While it is possible the god returns, it is equally possible these are mortal men dressed like the returning god to deceive us. They must be tested. Send ambassadors, magicians and priests. See whose magic is stronger. Pretend to welcome these strangers. Question and observe them all the while. Let us offer them food that has secretly been sprinkled liberally with human blood. Quetzalcoatl would know and refuse to eat. But we have no proof this is Quetzalcoatl yet. Let us test their divinity."

Huitzilopochtli's priest agreed quickly. "They may be imposters, Great Moctezuma. They must be tested."

The Emperor nodded slowly and, for the first time since the audience began, Atlatzin was relieved to see the strain etched into his face lessen some. "Very well. We need to gain time and distract them. Have the gifts I ordered sent to them along with slaves to attend to their needs. Make sure magicians are concealed among them. If it is not the god, I want strong enchantments to make these strangers leave my land. I want spies to watch and report their every move." This was directed to Atlatzin. "I want to know the smallest detail of their behavior. If their sleep is restless, I would know of it. If they indulge in pleasure, make sure I am told. If they defecate frequently or if they do not defecate at all, report it to me. I want information daily. It will be difficult, this testing. And it must be discreet. If Feathered Serpent is among them, he may take offense."

"If they are mere men, they will never know they have been tested, my Lord." Atlatzin made his obeisance and Moctezuma returned to the Black Room to pray.

As the nobleman passed through the *zócalo* on his way to implementing the Emperor's orders, he came upon a small crowd cheering on a group of boys playing ball.

How strange, Atlatzin thought as he passed them. Life goes on as usual when there are such momentous doings afoot.

It was late at night when the messenger arrived from the coast. Moctezuma was awakened from a fitful sleep and ordered that his advisors and the messenger gather atop the great staircase of the twin temples. There the messenger was blessed and sanctified with the blood of fresh sacrifices, for he was witness to portentous events. It was possible he had seen men from a distant and unknown tribe, but it was also possible he had rested his eyes upon the god and heard his divine voice, so offerings were also sent to Feathered Serpent's temple. Atlatzin stood by the Emperor in the shadow cast by the resin torches as the messenger told his disturbing news.

The arrivals on the coast were dressed in black. Some wore strange metal on their chest and head. Only their faces were visible, and they were the color of pale maize dough. Some had black hair, some yellow like the sun. There were even those among them who appeared to have black skin like the fearful Night Gods! When the strangers mounted the huge hornless deer they brought with them, they were roof-high and ran like the wind itself.

At this point, Moctezuma gave Atlatzin a significant look, and the nobleman knew what he was thinking. It was no wonder the strangers rode so quickly. Quetzalcoatl was Lord of the Winds. It was yet another reason for the Emperor to believe the god had returned. Moctezuma signaled for the messenger to continue.

"The strangers had with them dogs of monstrous size. These had long folded ears and tongues that lolled out from between great hanging chops. Their eyes were yellow and gave off sparks of fire, and their coats were spotted, almost like that of a jaguar's. The strangers took a wooden figure of a goddess from one of their floating temples and performed a religious ceremony before it. They called the goddess Our Lady, but it was not Tonantzin, Mother of the Mexica. Still, not wanting to appear rude, we Mexica joined in. Then the leader of the strangers nailed two crossed pieces of wood to a spiny ceiba tree, as if they knew the tree was sacred to our ancestors. They bowed before the tree as well.

"After their religious rites were done, our ambassadors welcomed the arrivals with a feast. Turkey roasted in chili sauce was spread out before them, with eggs, tortillas, avocados, potatoes, and fruits of differing sweetness. They ate the eggs and fruits without hesitation. The woman translator ate the turkey, but when the one who is the leader tasted the meat, he spit it quickly out and appeared very angry. His men seemed to find it humorous, but after that, they too turned up their noses at the turkey.

"Had blood been sprinkled on the food?" demanded Atlatzin.

The messenger looked up in fear and explained that it had only been sprinkled on the turkey and then covered with the chilies it had been cooked with so the strangers would not see or smell it.

"It is Quetzalcoatl, then," cried Moctezuma in anguish, "the god or his emissary. His magic told him about the blood!"

"My Lord, it still could be a man dressed as the god," insisted Atlatzin. "This was no true test of divinity. Perhaps they had never seen a turkey and did not know what they were eating. Or perhaps the chilies were too strong for them. This alone proves nothing!"

But the rest of the messenger's news did nothing to calm the Emperor. After the turkey was refused, the strangers took out a log made of unknown metal and lit a flame at one end. The log belched thunder and lightning! One end seemed to explode and something hit a tree in the distance, turning it to dust! The smoke was so thick and bitter that the ambassadors choked and got dizzy. They were given a sweet red drink that seemed to clear the throat, but it quickly confused the tongue. After drinking more, the feeling of well-being dissolved and one of the men fell down as though he had been drinking *pulque*.

After this, the leader of the arrivals dressed himself in hard and shiny clothing and challenged the emissaries to combat. Naturally, the Mexica could not respond. How could a mortal fight a god or his emissary? And if the leader were not the god or his emissary, he was still someone the Emperor had ordered them to welcome with great hospitality. The magicians might be testing his divinity, but the ambassadors were to act as though it had been proven. Seeing they refused to fight, the leader of the strangers threw back his head and laughed, and the ambassadors were sent on their way home.

"You saw them all. Is the leader Quetzalcoatl?" demanded Moctezuma of the poor man.

He shuffled his feet uncomfortably on the stones and looked around himself as though seeking help. Finally, he said, "Great Moctezuma, if he is, something most strange has happened. He has forgotten how to speak Nahuatl. He uses a barbaric unknown tongue to his men. He uses the slave woman to translate his language into Nahuatl."

Moctezuma stared at the man in surprise. How could the god forget one of his own languages?

"There is more, my Lord. He says there is only one true god and all the others are lies, but he worships before a goddess. He never mentioned the name Quetzalcoatl. He calls himself Cortés."

"Cortés." Moctezuma tried the strange name. The sound of it was harsh against the stone walls of the temple and seemed to fade into a serpent's hiss. The Emperor looked around himself nervously and the torchlight gleamed in the sweat that suddenly covered his body.

"*Tlatoani*, this leader must be tested more fully!" Atlatzin spoke forcefully, willing the strength in his voice to reach the Emperor. "Perhaps you might welcome this Cortés as a god but continue to test him like a man."

Moctezuma nodded wearily, and the hand he raised seemed suddenly old. "Send him the jewels and clothing of Quetzalcoatl I ordered prepared with great courtesy. Let him wonder at our wealth and generosity. If he is a god, he will accept the gifts as his due. If a man, he will realize our magnificence and polite manner are signs of our superiority and be afraid of our strength. At the same time, send twenty cages of butterflies to Quetzalcoatl's main temple, Atlatzin, the rarest to be found. You take charge. I need to seek a vision to explain these events." The Great Speaker dismissed them and entered the Black Room to pray.

CHAPTER TEN

Two thousand Mexica servants were sent to wait upon the strangers. Among them were the magicians, spies, and priests. The attendants built a camp for Quetzalcoatl-Cortés and supplied food and necessities for him and his men. He was given a turquoise serpent mask with jade earplugs and a leg band of green stones and golden shells. A cape of quetzal feathers was placed on his shoulders and pearl-studded sandals on his feet. In return, the stranger sent Moctezuma a throne of wondrous dark blue stones flecked through with gold, a golden medal of a man mounted on a great deer and fighting a great winged snake, and a crimson hat of unknown cloth. He also sent him a metal headpiece called a helmet and asked that it be filled with gold dust.

"Hardly the demand of a god," Atlatzin pointed out in council, but Moctezuma shook his head and measured out the fine dust himself.

Among the servants, spies and enchanters was an Indian slave who was the same height and build as the one called Cortés. The slave fell sick and died, and Atlatzin's spies told him the magicians smiled at each other from behind their fans, thinking their magic was potent but mistook the target. But the pale man who was the leader of the strangers remained unaffected, and word was sent to Moctezuma that his magic was surprisingly strong.

"He may be a magician himself, as well as a warrior," insisted Atlatzin. "But I cannot believe he is a god. His appetites are too mortal. I hear the female slave who is his translator is also his concubine. Quetzalcoatl went into exile because he broke his vow of celibacy. The god would not take a woman on his return. And he drinks their red *pulque* to excess, my Lord. These things prove he is no god. We should fall upon them and destroy them now, before they grow stronger."

"And if he is Quetzalcoatl? Would you have us try to destroy the Lord of the Wind? The Breath of Life? I have no choice but to wait and see what will pass. It is the fate the stars decided for me on the day of my birth." Moctezuma withdrew again into the Black Room and Atlatzin was left to curse with frustration. He could not act directly without Moctezuma's orders. But, upon receiving the next intelligence report, he sent word to the princes of the Triple Alliance. They came to the Palace at once to confer with the Emperor.

"This Cortés has declared his desire to come to Tenochtitlan," Atlatzin informed them in a voice full of quiet anger.

"No!" cried Moctezuma when he heard. "I will not see him! Make him go away!"

"If he is the god and so determined, nothing we can do will stop him," said the Prince of Tlacopan in resignation.

Cacamatzin, Prince of Texcoco, was persuaded differently. "He has never said he is Quetzalcoatl, but he might be the ambassador of some foreign lord, as some say he once confided. If that were true, courtesy demands that he be allowed to enter the city. Remember, the strangers are few and we are many. It would be safer to have the strangers here where we can control their actions than on the coast where we cannot. What can they do to us here?" He smiled at the others' fears before bending his head to smell the cone of roses in his hand.

"One should not admit to his house the very person who intends to take it from him. Perhaps we can dissuade him from coming." The Prince of Tlacopan looked from one ruler to the other. "Has anyone asked him to leave?"

Atlatzin snorted in disgust. "Throw them all back into the sea that brought them to our shores, my Lords. Texcoco is right about our numbers. They are only four hundred men and we are hundreds of thousands. Every day they are allowed to stay on our soil is an extra day they have to spy out the land and discover there are conquered tribes who would rise against us if they dared. Every day gives them time to make allies and foment rebellion."

Moctezuma shook his head slowly. "We cannot understand the truth behind the events on the coast. Whether the strangers' leader is Quetzalcoatl himself or just his emissary matters little," he told the men around him. "He had already assumed sovereignty on the coast where he landed. If he comes to Tenochtitlan, I will be blamed for permitting him to take over. I have no choice but to return the Empire to its rightful ruler. Still, some will call me traitor. My only hope lies in discouraging this Cortés from coming to the city. Perhaps he will be content with that part of the Empire on the coast. After all, we have conquered foreign territories and extended our boundaries to the seas, far beyond what Quetzalcoatl once ruled. It is not unreasonable to think that this stranger could be persuaded to leave Tenochtitlan alone. And if not, and if he is indeed the god, he will certainly not allow the conquered tribes to revolt against the city he is coming to claim. It would not make sense.

"Think, Atlatzin. Why should the god encourage or even tolerate rebellion in his own empire?" asked Moctezuma with a forced smile. "There is no logic in that. I fear you are obsessed with the idea that this stranger is an ordinary man."

"It has not yet been proven otherwise, my Lord," the counselor insisted stubbornly.

"Then we will continue the testing. And we will ask this Cortés to leave as Cacamatzin suggests. Who knows? If we are courteous enough, perhaps they will return to their floating temples and take them elsewhere."

Atlatzin caught himself staring at his ruler in dismay and quickly dropped his eyes before his gaffe was noted. Moctezuma seemed to be alternating between fear and fantasy. And there was nothing Atlatzin could do but follow the Emperor's orders.

Envoys politely told the strangers that the journey to Tenochtitlan would be long and arduous, and food difficult to obtain. It was all together impractical for them to trouble themselves with the journey. They were informed that they might stay where they were until rested enough to continue their travels.

Atlatzin was not surprised by the reply. Cortés assured the envoys that the trip to Tenochtitlan would be no trouble and that the lord he served would be sorely disappointed if his representative failed to meet the Lord of the Mexica face to face.

"Who is this lord?" demanded Moctezuma, "Was he named?" The messenger shook his head. That had not been part of the message.

It was the other part of the response that sent Moctezuma scurrying to the Black Room. There must be an end to human sacrifices, announced the message from Cortés. Huitzilopochtli was an evil god and must be replaced with the son of the goddess they called Our Lady.

Atlatzin could see that the Great Speaker was not greatly surprised at the message. Whether the stranger was Quetzalcoatl's servant, his messenger, or the god himself, it made little difference to the Emperor. Feathered Serpent forbade human sacrifice.

"This is the day foretold. I must return the land to the god who refuses sacred fruit. I will have no choice, though I live in history as a traitor to my people. All I can do is delay the inevitable. But though I lose my throne, I will not make it too easy for the god.

"All supplies we are giving to the strangers will cease today. Those who serve them will disappear during the darkness of the night. Let this Cortés find his own food and his own way to Tenochtitlan."

Cortés' response was swift in coming. Spies reported that he ran his floating temples ashore and put the splintered wood to flame. Finally it was clear he had no intention of leaving, not then, not a year from then. The action had been bold and daring. Atlatzin had to admire it, even though he knew it meant the strangers had no intention of retreating. This Cortés would come to Tenochtitlan. Man or god, he was a formidable warrior.

The Emperor's advisor was not surprised to discover the strangers formed an alliance with Cempoala, capital of the Totonacs. He was present when two of Moctezuma's tax collectors arrived with their shocking tale. Five of them had gone to collect duties from Cempoala. Instead of showing their usual fear and respect, the vassal tribe had turned on Moctezuma's representatives and thrown them into prison! The Totonacs would never have dared to commit such an outrage had they not been encouraged by the strangers. As he listened, Atlatzin suspected the two men had been allowed to escape so they could carry a message to Moctezuma. Cortés had made a point of telling them his intention to see Tenochtitlan.

The taxmen brought other news with them that made Moctezuma shrink back farther into his feather cloak. Cortés had sent fifty of his men to smash the sacred images of the Cempoalan gods. They set their own altar to Our Lady on top of the temple where Huitzilopochtli had claimed his sacred fruit. The god's priests had been forced to cut their hair, dress in white, and serve as acolytes to the wooden goddess!

Atlatzin struggled to hide his impatience when he finally realized that Moctezuma would not, could not act, and it would not matter what his counselors advised.

"It is to be expected that Quetzalcoatl's emissary would want the images of other gods destroyed. Our Lady must be Chimalma, the god's mother," he told Atlatzin. "It is a mystery why Cortés has asked the Totonacs to worship her and her wooden cross, but who are we to understand the ways of the gods? To attack him would be to invite disaster," he said plaintively.

But when it was announced that the strangers had begun their march inland, the Emperor changed his mind again and was more willing to listen to his advisors.

"If you will not order your armies to attack, let us encourage your allies to do so, my Lord," pleaded Atlatzin. "The strangers take a path through the lands of the Tlaxcalans. Let the Enemies of the House try to destroy them. If Cortés speaks for the god or if he is the god's emissary, Tlaxcala will pay for the attack, not the Mexica.

"I find it strange that he has never named the lord he serves. If he is but a man, he will be destroyed by the Tlaxacalans and our problem will be solved."

"Why would Tlaxcala take so great a risk?"

"We could promise them lower taxation, *Tlatoani*. Perhaps we could exempt them from their usual tribute of sacrifices for Hummingbird if they succeed."

"That will interfere with the proper celebration of the feast days, Atlatzin."

"Great Moctezuma, if these strangers are not stopped, there may be no more feast days!" Atlatzin pointed out bitterly.

"Very well," said the Emperor wearily with a wave of his hand. "Send word to the Council of Four in Tlaxcala." He sipped his cacao through a golden straw and Atlatzin knew he had been dismissed.

On his way to the *telpochcalli*, the nobleman decided to increase his network of runners. He wanted news of the strangers three times a day. If there were tribes that aided them, if skirmishes were fought, if the Tlaxcalans were punished for victory over them, Atlatzin wanted to know as soon as possible. Quetzalcoatl might be Lord of the Winds, but the Jaguar Runners were the fastest humans alive. In the meantime, he decided to select a young student to personally attend the Emperor night and day. There was one he had sponsored at school who had an excellent memory and could recite long verses after hearing them just once without coaching. The boy Tepin was quick and was especially loyal to him. He could be with the Emperor when Atlatzin could not, and, as a servant, could come and go unseen. Since he was small for his age and looked younger than he really was, it would never occur to anyone that he was a spy.

Not a spy, Atlatzin corrected himself quickly. Moctezuma was the Great Speaker and his word was law, but Atlatzin was decidedly uncomfortable with the way he had been acting regarding the strangers. Tepin would not be told to spy on the Emperor; it was not a question of that, Atlatzin told himself. But the nobleman was convinced he could be of greater help to the Emperor he served if he had more information about what the man was thinking. The boy could help with that.

CHAPTER ELEVEN

The runners brought news that the Tlaxcalans had met the advancing strangers halfway between the coast and Tenochtitlan. Three thousand warriors had surprised the strangers in ambush. But the warriors' obsidian clubs and leather slings were a poor match for the sticks that spit fire, the strange sideways bows, the thunder logs, and the long knives of magic metal. The Tlaxcalans fought bravely until nightfall, when their religion forbade them to continue fighting.

The next day, the news was even worse. An advance force of six thousand Tlaxcalans attacked, but the strangers quickly formed a square, which opened only to allow the charge of the frightful giant dogs and riders on the magic deer. One of the hornless beasts was killed and the Tlaxcalans were elated. It proved that the terrible creatures were mere animals. Its head and hooves were offered to the gods as the battle continued. But the strangers must have realized that the warriors in the brightest capes and feathers were leaders. As they rushed in to take prisoners, the firesticks exploded and the Tlaxcalan leaders died in disproportionate numbers. The metal logs thundered death into the midst of the warriors, who grouped together in masses, as was their custom. Word spread that the strangers knew no fear and were impervious to magicians' spells and warriors' knives alike. Even the leader's concubine carried a shield and weapons of the magic metal into battle.

The runners reported that there were those who said the strangers' numbers were decreasing and argued they could be killed like any warriors. It was even whispered that they must bury their dead secretly at night so the Tlaxcalans would believe they had not died. Atlatzin's spies told him the Lords of Tlaxcala were divided on this. Some argued that the strangers would surely honor their dead if they had any! They would not bury them secretly at night and so shame them. No one could be that dishonorable! It was confusing that the strangers took no prisoners. It was as though they preferred to kill their enemies needlessly, rather than taking them for sacrifices. It appeared they had never been taught the rules of correct warfare.

Atlatzin stood with Moctezuma and his council as they heard that the Lords of Tlaxcala themselves had led sixty thousand warriors into battle. They fought honorably, but there was division in their command. Two of the Council of Four decided Cortés was indeed Quetzalcoatl and withdrew their troops. Another had his magicians cast spells on the invaders. When he saw Cortés had no fear of magic, he decided that the stranger must have greater magic of his own. Why else would he be unafraid? The third lord withdrew from the battle. The final Lord of Tlaxcala fell in a mass of bloodied feathers and the battle was over.

The last runner reported that Cortés met with the remaining members of the Council outside the city. He spoke of the great lord he served across the sea. The Council announced they realized that they had risen against Quetzalcoatl's emissary, and were quick to swear allegiance to the god and the man who served him. They paid obeisance and invited him into their city. Everything they had was at his disposition, they said: their homes, their food, their treasures, their armies.

"But before he entered the city," the runner told Atlatzin and the Emperor, "the Tlaxcalan Council confessed that *Tlatoani* Moctezuma had offered to reduce their taxes if they attacked the strangers.

"The one called Cortés grew very angry when he heard this," the spy reported. "And the Tlaxcalan Council was pleased to see it."

Atlatzin swore silently. Of course. The Tlaxcalans had always resented the taxes levied by Moctezuma. If they had defeated the strangers, all would have been well. Now, however, it would be open rebellion. It had not seriously occurred to him that Tlaxcala would be defeated. They were sixty-six thousand warriors strong and the strangers four hundred! Now, their surrender was throwing the Emperor into a panic. Atlatzin could hear it in his voice when he ordered a message sent to the strangers.

Moctezuma sent congratulations to Cortés on his victory and pointed out that the Mexica and the Tlaxcalans had long been enemies. The defeated tribe was made of treacherous liars, the Emperor stressed in his message, and Cortés was advised to deal with them very harshly.

Atlatzin was not present when Moctezuma sent a second message, but the young student he had installed as the Emperor's attendant was. Through him, Atlatzin learned that the Great Speaker sent word to Cortés that the Mexica would pay an annual tribute in gold, silver, precious stones, cotton, mantles, and *cacao* if he would stay away from Tenochtitlan. He promised to give all that was asked if the strangers would go away and not return.

A response came quickly. Cortés thanked the Emperor for his offer but said he had to postpone any decision until after settling affairs with Tlaxcala. Word soon came that he had again started to march and would soon arrive in the city of Cholula.

Still Moctezuma held his warriors in check. Atlatzin doubled his runners and spies.

His frustration doubled when he learned that the stranger had taken with him six thousand Tlaxcalan warriors. These he left at a distance from the city, knowing that the Cholulans and Tlaxcalans were sworn enemies. The Lords of Cholula sent to Tenochtitlan for help, but in spite of Atlatzin's advice, Moctezuma refused to raise his hand. The city was forced to welcome Cortés and his followers. The Cholulans continued to take defensive measures against the Tlaxcalans, who camped outside their walls. Atlatzin learned they had blocked many of their streets and dug hidden pits filled with spikes. They brought in supplies of stones, and women and children were sent out of the city. Cortés was treated as a honored guest, but the Cholulans refused to trust the Tlaxcalans.

What happened next was terrible and convinced Atlatzin more than ever that Cortés could not possibly be representing Quetzalcoatl. The stranger called the Lords of Cholula together to discuss his departure. Without giving them a chance to say a word, he ordered them seized and bound. His soldiers fell upon the servants in the courtyard and signaled to the waiting Tlaxcalans beyond the gate. The enemies of Cholula poured into the city and, within a few hours, three thousand people lay dead. After the town was looted, the imprisoned lords were set free and ordered to call the people who had escaped to come back into the city. They returned quietly and went about their business, as if grateful that the god was no longer angry at them.

The massacre at Cholula did not horrify Moctezuma. He explained to Atlatzin that he had always suspected that Quetzalcoatl must have a dark side as well as one of light. Although Cholula had welcomed Cortés and given him all he asked for, somehow the people had incurred the god's displeasure. They had been forced to pay the penalty demanded by his divine wrath.

"Cortés will march on us with Tlaxcalan and Totonac warriors, my Lord," warned Atlatzin. "If you will not allow us to attack, we must at least do something to protect the city." Moctezuma was deaf to his words. He seemed to be unable to see beyond the walls of the Black Room. Then Hummingbird's High Priest added his voice to Atlatzin's. Huitzilopochtli's statue had been thrown down in Cholula. A wooden cross stood where the sacrificial stone had lain.

"Invite this Cortés to Tenochtitlan, *Tlatoani*. Once he enters the valley between the volcanoes without his allies, Huitzilopochtli will destroy him," the priest promised. "Hummingbird has always protected us. He led us here and claimed this land, this city, as his own. We are his people and he has never been defeated."

Six noblemen delivered Moctezuma's invitation. The slaves that followed them carried baskets of gold and jewelry and rich mantles. Atlatzin's spies were among them. The aristocrats bent down, touched the ground, and lifted the dust to their lips. Their faces were strained, but they bore themselves with dignity as they handed Cortés roses.

"Our Lord, the Great Moctezuma Xocoyotzin, Ninth Ruler of Tenochtitlan, sends these gifts with affectionate regards to you," said the man whose gold and feathered lip plug proclaimed him the group's leader. "He much regrets that the Cholulans have annoyed you. They are a tiresome people and you have not punished them enough. Count on his friendship. He invites you to the capital. Come when you like and he will do his best to entertain you. I am instructed to guide you by the shortest route. Food and drink will be provided at the stopping places for your comfort."

Word arrived at Tenochtitlan that the invitation had been accepted. To Atlatzin's relief, most of the Tlaxcalans and Totonacs were sent home. At least most of the enemy warriors would not be heading toward the capital. The conquerors of Cholula and their small escort marched through the pine forests and into the scrub belt between the two volcanoes. It began to snow as they reached the pass into the valley. The crater of Popocatépetl belched smoke and flames and an icy wind moaned below in the pines. True to Moctezuma's word, food and warmth awaited the strangers each night at rest houses inside the valley. So did Atlatzin's runners and spies. The strangers reached the southern shore of the great salt lake, from where they could see the temples of Tenochtitlan.

They were met by a rich procession. A golden litter was lowered and a figure in quetzal feathers stepped out. The turquoise hanging from his septum proclaimed him the Great Speaker. Next to him stood the High Priest of Huitzilopochtli. The priest and Atlatzin had planned this last test carefully. The man who stood in the Emperor's cape was a magician. It was his intention to draw the stranger into a conversation, the words of which would create an enchantment. The conqueror of Tlaxcala and Cholula would be forced to return to the sea that delivered him, and the Mexica would be safe. The envoys, who had been alerted to the plan, dropped to the ground before Cortés. The High Priest made sure all was in order and then caught the imposter's eye and signaled to him to begin. But the woman who stood by Cortés' side suddenly pulled on his sleeve and whispered something in his ear. He stared at the magician angrily.

"Do you think me a fool? You send me an imposter and pretend he is the Emperor!" he roared. "I will meet the Lord of the Mexica in his city. The Great Emperor Carlos demands it! Tell that to your lord and do not annoy me with any more trickery!"

The High Priest abandoned the pretense and headed back to Tenochtitlan. But, as he informed Moctezuma and his counselors when he arrived, there was more to come and it was much worse.

"Last night as I prayed, I had a vision. A figure approached us as we were returning to the city. It wore only a loincloth tied around the waist by a grass rope. It halted in front of me and screamed like a man drunk with fury.

"'What, you have come again?'" The priest tried to imitate the figure's voice. "This time what is your errand? More gifts? Or has Moctezuma come to his senses? His errors, his guilt, all are past counting. He has given my people over to death! He has wrapped them in their shrouds!'

"Forgive me, Great Lord, these are his words, not mine," cried the High Priest in fear. "And then I saw he was no man but Huitzilopochtli himself who stood before me. I threw myself on the ground and prayed, but he continued to rant at me. I made a mat of grass for him and begged him to sit there while I offered him my blood. He would not even look at me!

"Opening his great mouth, he cried, 'All is over. The empire that was, is no longer and shall never be again. Too late! Too late! Look what is happening!'

"He pointed toward Tenochtitlan, and I thought I saw the city in flames. The temples of the gods were on fire and there was a terrible battle going on. I looked back and Huitzilopochtli had disappeared. He who had spoken was no more.

"Forgive me, *Tlatoani*." The High Priest rubbed his hands nervously in his black robe. "I must speak out and tell you what this means. Hummingbird, who once drove Quetzalcoatl from this land, is enraged at you for having allowed his emissary to return. By refusing to fight Feathered Serpent, you have gravely insulted the god who guides us. He has withdrawn his protection and is leaving the Mexica to our fate. The cosmic balance is no longer. It is over."

Moctezuma could not speak. He stood with his head down and his shoulders bent with a terrible weight. Atlatzin could tell what the Emperor was thinking. Although he was treated like a god, the man had been born a mortal. How could a mortal fight against the gods? Moctezuma had grown comfortable with the idea of his own divinity and suddenly he was being forced to face his own human frailty. If the Mexica had been abandoned, they would fall like crushed petals before the advancing god. There was no longer any hope. The Emperor's next words told Atlatzin he had guessed correctly.

"Perhaps he will not settle long in Tenochtitlan," Moctezuma finally said as he turned away from the tight lines of anger and disappointment etched on Atlatzin's face. "Cortés spoke of his leaving to my envoys, perhaps his presence will be a temporary thing. It would appear I have no recourse. I will attire myself to greet the god and welcome him personally to the city.

"Increase the sacrifices to both Huitzilopochtli and Quetzalcoatl in their temples," he said with great weariness. "Let blood flow without ceasing and a multitude of flowers cover the stench. I know not what else we can do."

The Lord of the Mexica walked slowly down the temple steps, his cape dragging behind him. A lone feather escaped its woven bed and drifted lazily in the air. In helpless resignation, Atlatzin watched as it floated down onto the sacrificial stone, and the blue plume turned dark with blood.

Atlatzin paced back and forth in front of the school for warriors but could not bring himself to go inside. He couldn't decide if he was angrier at the High Priest or at the Great Speaker. Both of them had decided to simply give up, to hand the Mexica Empire over to this Cortés. They could not even wait for Atlatzin's spy to arrive and give his report about what had occurred. What if the female translator had caught some kind of signal between the priest and the magician pretending to be the Emperor? What if there were a human explanation for Cortés knowing it was a trick? What had happened to the warrior Moctezuma had once been?

Abruptly, the nobleman wheeled around and headed for Xochiquezal's small temple. He would speak secrets with the goddess about all this. Last time, he was urged to test the strangers. Perhaps she could give some good advice again.

When he arrived, the temple seemed empty. He looked around for the young woman he considered "his priestess" but only saw a girl sweeping the flagstones before a side altar. Impatient, he turned to leave when he noticed a shadow against the wall in the temple patio. There she was, his priestess, weaving thread into fabric. When she saw him, Papalopil started to get up, hampered by the backstrap loom that anchored her to a post. He stopped her with a gesture.

"No need to rise. I would speak secrets."

"Forgive me, Lord Atlatzin, I cannot. I have a quota of weaving I must fill. I cannot stop to serve you today." She seemed nervous, but he dismissed it.

"Then I will sit here next to you and you continue to weave as I speak." Without waiting for her response, he flipped his cape out behind him and folded his long legs so that he sat close by her side. She seemed startled, but after a moment resumed rhythmically passing the shuttle through the threads on her loom.

"Things have gotten much worse since last I was here," he began. "We tested the strangers again and again, and each time they passed. Yet each time it could have been because the test was faulty or because we overlooked something. The Emperor first sent priceless gifts, basically bribes to keep the strangers away from Tenochtitlan. If anything, they served to whet the appetite of this Cortés. He became even more determined to come to the City." He paused to look at Papalopil, to see if she reacted. But she kept her eyes fixed on her weaving, so he continued.

"We got the Tlaxcalans to attack them. The strangers number only four hundred, yet they defeated thousands of Tlaxcalan warriors! I fail to understand how this could happen! Did I tell you they burned their floating temples that brought them here before they marched inland? They have no intention of leaving our land."

He knew the frustration was clear in his voice and this time she looked at him for a long moment. But she said nothing and resumed the slight rocking movement that tightened and loosened the threads of the loom so the shuttle could slip through.

"The Tlaxcalans told them we arranged the attack, and now they are allies of the strangers. They marched with them to Cholula and captured the city. And still the Emperor would not let my warriors attack!

"Finally, I managed to convince him to allow one last test. The High Priest and I sent someone, a magician, to pretend he was the Emperor, to confuse and bewitch him. But somehow Cortés saw through the pretense. And now the Emperor has given up! The High Priests had a vision that Huitzilopochtli has abandoned us because we did not fight. Whether this is true or not no longer matters because Moctezuma believes it! He has decided to welcome the stranger as Quetzalcoatl, to give him the Mexica Empire. No more tests, no tricks. Just surrender.

"I am a warrior who is not permitted to fight, an advisor whose advice is ignored! I have been proud to serve the Great Speaker. All I ever wanted was to be the perfect warrior for my emperor. But my emperor has grown old and weak, even more, he is afraid. And there is nothing I can do to help him now, nothing I can do to protect him from his own fears. I am helpless."

Papalopil's rocking ceased. She reached out and placed a gentle hand on his knee. He stared at it for a moment, not really seeing it, but feeling its warmth. Then he raised his eyes and for the first time looked into hers. He made no attempt to read the meaning of her gesture; he just looked into the dark pools that were her eyes.

And was abruptly pulled back at the sound of a woman's voice calling, "Papalopil?"

He sprang to his feet as a priestess came onto the patio.

"Here, Cuicatl," responded the young woman at his feet.

"My I help you, my Lord?" asked the newcomer courteously.

"No," he responded very quickly. "I have a gift for the goddess. I will put it on the altar on my way out." As he tossed a small bag of cacao beans on the altar, he thought he smelled a wisp of deer musk. What strange incense for a temple! The voice of the unknown priestess caught his attention.

"Papalopil, what did Lord Atlatzin want?"

"He brought a gift for Xochiquetzal," was all his priestess said.

Atlatzin smiled. She would keep his secrets.

CHAPTER TWELVE

Cacamatzin, Prince of Texcoco, was sent ahead to greet the new arrivals and bring them into Tenochtitlan. He was joined by his brother Cuitlahuac, Prince of the causeway town of Iztapalapa where the travelers rested. Dense crowds lined the way, staring at the extraordinary strangers with amazement and fear, and not a little excitement. They fell back before the huge dogs that ran ahead of the column of soldiers riding the great deer they called horses, but quickly regrouped as they passed. Some of the Mexica threw flowers in welcome, others sang chants of Quetzalcoatl's return. Rumors ran faster than the giant dogs. This was the god. No, it was the god's emissary. It was a warrior preparing the way for the god. It was a god/man. It was whispered that not even the Great Speaker knew for certain if this stranger were a god or a man. Since no one knew the truth, some in the crowd cheered, while others stared in silent terror as the procession began its march across the causeway to the city. The lagoon was filled with canoes; the strangers were a small island in a sea of Mexica. A ripple stirred the flowers, feathers and brightly colored cloth. Moctezuma was coming. The two princes hurried to reach their uncle's side.

Moctezuma's litter and canopy were richly worked in green feathers. Its silver borders were lush with pearls and jade, shaped full and ripe like hanging fruit. The eight noblemen who bore the palanquin cautiously lowered it to the ground, careful not to jostle him. Cacamatzin and Cuitlahuac helped Moctezuma from his litter and supported him as he approached Cortés. In the background stood Atlatzin and, behind him, the proudest warriors of the Mexica, dressed in the skins of jaguars and eagles.

The god/man Cortés dismounted from his horse and stared directly into the Emperor's eyes. The woman at his side translated into Nahuatl the strange sounds that fell from his lips.

"Is it you?" he demanded. "Are you really Moctezuma?"

The Emperor made a deep bow. Cortés acknowledged it by bending slightly at the waist and then stared at the brightly dressed man in front of him. Moctezuma struggled to master the shock of being stared at boldly for the first time since he had donned the turquoise crown seventeen years earlier.

"It is so. I am," he managed to say.

Cortés stepped forward and made as if to embrace him, but Moctezuma stepped back. To be stared at was one thing, but to be embraced was too much. The two princes immediately moved to put their bodies in front of their lord, preventing the embrace. They did not object, however, when the stranger took off a necklace he was wearing and offered it to the Emperor. Moctezuma fingered the strange shiny colored beads and finally collected himself. Speaking slowly enough so that the woman could translate his words, he welcomed the stranger to Tenochtitlan with dignity and grace. His exaggerated courtesy demonstrated his power and position.

"Our Lord, you have spent yourself and suffered fatigue on your long journey. Now you have arrived again on earth and reached your own land," said Moctezuma, deciding it would be wiser to treat the stranger as the god, not the emissary. "You have come to your noble city to occupy your throne and sleeping mat. I have guarded the land and watched for you. The rulers of time past have protected and guarded Tenochtitlan on your behalf. Beneath your hand and under your protection the common people are now placed.

"I do not dream now. I do not see this as if in a trance. I have in truth seen you and set eyes upon your face. And today you are here. For days I have been in anguish. I have gazed into the unknown, the Place of Mystery in the East. You have come to us from that direction, from between mists and clouds.

"The rulers of old have gone, saying that you would return, you would come to your city, you would descend to your throne and sleeping mat. Now it has come to pass. With toil, with weariness, you have reached us at last. Welcome to this land. Come now and rest. Take possession of your royal houses. Give comfort to your tired body. With your companions, your faithful lords, take your rest with us."

Atlatzin tasted hot bile in the back of his throat as Moctezuma presented Cortés with a necklace of golden shrimp and shells. He saw the angry look that flashed across Cacamatzin's face when the Emperor announced the arrivals would be given the palace that had belonged to the prince's father. But Atlatzin took care not to let his feelings show. Moctezuma was the Great Speaker and his word was divine. It could not be questioned. The Emperor himself led the strangers into the city and to the palace next to his own on the *zócalo*. He took the stranger by the hand and begged him sit on a draped dais where servants awaited him with dishes of gold piled high with delicacies prepared by the royal chef. No courtesy was spared. As the strangers withdrew to rest, Atlatzin made sure some of his own spies were among the servants before following Moctezuma back into his own residence.

When it was reported that the strangers were fed and rested, Moctezuma returned to the guests' palace with a group of important Mexica lords. Each in turn dropped to a crouch before Cortés and paid homage. Servants brought a second dais and placed it next to the Emperor's. Moctezuma and Cortés sat side by side on twin thrones while the nobles and soldiers formed uneasy groups around them. The Lord of the Mexica was the first to speak.

"We know from the scrolls of our forefathers that we are descended from strangers who came here from distant lands. It is written that our race was brought to these parts by a great lord, who returned to his native country, the land where the sun rises.

"You have told our emissaries you serve the great god Emperor Carlos, who lives in the Land of the Rising Sun. Is this what you call the great Quetzalcoatl? Did he send you to us? Are you his messenger? His kin? Tell us who is the one who calls himself Cortés."

Cortés cleared his throat and looked around at the group of nobles. It seemed to Atlatzin that he swallowed nervously, but he could not be certain. The woman who translated was obviously afraid, but that was to be expected. Spies had told Atlatzin that she was from a conquered tribe and given to the strangers as a slave. Cortés had freed her and dedicated her to their new religion. But Atlatzin knew she had been raised to hold the Mexica in awe, awe and fear. He suspected she still did.

"I am Cortés and I am the voice of the great and powerful Emperor Carlos. He may indeed be your Quetzalcoatl, he is most certainly the greatest ruler of all time. He sent me here to speak with you." When he spoke, his words rang loud and Atlatzin could hear no sign of weakness in the man's voice.

Moctezuma nodded thoughtfully. "We knew that you would come. If the one you call the great Carlos is your sovereign lord, then he is ours as well. You may be sure we will obey you and hold you as his representative." He gestured and servants appeared bearing gifts of feathered mantles and gold chains. They were followed by a small group of young women, *auianimes* whose services were to be given as gifts as well. Cortés' companions were laughing and making comments that were not translated as they realized the females' services were gifts for them as well. But Cortés motioned for silence and continued the discourse.

"My Spaniards," he said indicating the men, "and I have come across the water at the bidding of the greatest lord of all. He has ordered that you be instructed in the ways of Christianity so that your souls might be saved. Your gold and jewels will not save you from the eternal flames of Hell. Only the one true god can do that." As his words were being translated, Cortés appeared to study Moctezuma's face intently. Already perspiring under his steady gaze, the Great Speaker began to lose his composure at the mention of a new deity.

"I know my enemies the Tlaxcalans have lied about me," the words started slowly but gained speed until they came pouring out. "They have told you the walls of my houses are made of gold and that I make myself a god. They lie! You have seen my houses. They are lime and stone and earth. My causeways are lined with stones not pearls! I myself am made of flesh and blood!" The Emperor stood abruptly and threw back his feathered robe, so that his body was covered only by his ornate loincloth. "Look at me!" he demanded. "I am as mortal as any man. Look how they have lied to you!"

Cortés simply stared. Moctezuma appeared to realize that his panic was visible and close to overwhelming. He gathered his robes about his thin body and sat down stiffly. The nobles shuffled their feet in embarrassment that was not untouched by fear. Atlatzin's jaw was clenched so tightly that tiny fingers of pain clawed at his temples. He shook his head and the feathers in his headdress flopped angrily. The Emperor sank back into the safe embrace of his throne.

"It is true that I have some things of gold which have been left to me by my forefathers," he said weakly. "All that I possess you may have."

The interview was over. Moctezuma had offered his gold, his throne, his people. Atlatzin followed him with the rest of the nobles as they filed out of the room and returned to the main palace in silence.

It was one of Atlatzin's spies who explained the terrible thunder that shook the earth that night and caused the palace walls to rattle. The strangers had made one of their metal logs explode. They had laughed when the terrified servants fell to the ground. No one had been injured, but the smell was that from mountain Popocatepetl when it belched smoke. There was no question but that the explosion had been a warning. Gods or men, the strangers possessed a power Atlatzin did not understand.

Shortly after the morning sacrifice, Cortés, his translator and some of his men arrived unannounced at Moctezuma's palace. Atlatzin arrived in time to hear the Emperor offer him a seat on his right and tell his assembled counselors they might stay and listen to the conversation. He clapped his hands and ordered drinks of chocolate, but Cortés came abruptly to the reason behind his visit.

"Yesterday you acknowledged the Emperor Carlos as your sovereign. This obliges you to accept him as your spiritual guide as well. To call yourself vassal and friend of His Most Christian Majesty and not to embrace Christianity is a fatal contradiction. I am here to instruct you in the true faith."

Moctezuma stared at Cortés as the woman translated his words. Atlatzin noticed there was a light in the stranger's eyes like that of Huitzilopochtli's High Priest. He distrusted it. He knew the Emperor believed it was difficult to understand the ways of the gods and their chosen messengers. Could Moctezuma be thinking that, if the Emperor Carlos were not Quetzalcoatl, he was an even more powerful god as yet unknown? Atlatzin was convinced Cortés was no deity. But was Cortés the bearer of the divine word rather than its origin? What did Moctezuma believe? It was difficult to know, and Atlatzin suspected the Emperor himself was not certain what he believed. Regardless, the stranger was demanding the same respect as the god and was insisting that the Great Speaker learn about his religion. Moctezuma appeared to be willing, even if it involved learning how Emperor Carlos wished to be worshipped.

Atlatzin stood with the Council listening politely as Cortés described the creation of the earth and a long story he called Genesis. Moctezuma nodded slightly at the story of the evil snake. The Mexica were very familiar with the dangers serpents posed. Even Atlatzin had to admit that a snake was a prominent feature in the story of the founding of Tenochtitlan. One of the priests smiled at the story of the virgin birth, while a nobleman elbowed the man at his side when they heard about the omen of the star at the divine birth. These things appeared in Mexica stories as well. Atlatzin subtly shifted his weight from one leg to another as the story went on. It was unclear if the man-god called Jesus and the evil Lucifer who was his enemy were brothers like Feathered Serpent and Hummingbird. They clearly competed for worship. Finally Cortés seemed to draw the stories to a conclusion, as his words painted a vision of a place consumed by an undying fire and pain.

"The worship of idols leads directly to Hell, Moctezuma. Through Adam and Eve, all men are brothers. It was as an older brother that the Emperor sent me here to guide you, to help you put down your false gods, to end the hideous human sacrifices and cannibalism, and to do away with the shameful practice of sodomy." Cortés was flushed with emotion by the time he finished, and Moctezuma, noting this, appeared to choose his words carefully.

"I understand much of what you say. Much is familiar to me, especially what you say about the three gods and the cross. I even understand what you say about Our Lady. We too have a great goddess and similar stories, so I know they are true. Both Quetzalcoatl and Huitzilopochtli were born of virgin mothers. We have long understood the creation of the earth. Our beliefs are not exactly the same, but they are close enough." He smiled politely.

"As for putting away our gods, the request seems strange to me and I do not think the gods will like it. Our religion is no false delusion as you claim. It works. Proof of this is that our gods told us the exact year and day you would appear." Moctezuma smiled as though to a child who was too young to fully understand. "You are free to worship Our Lady, His Most Christian Majesty Carlos, and the one you call True God. We will not interfere. As our gods are good and true, we will assume the same for yours. But you must understand that if we were to ignore our gods and give up our sacrifices, the universe would come to an end. You cannot want that.

"Now, do not speak to me any more about this." The Emperor waved his hand and more chains of gold were given to the visitors. Atlatzin watched carefully as Cortés rose to take his leave. It was obvious to him that nothing had been settled. Cortés might bide his time, but he would broach the subject again. Atlatzin knew a fanatic when he saw one.

"He will not give up, my Lord. He will bring up his religion again in spite of your dismissal of it," he told the Emperor later.

"Perhaps. If this Carlos whom he serves is Quetzalcoatl, it may be that the translator has confused his message and that affects our understanding. Perhaps it means that Feathered Serpent and True God and one and the same. Time will tell."

"So you still believe Cortés speaks for the god?" asked the nobleman.

"It is a belief you obviously do not share, Atlatzin," Moctezuma said wearily.

"I do not, my Lord. Killing warriors in battle is one thing, but I do not believe a god would have his messenger kill innocent tradesmen and women, not to mention children, as Cortés did in Cholula. Besides, his translator is his concubine. Would the messenger of a god travel with a concubine?"

"Yes, you told me before that he shares his sleeping mat with her, Atlatzin. Why is that not fitting? Once an oath is broken it cannot be mended. It was Quetzalcoatl who broke his oath of chastity and was forced into exile. Why should his messenger be chaste? Or is it that you are offended that our guest keeps a woman and still has a warrior god's strength?" Moctezuma gave his counselor a penetrating look. "Is that it? Do you take personal offense because he has done what you have sworn not to and still wins against overwhelming odds at battle?"

"My Lord, the vow I took has added to my strength as a warrior. It has given my blade its biting edge and has nothing to do with this," the nobleman replied. "I simply doubt that the god's messenger would trifle with coupling when such momentous doings are afoot." Atlatzin watched Moctezuma pull absently at his crystal lip plug. Words of frustration held back for months welled up within the counselor and suddenly spilled out.

"Do you not see the way he looks whenever gold is mentioned? He can hardly tear his eyes from the emeralds around your royal neck, *Tlatoani*. Such greed is unheard of among the gods and not befitting their messengers. He is no better that the gamblers who wager their children on the ball game. He has the same kind of fever that possesses them. It is called greed!

"And the odor about his body offends us all! I will not believe the gods allow their messengers to fail so in cleanliness. My informers tell me that our guests have not bathed since they arrived several days ago! They are filthy! If they were Mexica, they would be shunned in the *zócalo*!"

"They are not Mexica, and I grow tired of this, Atlatzin," interrupted Moctezuma sternly, his voice stronger than before. "Perhaps, like our traders, Cortés has taken a vow not to bathe until his task is accomplished. If so, he must be suffering grave discomfort. I cannot pretend to understand what goes on in his mind. And I will not attempt to explain it to you. He has met every part of the prophecy. Do not forget that he defeated an army of sixty thousand Tlaxcalans with only a few hundred warriors. How do you think he did that? Do you really think matters who he is – god, emissary, or adventurer? Do you really think the outcome will be any different? Did you feel the thunder when they lit their metal log?" The Emperor shook his head in mounting frustration.

"If I decide our fate is to fully accept this Cortés as the god's messenger, it shall be done! If I decide the Mexica need to worship Emperor Carlos and build him a temple on the *zócalo*, it will be done. I do what I must do. Your duty is to accept my decisions, to follow me, and to cease your questions!" He caught an angry look exchanged between his counselor and Prince Cacamatzin.

"Withdraw your spies from among the strangers' servants, Atlatzin. And take care, Cacamatzin. Though you may be my nephew and Prince of Texcoco, I am your sovereign lord and your first allegiance is to me."

Atlatzin bowed obediently, because he had no choice. He caught himself grinding his teeth and forced his jaw to relax. Silently, he vowed to delay withdrawing his spies as long as he could. He could not truly help the Emperor without the information his spies could give him. Moctezuma might believe he knew what he final outcome would be, and the priests might teach that outcomes were always preordained, but no one knew for certain exactly what the outcome of the encounter with the Spaniards would be. Not yet, anyway. As he turned to leave, he caught the eye of the boy Tepin he had placed in service to the Emperor. Tepin nodded slightly and Atlatzin knew the boy understood how important it was to keep him aware of everything that occurred concerning Moctezuma. Especially now.

CHAPTER THIRTEEN

Papalopil was in the crowd when the strangers entered Tenochtitlan. The giant dogs frightened her, but the figure they called Cortés seemed like an ordinary man, except for the unhealthy color of his skin. Although she, like the other temple dancers, had brought bouquets of passionflowers to throw at the arrivals' feet, something made her hold on to hers at the last moment. Maybe it was the look of anger on Atlatzin's face. She had managed to slip into a position in the crowd where she could see the nobleman. He was so focused on the drama being enacted between the leader of the strangers and the Great Speaker that she managed to get fairly close to him without being seen.

What was it that angered him so? Even though he tried to hide it, she knew his face well enough now to see that he was very angry. She knew he was frustrated with the Emperor. But this seemed to be more than that. Was it at the man/god? Was he angry that the stranger was less than truly respectful of Moctezuma? Was he angry because he felt helpless to protect the Great Speaker as he wished? Was he angry at fate itself?

The crowd followed the strangers and the Emperor's entourage through the city and into the *zócalo*. Papalopil felt a twinge of pride as she watched the strangers stare about them, as though they had never seen anything quite so magnificent. She wondered if they were not just a little afraid. If Cortés were a god, he would have no fear, of course. But the men with him might be afraid, she reasoned. Traders who came to the city for the first time often had similar looks on their faces. Tenochtitlan was the most magnificent city in the world. It stretched almost as far as the eye could see, and the many canals and streets seemed to weave in and out like the finest of tapestries that could be seen in the market.

She followed the procession until it entered the grounds of Moctezuma's palace, and then she returned to the little temple where she served Xochiquetzal. She was arranging the passion-flowers on the altar when an excited group of *auianimes* burst in, led by Mama Amoxtli.

"The Emperor wants to offer women to the strangers," she announced. "Not to all of the men, of course. But he wants a group of *auianimes* for all the important warriors under the mangod. He promised that whoever volunteers will be well rewarded. If you are willing, go bathe and prepare yourselves. You will be called upon this evening."

Papalopil sighed unhappily as she carefully put her last flower at the goddess' feet. Her monthly blood had come upon her that morning, so she could not answer the Emperor's call. She could have used the payment the Emperor promised to help lower her freedom debt.

Mama Amoxtli heard the sigh and came over to her. "Perhaps you should thank Xochiquetzal that this is your bleeding time. Assume she has other plans for you. If the girls come back and say all is well with these strange men, you may yet have a chance to earn a reward. If they say otherwise, well, this is a time of great change. Who can say what will be the outcome? What will be of any of us as the wheel turns?"

Days later, when the *auianimes* returned to the house, Papalopil had to admit she was glad she had not gone with them.

"They stink of sweat and filth," one of the girls proclaimed loudly. "They refuse to bathe every day. In fact, they bathe only infrequently and the man I was with did not bathe the whole time I was there! The woman who speaks for them says they believe bathing allows disease to enter the body!"

"I tried to explain about soaproot, but the one I was with was horrified at the idea of scrubbing his skin with plant roots and would not even touch it! There was food matted in his beard. He let me comb it out but refused to let me wash it!" said another.

"Their clothing is so filthy it is stiff. If you touch it, it feels like the bark of a tree," said still another. "When they take off the long cloth coverings on their legs, the material stands up all by itself, as though their legs were still in it! I think they must wear it until it falls off from rot."

"Mine had bugs living in his hair!" chimed in another.

"I burned incense the whole time I was there. He thought it was one of our customs, but it was because I could not stand the disgusting smell," said the first, anxious to tell her story.

"But that is not the worst thing," interrupted a third. "They clean their teeth with their own urine!"

At that, the girls broke into gales of horrified laughter, as one tried to imitate a man urinating into his own mouth while another pretended to choke as she cleaned her teeth. Even Mama Amoxtli had to laugh.

The *auianimes* declined to go the next time the request came for women to attend the strangers, so slave women were sent instead. Mama Amoxtli made sure Papalopil was not among the women forced to go. The strangers seemed not to notice the difference between trained courtesans and slaves, a fact that became another reason for ridicule among the *auianimes*.

In the months that followed, it seemed to Papalopil that the people in the city became accustomed to the presence of the Spaniards, as the Mexica learned to call them. They never accepted the Tlaxcalans that stayed on camped beyond the causeways, however. There were far too many of their enemy on the shores of the lake for comfort. So even though the tension was not directly attributed to the presence of Cortés and his men, Papalopil could still feel it in the market. It was reflected in the increase in sales of weapons, *maquahuitls*, wooden clubs studded with jagged pieces of obsidian, decorated dart-throwers, and knives. Some tradesmen from outside the city were reluctant to pass through the Tlaxcalan camps, and some of the foodstuffs that usually were available in the city became scarce. But by and large, people began to grow used to having the Spaniards there.

However, Papalopil noticed how the vendors took pains to cover up the gold and turquoise jewelry when the foreigners came into the market. There was no report of theft and no one would insult the Emperor's guests to their faces, but there was no point in inviting trouble. The Spaniards followed their own laws, not those of the Mexica. And, as those who served the foreigners told their stories, it was clear that the strangers' customs were very different from their own.

It was reassuring when it was announced the Festival of Toxcatl, celebrating the end of the dry season, would go on as usual. Things might have changed, but they had not changed too much, thought Papalopil, as she was sweeping up the jacaranda petals in the temple patio. She turned when Cuicatl rushed in with the news.

"Moctezuma says we may have the festival the way it has always been done, with the huge serpent line where everyone dances for hours and hours and the marriage of the four maidens! I have been chosen to represent Xochiquetzal and marry the god!" She was bubbling with joy, and the temple girls and younger priestesses rushed to congratulate her. Even Papalopil laid the broom she was using against the wall and joined the small group around her.

"You know the war captive who will be sacrificed was chosen at the festival a year ago, but none of us knew if the ritual would happen with the Spanish among us. But it will! He has been walking through the city all this time dressed in jewels and the finest cotton, playing the flute and speaking poetry. He has done a wonderful job of embodying the god. And I will embody a goddess!"

"I saw him yesterday walking through the *zócalo*," said one of the young priestesses, putting down her spindle dreamily. "Even though he has a black band painted across his eyes and nose, I could see how handsome he is. How fortunate you are, Cuicatl!"

"I know! Is it not wonderful? We have the marriage and then the other wives and I spend twenty days and nights with him in our own rooms in one of the palaces!"

"And then what happens?" asked the youngest temple dancer.

"Then he is taken away to die and we come and join the great dance," Cuicatl happily.

"Does he not mind that he is to die?" asked the young girl.

"I imagine he will have accepted his fate," commented Mama Amoxtli dryly. "A year ago he was given the choice between being sacrificed immediately or living a year honored as a deity, passing the time in luxury, having four beautiful wives, and then dying an honorable, even glorious death."

"I saw him too," said another. "I listened to him play the flute. He does it beautifully and wears wonderful little gold bells around his ankles. Sometimes he dances as he plays and the little bells jingle in time with the music."

"The bells will be given to the captive who takes his place next year, once the rains have come. The flute will be broken though. The next man will be chosen after the women do the Corn Dance and he will get a new flute. All of us will need to make necklaces out of corn to wear. I will show you how. And, Papalopil, I want you to help me make the figure of the god that will stand in the *zócalo*. We will use the amaranth seeds we have been saving for months." Mama Amoxtli nodded toward a large basket that Papalopil knew was stored behind the altar. "The elder priestesses at other temples have been saving them as well."

"Who are the other maiden-brides?" asked one of the dancers with curiosity.

"Oh, I forgot to ask, probably priestesses from other temples," said Cuicatl. "I think they pick a priestess from each of the four goddess' temple to embody that deity. This is a tremendous honor for my family. They will be so proud." She turned to Papalopil. "I must look perfect! Help me fix my hair like Xochiquetzal for the marriage ceremony. I love the look, with the hair tucked under at the neck and coming up into little horns of love on top of her head. Teach me how to do it so I can do it every morning for the twenty days I am the goddess.

"Mama Amoxtli," she turned in sudden panic, "what shall I wear? I have no embroidered cloth or jewels befitting a goddess!"

The elder priestess smiled at her from a mat in the shade, where she was taking an unusual mid-day rest. "The temple will supply what you need. We have feathers and jewels and intricately stitched cotton put away for these joyous festivals. This is one of our special days, and we all honor our goddess."

Later, when Papalopil found herself alone with Cuicatl, she could not keep back a question. "Forgive my asking, but does this not put you in a delicate position? What if the man embodying the god realizes you are no maiden? Will you be safe?"

Cuicatl dismissed the question with a wave of her hand and

a just a touch of condescension. "Mama Amoxtli assured me that he is always given a mild drug before the ceremony. Besides, there will be four of us women as his brides. He will be far too busy to focus on just one of us. And afterward, I'll be able to leave the temple with full honor and marry a man of my choosing. That is why Mama Amoxtli arranged all this. Who wouldn't want to marry a woman blessed by the love of a god?"

Papalopil assumed Cuicatl was correct and returned to her sweeping. Hers was not to wonder at the ways of the gods. They had never made much sense to her any way.

She was in the marketplace buying combs for Cuicatl's hair and had just finished handing the tradeswoman the price Mama Amoxtli had given her, when she caught sight of Atlatzin coming toward her. She bent low over her basket, acting as though she were studying its contents, hoping he would pass her by. Pretending to be a priestess had gotten out of hand and was dangerous, but she did not know how to stop it without making the situation even worse. Here was the nobleman again bearing down on her. She sent a brief thank you to the goddess that she had not used the yellow power on her face that morning. That would have betrayed her real status immediately.

"There you are," said Atlatzin, stopping in front of her. "I was just going to the temple to speak with you, speak with the goddess," he corrected himself.

"I am very busy today, Lord Atlatzin. Forgive me, but I must return to the temple immediately for...prayers," she finished lamely.

"I will walk with you," he announced, and she had no choice.

"I have a foreboding." He said it softly so no one could overhear, and it caught Papalopil's attention.

"I have a feeling something terrible is going to happen."

"To you?" In spite of her resolve, Papalopil found herself asking the question.

"To me, to you, perhaps to all of us. Something huge and terrible, I know not what, but it has to do with the strangers." Atlatzin looked around and saw the market crowd had thinned out. If he spoke carefully, it would be safe.

"The one I serve seems to be lost. He begins to accept a defeat he believes inevitable, but it is an ending that need not be. I fear he will adopt the new god and swear loyalty to those who bring the god's message. Then he will demand the same of those of us who serve and protect him. But how could I take that oath? I would be betraying all I believe in. How then could I believe in him as my lord and ruler?"

"You could not," said Papalopil, forgetting for an instant she was supposed to be a priestess and was not in normal conversation with an equal.

"What?" He swung her around to face him.

Flustered, she remembered her place but realized at the same time that she had to answer. "I just meant that you could not be disloyal to yourself and what you believe in and then be truly loyal to anything else.

"Forgive me, Lord. I cannot do this here. Speaking secrets must be done in the temple, not in the street. And I must get back." She turned and walked quickly toward the temple that was now in sight.

He ignored what she said and followed her. "I feel something terrible coming. I have no idea what it is, but I feel it. I do know there is something Hummingbird wants me to do, something important that will be part of the terrible that awaits. The problem is that I know not what it is, just that I will do it when the time comes. And it come as surely as the wheel turns."

She could hear despair in his voice.

"How do you know?" Papalopil forgot herself a second time.

"I just do." He looked at her strangely and she again had the feeling that there was something he was hiding, something important.

Then she saw that they had reached the entrance to Xochiquetzal's temple and Mama Amoxtli stood there with her arms crossed and a frown on her face.

"Papalopil, go inside immediately and wait for me," the Elder Priestess ordered.

Papalopil slipped inside and leaned up against the wall where she could hear without being seen. Mama Amoxtli stood there in the large doorway, her arms crossed and her feet spread out, as though her small form could bar the way against the leader of the Jaguar Warriors.

"Lord Atlatzin, forgive us, but we have special religious observations we must do now. We cannot receive supplicants today."

"Very well, Mother," said Atlatzin respectful of her age, "I will return tomorrow to speak with my priestess."

"Your priestess?"

"The one who just entered. Of course, it is the goddess I speak to, not the woman." Atlatzin made haste to correct himself.

"If you are speaking secrets, perhaps I can help you. As Elder Priestess, it is part of my service here at the temple. Papalopil is too inexperienced to do this task well." From where she stood in the shadow, Papalopil could hear the tightness in her voice and knew she was angry. Atlatzin seemed not to notice.

"To the contrary, Elder Priestess. She may be inexperienced, but she has given me some good advice."

"Has she?" The words were a question but it did not sound like a question to Papalopil.

Nor did it to Atlatzin apparently, as he simply indicated he would return the next day and departed. Papalopil darted to a side altar so it would not be obvious she had been listening and waited for the storm she knew was coming.

"Papalopil, you are a fool!" Mama Amoxtli bore down on her,

"a fool and an imposter! Speaking secrets? The Lord Counselor and Leader of the Jaguar Warriors? How could you be so stupid?"

"It was not my intention to deceive," said the girl. "Well, it was at first, but he just assumed I was a priestess. I never lied to him."

"Whether you lied to him or not he still might kill you when he finds out you are nothing but a slave." It was said harshly and Papalopil felt it like a slap.

"I tried to stop, but he would not let me. He kept coming back and insisting."

"And you let him."

"I did not know what else to do, how to stop it. Please, Mama Amoxtli, help me."

"Help you? You still fail to understand. If he finds out, he may kill me as well! I am the Elder Priestess of the Temple. You are my responsibility. Everything that happens here is my responsibility."

"Forgive me. Please. I will go to him and tell him it was my fault. Please."

"You will do no such thing! You will hide away and never see him again. I forbid it! The last thing I need is for you to go confess and bring the authorities down on us." Mama Amoxtli slapped her fan open and flipped it back and forth so rapidly that petals on the altar scattered the air. "This is what you will do. The next few days you will stay away from the center of town. In fact, you will stay with the *auianimes* until I tell you it is safe to leave. It is the one place Lord Atlatzin will never look."

"Thank you, Mama Amoxtli," she said gratefully.

"Once I tell you it is safe, you will look out for Lord Atlatzin every moment you take breath. If you see him, you will hide; you will disappear! You must take pains to avoid him, to avoid ball games and any event he might attend. If he comes to the temple, you will hide and I will tell him you are gone, ill, something. He is dangerous now. If he finds out the truth, I will be unable to help you. You have been a fool, but you must remember that."

"I promise," Papalopil tried to reassure her. Mama Amoxtli did not seem much comforted, and so she added, "Lord Atlatzin left gifts each time he came. I put them in the storeroom. I did not even take a tiny bit for myself."

"And you think that makes it acceptable? His priestess indeed!" She shook her head and turned away, murmuring, "You girls will be the death of me."

With that, Papalopil knew the Elder Priestess, at least, would forgive her.

CHAPTER FOURTEEN

A tlatzin wrinkled his nose in distaste as he led Cortés and his men through the *zócalo*. He could not abide the smell of the unwashed. Even the poorest and most ignorant among the Mexica knew enough to bathe daily. But spies told him that the foreigners reacted as though a little water and soaproot would wash away their manhood. It was disgusting.

Cortés had requested permission to visit Huitzilopochtli's temple that morning, and Moctezuma had ordered his counselor to accompany him and his men. They passed by the dealers in jewels and precious metals and those who traded in skins and cloth of varying degrees of fineness. The nobleman was appalled by the foreigners' fascination with the stalls built for public conveniences, especially when their translator explained they had no such thing in their homeland. Where did they relieve themselves when out in public? He wondered, but did not lower himself to ask.

Cortés stopped beside a canal filled with *chinampas*, and Atlatzin was forced to explain how the rafts were woven, filled with dirt, and planted in order to increase the amount of arable land. He wondered briefly where these men grew their vegetables and flowers. Did they not have lakes to provide water and grow food? No lakes and no public conveniences! What a strange, barbaric country theirs must be!

Once inside the Serpent Wall around the Temple, the party was met by six priests who waited to escort Cortés to the summit platform. Slowly they climbed the huge stairway until they reached the twin temples. The lower of the three stories held the temples; the upper two tiers were of intricately carved wood and served as burial vaults that held the ashes of cremated emperors, they explained to the strangers. In front of the temples stood a large snakeskin drum and two sacrificial stones, wet with fresh blood. Moctezuma stepped out from between the two stones and greeted Cortés graciously.

"From this point, you can see land several days distant," he said after the exchange of niceties. "There is the aqueduct that brings fresh water from Chapultepec and there is the causeway of Iztapalapa which you crossed in coming to Tenochtitlan. To the north is the causeway of Tenayuca and to the west is Tlacopan."

Cortés stared down at the whitewashed city below him. His face gave no sign of what he was feeling, but Atlatzin got the sudden impression that the man had never seen anything quite so grand.

"How many people live in the city?" asked the translator softly. Atlatzin looked at her carefully and realized this was her question, not one prompted by Cortés. Clearly she was impressed as well. Well, it was to be expected. The people she came from lived by the coast. They would have heard of the city, but never seen anything as impressive. There was nothing like Tenochtitlan in the whole world.

"People come and go. Scribes say there are close to three hundred thousand in the city proper, though it is difficult to be exact," he answered.

Cortés interrupted and asked to be shown the inside of the buildings. Moctezuma hesitated but, after conferring with the black-robed priests, agreed. Leaving Atlatzin and the woman behind, they entered one of the temples.

Atlatzin knew that inside the building dedicated to Hummingbird there were two altars, each of which held a huge statue. There, in his two manifestations, sat Huitzilopochtli, the statues' broad faces partially hidden by golden masks. The foreigners would be looking at both of the god's polished stone bodies that were encrusted with mother of pearl and precious stones. Thick serpents of gold girded the two bellies. They would see that one statue held arrows made of gold in one hand and a bow in the other. A necklace of silver hearts lay about the other's neck, a strange metallic reflection of the fresh hearts that were piled in a brazier at the base of each statue, sacred fruit for the god.

The walls were deeply sculpted with more figures of the gods. Their gaping mouths were filled with dried blood built up by repeated feedings over the years. The stone floors were thick with the blood of two centuries of victims. Atlatzin knew that a constant flow of dark red ran from each brazier and ended in a wet pool at the god's feet.

A yellow-haired Spaniard came running out of the temple gagging. Others quickly followed and Atlatzin saw with satisfaction that one vomited violently, while the others tried to breathe deeply of the fresh air. Hummingbird was a god of war, full of awe and terror. It was only fitting that these strangers were afraid.

Cortés turned to Moctezuma, who had followed his guests out of the sanctuary, and forced a tight smile. The smile reminded Atlatzin of an animal baring its teeth, and he stepped forward in case he were needed.

"My Lord Moctezuma, I do not understand how a great and wise lord like yourself can believe such evil things are gods. They are clearly demons straight out of Hell! Let me prove this to you. Allow me to place a cross above this temple and give me this shrine for the Mother of our Lord. Cast down these demons without fear."

The effect of these words when translated was immediate. The High Priest spat deliberately upon the ground in front of Cortés. "A goddess in the temple of the war god? You are mad!" The priests around him angrily agreed and the small group of pale men seemed to shrink before their fury. At Atlatzin's gesture, priests surrounded the offenders and waited for Moctezuma to order their death.

But the Emperor made a last attempt to maintain peace. "If the mother of your god died in childbirth, we will be happy to honor her. There is a privileged place in Mictlan for those women who die giving birth in blood and pain."

For some reason Atlatzin could not understand, the words seemed terribly offensive to Cortés, who narrowed his eyes in outrage. "The Holy Virgin did not die in..." He checked himself and swallowed with difficulty. "Your Hummingbird is Lucifer himself! Throw down his statue and embrace Christ!"

"Enough!" cried the High Priest, and the priests raised their black knives. But Moctezuma held out his arms in restraint. They could not attack guests.

"Had I known the words you would speak, I would not have permitted you inside the temple. You must understand my position. I do not yet fully understand your god, but our gods are the powers of nature. If the world is to continue, our gods must be given their proper nourishment. Otherwise, the world will end. I have no choice in this matter."

Cortés seemed to know that he had gone too far and gave a tight nod, as he suggested that it was time to return to the guest palace. Moctezuma stared at him for a moment, as though he were trying to see if the man really understood, but then inclined his head and stepped aside.

"Yes, it is better that you go now. I must stay here and placate Huitzilopochtli. It will take many hearts to expiate the insult you have paid him."

Atlatzin saw the flush on the stranger's face and could not decide if it were anger or fear. On the way back to the palace, he resolved to lead the Spaniards the long way through the *zócalo* and past the rack that held the skulls of men who had been sacrificed. It could not hurt to remind them once more of the war god's power.

There was an uneasy peace in Tenochtitlan. Encouraged by the fact he had defied Cortés and nothing had happened, Moctezuma met with his advisors and members of the Triple Alliance.

"I have promised him everything, yet in reality, I have given him little – some jewels, gold and women, but no earthly power. He does not command the armies nor the tax collectors. He seems to have chosen not to use whatever power and strange weapons he has, or perhaps he is restrained from using them for some reason we do not understand. It may even be that he has less power than we feared."

"Then this is the time to attack him," urged the Prince of Texcoco.

"Think, Cacamatzin! Do not rush in to risk everything. We have no proof that he cannot call upon the god's power, only that he has not yet done so in Tenochtitlan. Have you forgotten the battles of Tlaxcala or Cholula? No mere mortal power sustained Cortés then."

"Since there has been no sign of his power since coming here, perhaps it has left him," suggested Cacamatzin reasonably. "Perhaps Hummingbird's power is too great for him here at the heart of the Empire." He looked to his fellow prince and at Atlatzin for support.

"Possibly," agreed Moctezuma slowly, "but until we know,

it would be folly to attack him openly. Atlatzin," he asked, "did Cortés not leave a garrison of warriors on the coast and another in Cempoala?" Atlatzin nodded in confirmation and the Emperor continued. "I shall instruct my tax collectors that it is time for the people in Cempoala to pay their taxes. When they repeat their refusal, send Jaguar Warriors to collect the taxes by force. If some of Cortés' men are killed in the process, I cannot be blamed. But take care it is not ordered in my name. It must look like the Cempoalans are to blame."

"Let me double the guard in Cortés' palace now, my Lord, and send my spies back in among their servants," asked Atlatzin. "I have heard disturbing things. Your guests sleep with all their weapons. Their animals are kept ready to attack at all times. They have not contented themselves with the generous gifts you have given them. I have learned the false wall in front of your treasury in the guest palace has been discovered. Cortés ordered the wall carefully resealed, but not before examining all that the secret chamber behind it contained."

"Let them believe their discovery a secret," ordered Moctezuma thoughtfully, "Let them delight in my treasure while we test them at Cempoala. Double the guards as you suggest. But I told you to withdraw your spies, Atlatzin." The Emperor stroked the long blue feathers in his fan. "I will not ask how you know these things, but you clearly fail to understand the delicacy of our position. There is much we do not understand. The Lord Carlos may not be a god, but the Spaniards have powerful weapons we do not and they arrived on the day foretold in prophecy. I do not wish Cortés to become suspicious. I shall continue to treat him as an honored guest and await the results from Cempoala."

Cortés reacted with a swiftness that took Moctezuma by surprise. One of his Tlaxcalan spies brought him the news that

Cempoala had been attacked and six Spaniards were dead. Exactly how Moctezuma was involved in their deaths was unclear, but Cortés knew somehow that the order for the attack had come from Tenochtitlan. Careful not to show his fury, he took his captains and translator and went straight to the Emperor, who was in session with his Council. Moctezuma was caught off guard. Cortés told him he knew what had happened in Cempoala and that he held Moctezuma personally responsible for the deaths of his men.

"It is not true!" the Emperor protested. Stripping Hummingbird's bracelet from his wrist, he flung it at the floor, giving great emphasis his words. He turned dramatically to Atlatzin and ordered him to send a message that the Mexica official in charge of the area around Cempoala present himself in Tenochtitlan.

"We need to speak in private, Moctezuma," Cortés announced. "I want to believe what you say, but there is danger here. Send your attendants away so that we may speak alone."

Moctezuma hesitated at the unusual request, but Cortés repeated himself.

"I want to believe you are not guilty of this horrendous act. If you are indeed innocent, there is danger around you and we must talk."

Atlatzin started to protest. The danger lay in leaving the Emperor alone with the foreigner. But Moctezuma silenced him with a glance, and the nobleman knew he dare not continue, as it would disrespect the Emperor in front of Cortés. As the nobleman and the counselors filed out, he noted that the boy Tepin remained behind unnoticed. It was he who later told Atlatzin what had happened.

"The Spaniards never left the room," he told Atlatzin. "The one called Cortés said that it was not enough to send for the Mexica official, that the uprising at Campoala meant that the Emperor himself was not safe. He invited Moctezuma to move to the guest palace where he could protect him with the magical weapons."

"He invited him?" questioned Atlatzin with alarm.

"The words the translator used made it seem an invitation, but it did not sound like an invitation to me."

"And the Emperor's reaction?"

"He protested and said the uprising was against the taxes, not against him. But he looked around the room as he spoke and all the Spaniards were fully armed. Their swords were not drawn, but they hand their hands ready to pull them from their belts.

"Then Cortés insisted again that the Emperor needed protection and said he should bring all his wives and concubines and move to the guest palace until the issue of Cempoala is resolved. He said the Emperor could hold council as usual and have whatever food and entertainment he desired. He promised the Emperor that he would be an honored guest, not a prisoner."

"A guest in his own city! In his own Empire!"

"Moctezuma refused, Lord Atlatzin. He said the Jaguar and Eagle Warriors could protect him and he did not need the Spaniards. But Cortés insisted that the news from Cempoala meant that there were traitors among the warriors. He said he believed the Emperor when he said he did not order the Spaniards to be murdered. But that meant that there were people among the Emperor's most trusted men who plotted to make the Mexica and the Spanish enemies.

"He promised again to make the Emperor as comfortable in the guest palace as he is at home, and said he would be treated with every respect. In the guest palace, the two could speak more easily and discuss the plans he had made to support the Mexica against all enemies and make us stronger than ever before.

"I could see Moctezuma look around the room again,' continued Tepin. "I saw that the yellow-haired one they call Alvarado had his sword half-drawn then, another man pushed back his cloak to show a dagger in his hand as the Emperor watched. Alvarado said something hurried in his language that was not translated, but it seemed to spur Cortés to action.

"'Tell your nobles that your god commanded you to come with me,' he said to the Emperor. 'Tell them not to interfere. There are traitors who would harm you and turn us on each other. If you do not let us protect you, blood will be shed here today. Let us avoid that.'

"That seemed to decide the Emperor. He stood up slowly and stared at Cortés There was a long silence, and finally, he looked away and ordered his litter. You saw the rest, my Lord Atlatzin."

Yes, thought Atlatzin, he had been there when they were called back into the room. The Emperor had underestimated Cortés and had surrendered. It did no good to protest when Moctezuma informed his nobles he was moving to the guest palace. He simply shook his head and informed them that it was Huitzilopochtli's will. The jeweled litter arrived and the Emperor gravely took his seat. His attending lords carried him silently to the palace where Cortés was lodged. Although they walked in silence, tears flowed freely down their dark faces and stained their bright capes. Atlatzin did not cry; instead, his eyes were cold with fury.

Atlatzin sent runners to the princes of the causeway towns to tell them what had happened. He paced the halls of the *calmecac* between the long shelves of painted scrolls. It was not his place to decide what to do next. That was up to the princes. All he could do was alert them and wait.

Or he could speak with the goddess.

But when he reached the temple of Xochiquetzal, the elder priestess stood in the entrance, and did not move aside when he wished to enter.

"I wish to speak secrets," he announced with annoyance.

"And I shall be happy to serve you," said Mama Amoxtli.

"No. I want the woman who has served me in the past. She

knows what this is about and has given me good advice in the past," he insisted.

"Yes, you told me that last time you were here."

Her response struck him as strange. He nodded curtly but did not reply. Why was this old woman blocking his way? It was ridiculous, really. She was so tiny, yet standing there with her arms crossed, she seemed to fill up the entire entrance.

"Papalopil has gone home to her village, my Lord. Her mother is very ill. She may stay there and not return. At any rate, I can serve you. As Elder Priestess, I am very skilled and have done this for years." Mama Amoxtli smiled, but there was something strange in her smile, almost challenging. Nevertheless, she stepped to the side so Atlatzin could enter.

He did not. Without saying a word, he turned and left. For some reason he did not stop to think about, the prospect of speaking secrets to the goddess no longer seemed to hold promise.

CHAPTER FIFTEEN

A fter the initial shock wore off, Moctezuma and his nobles discovered the Emperor was not as badly off as they had feared. Cortés treated him with the utmost of respect and dignity, as did his Spaniards. Although it was true that the Emperor was not free to leave, his nobles and counselors visited him as easily as before. To all outward appearances, it looked as though he had simply moved back into the palace of his youth. His nephews were not easily deceived though, nor was Atlatzin, who knew the truth. He could not understand why Moctezuma had not called in his guards when he was threatened, why he had simply agreed to move out of his own palace. It could not be that the Emperor had become a coward. Moctezuma had led warriors into many battles in the past, and his courage had never been questioned. What had changed? Was it prudence or fear? Atlatzin decided to say something when the Emperor was alone with his counselors.

"*Tlatoani*," he began cautiously, "your guards are many and the finest among your warriors. If it is your desire, we will move you back to your own palace immediately where you can entertain your guests more comfortably."

"I am comfortable here, Lord Atlatzin," came the answer.

"Surely you would be even more comfortable eating at your own table and sleeping on your own mat," he insisted.

Moctezuma sighed and shook his head. "I am here because Hummingbird wills it. I will stay here until the god wills otherwise."

Atlatzin stared at the floor in disbelief. He did not trust himself to steal a look at the emperor's face. It was not necessary anyway. He knew Moctezuma was lying, but he could hardly admit that he knew because he had placed Tepin in the royal household to spy! What was motivating the Emperor? Was he stalling for time? Did he still think he could convince Cortés that the attack in Cempoala was not his plan? If so, what was to be gained by cunning at this point? Or was Moctezuma so troubled that he could not even see what was happening? The next thing the Emperor said concerned Atlatzin even more deeply.

"When my official from Cempoala arrives, I will turn him over to Cortés and demonstrate that I am an ally, not an enemy. That will convince him of my innocence in the attack. Then we will barter for the man with gold and I will buy him back in the traditional manner. I know that you have underestimated Cortés and that the counsel you gave me concerning Cempoala should have been wiser. I should have realized he would have seen through my plan. But this will remedy the matter." He dismissed his worried counselors with a wave of his feathered fan.

The nobleman who gave the official order for the attack on Cortés' men at Cempoala arrived with his son and fifteen of his warriors. As he had planned, Moctezuma made them prisoners and gave them to the foreigners. But there was no bartering, no gold. Cortés condemned all seventeen men to death by burning. A pyre was built in front of the palace with weapons taken from Huitzilopochtli's armory.

Again, it was Tepin who told Atlatzin what had occurred.

"While the men were strapped to stakes and the fire lit, Cortés brought the Emperor to the palace window. He had his men tie the Emperor's hands behind his back and left him there alone, but for me, to watch the burning. I saw the tears on the Emperor's face, but he would not let me wipe them away.

"When it was done and Cortés returned, he told the Emperor he was free to go back to the main palace, but the Emperor refused. He said he could not leave, that his enemies would learn that he watched his own people burn and was helpless. He said that they would not rest now until they destroy the Mexica. And then he told Cortés that the Mexica were in his hands! Only he could protect them from their enemies now!

"Cortés embraced the Emperor, who did not even try to pull away. I think his spirit has surrendered, Lord Atlatzin." The boy looked at him with concern. "Shall I return to his side?"

"Yes. You have done well, Tepin," said Atlatzin, shaking his head in despair. "Continue by his side as long as you can. The information you gather is valuable to me." Atlatzin feared the boy was correct. Moctezuma had given up. What could be worse?

He was not long in discovering the answer. Before he could receive Atlatzin's message about his uncle, Cacamatzin sent the counselor a message. A junta of powerful nobles had formed and would soon seize control of the government. The Emperor would be rescued and the foreigners punished. All would be well.

But Cacamatzin had sent Moctezuma a copy of the message. His pride and trust in tatters, the Emperor had little faith in his nephew's plan and was frightened by what he saw as its possible consequences. Instead of waiting for rescue, he turned the message over to Cortés. Tepin hurriedly sent word to Atlatzin, but it arrived too late. Cacamatzin, Cuitlahuac and the leaders of the junta were seized and imprisoned. A puppet ruler was found for Texcoco.

In an attempt to maintain some semblance of order in the universe and pretend that nothing was amiss, Moctezuma continued to appear for worship at Huitzilopochtli's temple. Upon occasion, he slipped away from the Spanish escort that was provided for his "protection" and did small sacrifices, piercing his own tongue and foreskin. But, Tepin told Atlatzin, the Emperor avoided the Black Room where he used to meditate and returned to his escort and to the palace voluntarily when his sacrifices were done.

Of course, thought Atlatzin. There is no other place for him to go.

Cortés moved to tighten his hold on political control. He informed the Emperor it was time to swear fealty and pay tribute to Emperor Carlos. Moctezuma called a meeting of the *pipiltin* with resignation. Although many of the lords refused to appear, Moctezuma proceeded as though he had not noticed.

This time it was his sister Quetzali who told Atlatzin what had happened, as the nobleman was one of those who refused to swear loyalty to the Spanish. She had stopped by the house to check on her mother, and recounted what had occurred.

"The Emperor gathered us all together in the great hall and said that he was now certain that Cortés was the one we have been expecting since the time of our beginning. He said he knew because it was the only way things could have unfolded the way they have. Everything that has come to pass was at the god's behest, he insisted. The prophecy has been fulfilled and it was time to make formal the transfer of power.

"He then led us into the reception hall where Cortés waited on the jasper throne. The Emperor crouched and touched his fingers to the floor and then to his mouth, swearing undying loyalty to the Emperor Lord Carlos of Spain. Then he put the royal seal to a scroll saying the tribute going to the palace would now go to Emperor Carlos, and it was recorded in triplicate by the head of the palace scribes. One by one, we all followed his example: members of the *pipiltin*, his counselors who were there, his children, his wives and concubines. All of us. What else could we do?"

"Did no one refuse?" asked Atlatzin.

"No. Those who would have refused, like you, Brother, did not appear at the palace. They would not defy the Emperor to his face."

"Did he give up the throne?"

"No, he is still the Great Speaker. But he swore allegiance to Lord Carlos and to Cortés as his representative. Moctezuma is a different person now. He looked strange, almost confused, as though he did not fully understand what was happening. As though things were moving too fast for him to grasp. There is something wrong with him, I think."

"It is in the hands of the gods now," said their mother in resignation. "It always has been."

"But in the hands of which god?" Atlatzin mumbled darkly.

Cortés was not content with collecting the tribute that had previously gone to the Emperor. The oath of fealty was not enough for him. He announced that human sacrifice was an abomination and had to stop. The demon Hummingbird had to be overthrown. He presented Moctezuma with an ultimatum. His men would remove the statues of the Mexica gods and replace them with the Spanish ones. It would be done peacefully if Moctezuma supported them. If not, it would be done by force and would result in slaughter. One way or another, the old gods would be destroyed.

Moctezuma begged him to reconsider and argued that the entire city would be consumed by the violence that would surely be provoked. They would not allow the gods to be so offended. It was too dangerous. Cortés deliberated and offered a compromise. If a room in the great temple were scrubbed and painted, a large cross would be installed. Moctezuma readily agreed, after all, it was just a cross, not a new god.

Women from temples across the city were called to clean the room for the cross. Cortés' men watched as they hauled leather buckets of water up the many steps to the top of the pyramid. The buckets sloshed water on the stone steps, and more than one woman slipped while the men watched. Xochiquetzal's dancers joined the cooks and cleaners, scrubbing the floor and walls inside Hummingbird's temple with brushes of dried grasses. Some used small knives to scrape off the centuries of caked blood.

Papalopil was among the women. She had tied her hair back with a thong to keep it away from the filth, but her dress was stained with water and blood. As she began to descend the temple steps for more clean water, a movement down by the disk of the dismembered goddess caught her attention. She paused, whirled around, and went back inside the temple

Atlatzin had tried to avoid the scene at the Great Temple. He was ashamed of his Emperor and afraid for his people. For a moment he thought he saw his priestess. But, no, of course not. She had left the capital to take care of her mother. He watched briefly as the line of women carrying clean water wove its way serpent-like up the long steps. This is what his people had been reduced to – servants to stinking soldiers and foreign gods. He could not watch any longer, and he whirled around angrily and disappeared into the shadows.

Not just a cross but also a wooden goddess called Our Lady was taken to Huitzilopochtli's pyramid and placed in a white-washed room. Many baskets of flowers were delivered to mask the faint odor of blood that still lingered. Prayers to her were said every morning and armed Spaniards guarded the figure day and night. It seemed to go well enough. The Mexica did not challenge the addition of a new god.

But a few days later, Cortés interrupted Moctezuma at prayer in the temple. Tepin was crouched down next to the altar waiting for the Emperor to finish when the Spaniard appeared with several of his soldiers. Moctezuma was used to protocol being violated by the foreigners, and turned politely to greet Cortés just outside the entrance. It did not go well. Tepin moved just enough so he could hear both men without being noticed.

"Lord Moctezuma, you can see for yourself that nothing bad has happened since Our Lady has been installed. The sun has not ceased to rise nor the corn to grow." Cortés opened his arms and gestured dramatically. "The Mexica throne is held by the True God, not the demons you worship. It is He who has decided all that has come to pass. It is time for you to be free of your delusion. I will liberate you today. We can do it together by rolling down your idols that are fed with the blood of innocents. We will put an end to human sacrifice and clean this whole temple. Let us replace the statues of demons with an image of Christ the True God!"

The Emperor shook his head but Cortés continued. "It is time the Mexica learn who created them. Let Him redeem them! Become the first Christian in this land! If you convert, you will win your people over to the True God. It will be done peacefully that way. No one will resist."

Tepin moved closer as Moctezuma held up his hand.

"You still do not understand! The Emperor protested. "Your True God does not hold the Mexica throne. The throne is held for the god, for Quetzalcoatl. It has been since the god left us, vowing to return. Great Speakers sit on the jade throne, but it is the god's throne, not ours! If I accepted your True God, the *pipiltin* would not follow me and accept him as well. Can you not be made to see this? If asked to choose between the Great Speaker and Huitzilopochtli, the Mexica would choose the god. Great Speakers are elected by the council. Gods are born of miracles."

He began to pace agitatedly.

"Already the gods were angered by what was happening in Tenochtitlan. The priests tell me the gods threatened to withdraw from the land. If they do that, they will leave it dry, barren! If we stop the gift of sacred fruit, the sun will hold still in the sky and burn everything that lives. I have explained this to you before! Remove the statues, you say? We dare not! Instead, your cross needs to be taken from Huitzilopochtli's temple and Our Lady too! If we fail to do this, the gods will rise up, and the people will follow." He slapped his feathered fan against his thigh with such force that the quills broke and the feathers fell to the ground.

"We will both die then, Cortés," the Emperor warned, "and so will the Mexica. It cannot be helped."

Furious at the refusal, Cortés stormed into the Temple itself. He spat out orders that his frightened translator repeated in Nahuatl.

"Get water and start scrubbing the blood from the rest of these walls! Make them as clean as the room that holds the cross. My men and I will cast these demons from their thrones!"

Before anyone realized what was happening, Cortés seized a metal rod and slammed it against the god's head. The golden mask fell and landed in a bowl of bloodied hearts, gleaming like rubies in the torchlight. Enraged at such blasphemy, the High Priest sounded the conch for the Jaguar Warriors.

"Before the warriors get here, let us find a compromise. Please, Cortés, let us avoid a massacre. Please! We will do fewer sacrifices, and you will leave our gods alone."

"No sacrifices!" demanded the Spaniard loudly.

"If you will not agree, we need to return to the palace immediately before the Jaguar Warriors reach us. If not, war between our peoples will begin."

Tepin watched as Cortés fought to regain control of himself.

The Spaniard had come with only a few of his men and some of the Jaguar Warriors were at the bottom of the temple steps already. Even Tepin could see this was not the time or place for an armed confrontation. With great effort, Cortés let the rod fall to the floor.

"Look at your god now," he sneered. "You can see he is nothing but stone. He cannot even protect his statues from my attack." He turned and led his men down the many temple steps and past the ascending Jaguar Warriors, who were uncertain why they had been summoned. Moctezuma watched the scene in despair.

Atlatzin listened to the details of what had passed from Tepin. The boy's eyes took on an unfocused stare when he recited from memory. Even though he trusted Tepin's ability to remember exactly what he heard, the nobleman had to be sure.

"Please?" he questioned. "The Emperor said 'please' to the Spaniard?"

"Twice, my Lord," responded the boy.

After the Emperor had sworn allegiance to Cortés, Atlatzin had thought he could not be further humiliated. Clearly he was wrong. The Great Speaker, *Tlatoani* of the Mexica Empire, had been reduced to begging! Atlatzin spat deliberately into the dust.

He was in the crowd a few days later when the great idols were removed carefully from their altars. Using ropes, levers and rollers, the Mexica lowered them to the base of the great pyramid, gently laid them on huge litters, and reverently covered them with fine blankets and mats. Although the *zócalo* was crowded with people watching, the whole operation was carried out in deathly silence.

Cortés watched in satisfaction and then ordered the cleansing of the twin temples. When all had been scrubbed and then painted with lime, a new altar was built in each temple. The Mexica looked on in silent resentment as the True God was enthroned next to his mother, the pale goddess known as Our Lady.

CHAPTER SIXTEEN

"The gods have ordered the death of Cortés." Humming-bird's High Priest threw back his matted hair as he spoke the challenging words. With a weariness that had become characteristic of him, the Emperor buried his thin face in a nosegay of flowers. He inhaled deeply before replying.

"Would the gods have me commit sacrilege and insult the messenger from the Eastern Quarter of the Sky? Shall I destroy the one sent by the Morning Star that brings the dawn and the wind that is our breath?"

"The gods have threatened to abandon the Mexica, my Lord. Without the presence of Huitzilopochtli, there will be no sacrifice; the sun will rise but not move across the sky and everything beneath it will burn. If the god Tlaloc leaves us, there will be no rain, no crops of maize or fruit. All births will cease if the fertile Ayopechcatl goes. We have no choice. The strangers must die."

Moctezuma tossed the flowers aside. The feathers in his head-dress were bright in the sun that poured down at the top of the temple steps in contrast to the dull color in the monarch's face.

"Do you still think this man has the god's blessing?" demanded the priest. "Even after all he has done? Whether or not he is the messenger of the foreign god called Carlos, he is not stronger than Huitzilopochtli and all the gods combined, *Tlatoani*. He does not even dare to prevent your coming here to the temple to pray. He knows he lacks the power." The priest turned to the audience of lesser priests who surrounded them. "It is time to put an end to all this. Let us sound the drums of war."

"No! Even though they are few, the Spaniards have weapons far more powerful than ours. The gods will leave us? But the Spaniards have dethroned the god! And Hummingbird did nothing! Can you not understand how dangerous any action against our guests would be? Do nothing without my command!" Moctezuma waved the priests away and entered the temple. He knelt before the empty altar where the god of war had once stood and the Emperor prayed for peace.

Moctezuma knew he had to try one last time, but he wanted his counselors with him when he spoke to Cortés. If he was surprised to see Atlatzin among those who came when summoned, he did not show it. But Atlatzin noticed that he was the only man present who had reportedly not sworn loyalty to the foreign Emperor.

"I have news for you that is most distressing," Moctezuma said to Cortés, when the latter arrived at the meeting. "The gods have ordered me to make war on you. I do not wish to do this. I have spent hours in prayer and deep thought and decided you and your men should leave my lands at once." Moctezuma peered at Cortés for his reaction. Atlatzin had to admire how the Spaniard kept his face perfectly blank. Neither surprise nor emotion of any kind showed.

"I will not be able to prevent an attack if you remain here," continued Moctezuma. "Our gods are fierce gods. They have been gentle with you so far, but now it is a question of your lives. Nothing but your leaving can save them. There is nothing I can do now. You and your lords are in the gravest of dangers." Moctezuma leaned back in his wicker chair, both with relief that the words had finally been said and unease because he had dared to say them.

Watching carefully, Atlatzin could see Cortés swallow and take a deep breath, but the nobleman had to admit that the Spaniard did it as a warrior would, with intelligence and stealth.

"I thank you most sincerely for this warning," Cortés said with a half-smile, and Atlatzin again had to admire his skill. "Your advice is appreciated, but I am troubled by two things. First, I have no ships to sail away in. Of course, I will be glad to build some, but that will take time. My second problem is that when I leave, you will have to come with me, Moctezuma. Emperor Carlos will insist on meeting you and learning from your own mouth the story of the powerful Mexica."

Unlike Cortés, the alarm Moctezuma felt at these words showed on his face. No one there doubted that the Spaniard had the power to enforce this thinly veiled threat. The gods of the Mexica would not prevent him from taking the Great Speaker with him across the waters any more than they had prevented his being taken prisoner. He would be taken away, a new Emperor would be elected, and life would continue as before. Used though he was to human sacrifice, the idea that the Emperor himself would be a living sacrifice shocked Atlatzin. But if there were no choice? He quickly reminded himself that even Moctezuma must know he would have no choice when the time came, if such a sacrifice were the fate decided for the *Tlatoani* on the day of his birth.

Cortés read the look on the monarch's face and the half-smile spread into a cold smile of victory. "I will send word to my garrison in the village I have named Vera Cruz after the True Cross, and I will order them to build three ships. We can leave when they are completed."

Moctezuma swallowed painfully and nodded. "I will supply carpenters to help and order them to hurry and not waste their time. I will also command the priests and military not to stir up disturbances in the area and direct that the gods be appeased with sacrifices. Perhaps this way we can prevent a war and save both our peoples." Cortés bowed slightly and left the room.

The Emperor stared blindly at an ornate weaving on the far wall where bright threads and feathers formed fingers of color that pointed to a great eagle perched atop a cactus, a serpent writhing in its claws. Before his counselors could say anything, the Emperor pointed at the tapestry.

"Look at that weaving! Hummingbird led us during generations of wanderings. He told us to build our home where we saw the sight pictured there on the wall. We obeyed and where we saw it, we built Tenochtitlan. We have prospered under the god's protection. But whether it is Feathered Serpent or the new god who has the power now, the wheel has turned."

"My Lord, you cannot be considering going with them!" The High Priest interjected.

"Let me order my Jaguar Warriors to put an end to this now, Lord Moctezuma. They may have magic weapons but they are still only a few men. It is not too late!" insisted Atlatzin.

"No." Moctezuma picked absently at the embroidery on his belt. "It will take time to build three great temple-ships. Anything can happen during that time. Who knows? With enough sacrifices, Huitzilopochtli may be convinced to continue his protection. If there is no choice, I will go east with Cortés, over the waters to the Land of the Morning Star. Better the sacrifice of one man, even a Great Speaker, than a war between the gods that might tear the world apart.

"Leave me now," he ordered his counselors. "You, Atlatzin, stay a moment."

After the other counselors left, Atlatzin knelt before the Emperor. He had hesitated coming to the palace that day, unsure of his welcome. But a summons to the Council from the Emperor could not be ignored, regardless of the consequences.

"You did not swear loyalty to the Emperor Lord Carlos when I asked the *pipiltin* to do so."

"My loyalty and my life are always for you and the Mexica, my Lord," Atlatzin tried to assure him.

"Yet, even I took the oath," Moctezuma continued. "You did not come when I asked the *pipiltin* to gather. You willfully disregarded my call. Why?"

"Had I taken the oath, I could not be loyal first to you, my Lord. I fear you may still need warriors who honor the gods of the Mexica and put you above all others. Forgive me if I have offended you, but I cannot bow before some pale wooden woman or pledge my loyalty to some foreign emperor who rules over men who do not even know how to keep themselves clean! I would die for you, *Tlatoani*. Do not ask me to live for them."

Moctezuma studied Atlatzin's face. His counselor kept his eyes averted as protocol demanded. But out of the side of his eye, he thought he saw the Emperor nod his head.

"Very well, Atlatzin. I could have you thrown into prison, but you have served me loyally in the past, as did your father. I did not order the *pipiltin* to swear loyalty to the foreign Emperor. But I expected them to follow my lead. Nevertheless, should I order it in the future, I will expect you to do so immediately. For now, you are dismissed."

Atlatzin bowed respectfully. As he left, he heard Moctezuma send for a messenger and order that the sacrifices to Hummingbird be tripled. He knew the Emperor was right. Anything could happen in the time it would take to build three great ships the size of temples.

Atlatzin came to the palace with news that several new ships had landed on the coast where Cortés left his garrison. The ships were full of soldiers like Cortés' Spaniards and their horses. It was unclear if the arrivals were friends or enemies of Cortés, but they far outnumbered the men Cortés had brought.

"Perhaps Huitzilopochtli is pleased with the extra sacrifices and has sent enemies of the Spaniard to free us," said Moctezuma, and Atlatzin could hear the hope in his voice. "If these new arrivals should decide to attack Cortés, we could hardly be blamed."

"I think it more likely that they would join forces, my Lord. Especially when they hear about the gifts Cortés has been given."

"Be careful, Atlatzin. That might be considered criticism." Moctezuma frowned, but it was without energy. "Cortés is due here shortly. I will tell him about the arrivals. Watch his face carefully and judge his reaction. That will tell us how to handle this new landing of soldiers."

When Cortés arrived and Moctezuma told him the news, Atlatzin saw it was no surprise. Of course, the Tlaxcalans would have told him. The Leader of the Jaguar Warriors was not the only one with spies.

"I have ordered that the new arrivals be welcomed," announced Moctezuma, "as I thought you would want me to welcome your brothers. I encouraged them to stay in comfort there on the coast until you send word to them. I am delighted at their arrival, for now you have no need to build ships. You can all return to your home. The ships have been brought to you." The Emperor studied Cortés' impassive face.

"I know you have shared my gifts with your men," he added as an after thought. "You will need more for the new men. I will order more gold and jewels to be brought from the royal treasury for them and as special gifts for Lord Carlos. You just take them with you, along with all the other gifts I have given you when you go."

"You are most generous, great Moctezuma, and I accept your gifts with thanks," said Cortés though his interpreter. "But these new arrivals are not my brothers. It is true they are from the lands of the Emperor Carlos. But Narváez, the man who leads them, is a bandit and it is my duty to arrest him."

Moctezuma twisted the large gold bracelets on his arms, failing to hide his unease. "He has large forces and your men are few. I will provide five thousand Jaguar Warriors to accompany you. They will see you arrest these bandits without trouble."

Cortés smiled slightly. "Again, I thank you, Moctezuma. But I must refuse this generous offer. With God on my side and our Blessed Lady, my men and I will easily take Narváez."

"You will leave Tenochtitlan soon?" Even Tepin, sitting quietly behind the throne, could hear the hope in Moctezuma's voice.

"I will leave Lieutenant Alvarado in the city with a small force. I hope you will continue to stay here in this palace where my men can protect you. I fear it would be unwise for you to leave." Cortés said the words politely, but there was an edge to his voice. Moctezuma must have heard it, as he seemed to pale against the iridescence of his cape.

"You need not fear for us, Lord Moctezuma. We will return victorious. Stay quietly with Alvarado and keep the priests from causing trouble." Cortés moved forward and embraced the Great Speaker, who had no choice but to allow it. As he turned, the Spaniard came directly face to face with Atlatzin. Although the warrior could control his expression, his body radiated fury. It did not escape Cortés notice.

"I do not believe this counselor of yours was among those who swore loyalty to the Emperor Carlos, Moctezuma." He turned back and faced the throne. "We will need to take care of that when I return." With a nod to his men, he swept out of the room.

"You are trapped now as well, Atlatzin." Moctezuma pulled his cape tighter around his body, as though to ward off the coldness Cortés left in the room.

"I cannot swear loyalty to him, my Lord."

"And I cannot have you disrespect my order."

"You need not order me, *Tlatoani*. You could say I am forbidden to take an oath for some reason." Atlatzin desperately tried to think of a way out.

"I cannot have others see you as an exception, and I cannot allow Cortés to think me duplicitous." Moctezuma sighed and fingered his thin beard. "But in all other ways, you serve me well. And who is to say how the Spaniard will be greeted by these new arrivals when he arrives at the coast?

"Very well. For the love I bore your father, you may keep your position as head of the Jaguar Warriors. And you will continue to maintain your network of spies and runners and keep the palace informed of events. But from this day on, you are forbidden access to my presence until you swear loyalty to Lord Carlos. I will never contact you directly again."

Atlatzin bowed respectfully. If Cortés were killed in battle with the newcomers, all would be well and he knew Moctezuma would relent. In the meantime, he would offer a special gift to the gods in thanks for Tepin's presence at the Emperor's side. He would know what was happening in the palace, as well as have warning should things go against him on the coast.

CHAPTER SEVENTEEN

Atlatzin could tell from the tight lines around his mother's mouth that she was disturbed. He tried to ignore her and concentrate on the messages painted on the scroll that lay in his lap. The ships that he had warned Moctezuma about had brought nine hundred Spaniards. They had marched north and were camped in Zempoala. Cortés had about one third of that number and was marching south toward the town. The Tlaxcalans were not with him As Atlatzin thought about the implications of the message, his mother made it clear she expected his full attention.

"I have received a message from your sister," she announced. Atlatzin looked up as she knew he would, and she nodded grimly. "You would do well to tend to your duty to family and leave the priests to their plotting."

"My sister?" asked Atlatzin impatiently.

"Do you remember what happened to the foreign princess?" Atlatzin watched his mother pick nervously at threads from the hem of her blouse and knew that she was more disturbed than he had realized. He nodded his assent; she had his full attention now.

"The gods once told a prince of the Mexica to take a foreign princess as wife. When her father came to join in the wedding celebration, he found a priest dressed in his daughter's skin. She had come joyously, expecting a royal wedding. Instead she was sacrificed to the Flayed God." She shook her head at the betrayal in the story.

"I remember the tale, Mother. What did Quetzali say?" demanded Atlatzin in growing alarm.

"She sends word she is to be given to the one called Alvarado, lieutenant lord to Cortés."

"The yellow-haired dung eater!" Atlatzin leapt to his feet and the forgotten scroll fell to the floor.

"Moctezuma himself ordered this alliance. It appears that Alvarado set eyes upon her and demanded her for his own. Since she has still not been promised to a prince, Moctezuma agreed," the woman continued, and although her voice was low, it trembled with anger. "But before that creature will take her to his mat, Quetzali is to be dedicated to their white goddess! These strangers think this must be done to cleanse her! As if our women were not clean! The whole world knows they are the ones who stink of filth!"

"The Emperor would not do this! He promised to marry her to a prince!"

"He has done it. He has given two of his daughters to Cortés, including his favorite. Do you think he would hesitate to give away your sister?"

"Alvarado will never touch her," Atlatzin swore softly. "One thrust of my knife will speed his way to Mictlan."

"And will that save her, my son?"

Atlatzin looked at his mother strangely. He had always thought of her as frail, yet there was a strength about her he had not suspected. "If you manage to kill the yellow-haired one, another of the foreigners will want her instead. These are strange times. The Emperor has withdrawn his protection, and my poor daughter is a sacrifice to foreign gods. You must go to Moctezuma and prevent this."

"I cannot," he told her. "I refused to take the oath of allegiance. The Emperor will no longer see me. And if by some miracle he should? Has he ever refused anything these strangers have requested? He has given them the empire and all its riches! Do you think he would hold back a simple girl from the *pipiltin* after he gave his own daughters?"

"You must not let your sister be dishonored or sacrificed to strange gods. Find a way to stop this and spare our family that humiliation. Whatever it takes, you must do that." She reached up and touched his face with a small sad smile.

Atlatzin stared for a long moment at his mother's face. When had the frown lines around her mouth grown so deep? Why had he not noticed? He put his fingers under her chin and gently turned her face up to his before bending to kiss her swiftly on the cheek and leave. When he was gone, the old woman sent a servant to the market for *pulque*. She did not intend to wait for the news of how her son would save the family's name without its help.

Once outside, Atlatzin realized he needed an excuse to get into the palace. The guards there knew who he was and that he was not to enter the Emperor's presence. He needed to demonstrate he was there to see his sister, or they might block his entrance. He changed course abruptly and headed for the *zócalo*. A gift for Quetzali would be reason enough, he decided, to "celebrate" the coming event. Once in the market, he headed for a jewelry maker's mat. A small bracelet of silver and turquoise links caught his eye, but as he examined it, he caught sight of Papalopil.

She was crouched over a mat spread full of sweet potatoes near him. Her dress had been washed since he last saw her, and though it was clean, it was streaked and discolored. A lock of her dark hair had escaped its pinnings and hung loose along her cheek but did not hide the bruises that he thought he saw there, even from a distance. Without thinking, he crossed the space between them and brushed the hair away from her face so he could see her eyes. Startled, she stepped back and tried to smile. The smile failed miserably and, looking into her face, Atlatzin saw only another Mexica maiden betrayed and misused.

"You have returned," he said.

"I ... yes," she said strangely.

"Your elder priestess told me about your mother. These are sad days."

Her reaction seemed awkward, but he dismissed it. He had no time for speaking secrets.

"Is that bracelet for a sweetheart?" asked Papalopil, catching sight of the gleam of silver in his hand.

"For my sister," he said, for the moment forgetting the difference in their status. "She is being given as wife to one of the strangers." Papalopil gave a slight shudder.

"May the gods protect her," she said softly. "I will offer a sacrifice and dance a prayer for your sister tonight."

"No!" said Atlatzin, more harshly than he intended. "Forget the sacrifices and the dancing of prayers! Not tonight or any other night. Do not dance! Make no sacrifices! They are a waste. The festivals are foolishness! The gods are not listening to our prayers or watching us dance any more."

Papalopil looked up in shock and then looked around quickly to see if anyone had overheard the blasphemy. But Atlatzin was not done.

"Do not waste your time in dancing. Leave the city! Go back to your village where they have never heard of the Spaniards and live your life there. Leave while you can. All is lost here!" He turned and threw a few *cacao* beans down on the jeweler's mat in payment for the bracelet and pulled his cape around him as he strode off. The temple dancer stared after him in concern.

Atlatzin slipped into his sister's chamber without arousing undue attention. He hid himself behind a thick hanging and watched as Quetzali was being groomed for Alvarado. Servants rubbed her skin with rose petals and brushed the shining hair that hung full about her waist. The women worked in silence. This was not a moment for joyful chatter, and each was secretly glad it was Quetzali who was being given to the stranger and not one of them. It seemed to Atlatzin that it took forever for the thick black hair to be braided and wrapped in coils around Quetzali's head. Finally, he could wait no longer. Throwing caution aside, he whistled the bird call that had been their signal as children. It was the song of the quetzal bird; he had taught it to her himself. Quetzali looked up, startled. The call was repeated, and she crossed swiftly to a wicker cage. Slipping a finger between its thin bars, she chirped at the yellow bird within. Her maids were city born and she hoped they did not know one bird song from another.

"Leave me now," she said to them. "I would be alone with my thoughts. I will call you when I am ready." When they had left, she turned and called, "Atlatzin! Where are you?" He stepped into view and she ran into his arms. "You should not be here now; it is dangerous. But I admit I am glad to see your dear face."

"Mother received your message, Quetzali." He held on to her for a second before letting her go and crossing to check the door. "When are you to be handed over?"

"As soon as I am dressed. They will take me first to the white goddess and bless me and then to Alvarado. You must help me,

Atlatzin. I know Moctezuma is my lord and he commands it, but I cannot do this. Alvarado smells like human waste. They all do. It is the smell of death, Atlatzin.

"But it isn't just that," she rushed to add, lest he think she did not understand the seriousness of the act. "I cannot bear the shame of it. It is an insult to our family, a family whose bloodline is as old as Moctezuma's. And if they dedicate me to Our Lady, I will never reach Mictlan. I'll die foresworn and forsaken. You must help me."

"I can try and help you escape, Quetzali. We can leave the city," Atlatzin offered, knowing at the same time that escape was impossible.

"There is only one thing to do, dear brother, and you know it. If we escaped, they would find us. You are not unknown and Moctezuma would be enraged at the insult. We would be captured and brought back to die like common criminals. Our mother would die of shame. You know what must be done."

"No, Sister. Don't ask me this."

"I tried to do it myself," she said urgently. "They took everything that cuts away from me. I thought I could swallow my earrings; the hooks are sharp. But I realized it would take me too long to die. And then I heard your whistle."

"Sweet Quetzali, I cannot do this," he whispered.

"If you fail me, I will do it myself the first chance I get, I swear. But by then it will be too late. I will have been given first to the foreign goddess and then to the foreign dog. We will all be shamed. You have to help me, Atlatzin. If you love me, you will. You have to."

Atlatzin shook his head. Quetzali was almost like a stranger, too adult, too calm, too self-assured. He had expected to find her in tears. And instead she was coolly asking him to kill her.

"I had given up until now. When I realized I could not end my life myself, I prayed. And the gods sent you to me."

"Quetzali," he tried to interrupt her.

"Remember the last five days at the end of the calendar wheel we learned about when we were young?" She smiled up at him and suddenly was the child-woman he knew. "Chimali was with us the night Mother told us the story. It was the last of the five nights at the end of the great cycle of fifty-two and she was just a child. Her mother was inside with that mask of agave leaves over her face to keep evil from befalling the child she carried. Remember? Mother told us that her father took her by the hand and led her out of the city to the Hill of the Stars. She was terrified. Her father explained how every fire in the entire world had been extinguished and how that very night the world might come to an end. He made her look around as she stood there. She told us it was the blackest night she had ever seen. There was no moon and she couldn't see a single star. She said that the only light in the whole world came from fireflies that danced in ignorance on the hill. I remember that I started to cry at this point in the story. You squeezed my hand. Chimali said that if I cried at Mother's memory, I might drowned in tears when the wheel turned and the end of the cycle came in my own lifetime. He scolded me and said I must always face fear bravely. And then you laughed. 'It might be a new beginning,' you said, and you promised that you would take care of me, whether it was the end or the beginning. I have never forgotten it.

"Then the moment came and the cycle was complete. The priests on the Hill of the Stars sacrificed a warrior from the *pipiltin* and offered the gods the sacred fruit. Mother explained how they kindled a new flame in the man's breast where his heart had lain. When the spark took, she said a great shout of joy rose from the hill and all the fires of the Mexica were lit again from that small sacred flame. Her father cut her earlobes and sprinkled blood to the wind, and then they went home and ate quail and amaranth seed cakes spread with honey."

"Quetzali, this is not the time..."

"But it is, Atlatzin," she interrupted. "The story taught me to be brave, and I must be brave now. We both must be. It will be a beginning for me in Mictlan. You promised you would take care of me and I am not afraid."

"This need not be!" he whispered fiercely.

She smiled with such sweet sadness that Atlatzin knew he had lost. "Do not leave me here to shame our family. Do not let them take me from my gods. Do not let them condemn me to a criminal's death. If you love me, my brother, let the words on your lips remain unspoken. Embrace me for the last time and wish me well."

He opened his arms and she stepped into them. He held her tightly against him. There was no other way, but he had hidden that truth from himself, not wishing to admit what must be done. But Quetzali was right. There was only one thing that could save her and, painful as it was, he was now the only person who could do it. He gently kissed the top of her head and whispered her name for one last time.

And then it was over. The black handle of his dagger protruded from the whiteness of her dress. Blood oozed up around it like an exotic flower from the hot lands.

"Sweet Sister, my Precious Feather," he crooned tenderly, pulling his bright cloak around to cover both of them from the evening's chill. He lowered himself to her mat and sat rocking her lifeless body in his arms.

He understood something his sister had not. In killing her, he had sacrificed himself. He was a brave and loyal warrior, a leader of the Jaguar Warriors. He deserved to die a good death, to be killed in battle or be sacrificed to the sun, to live with the god in his shining abode for four glorious years and then to return to earth as a hummingbird. But in saving his sister and family from shame, the nobleman had thrown away his chance for a beautiful death. He would have to die like a criminal. No one was above the law.

He rocked his sister's body and waited for the guards to come arrest him. He raised his right hand and rubbed his pounding temple. The bracelet he had bought slipped out of his pouch and fell into the blood that seeped down to pool on the polished stucco floor.

CHAPTER EIGHTEEN

"Cortés has left the city," announced Papalopil, returning from the market. "They say he is going to arrest a new Spaniard who has landed on the coast. A criminal, according to Cortés, someone who is our enemy, as well as his."

"Has he taken all his soldiers?" asked Mama Amoxtli hopefully.

"No," she replied. "The yellow-haired one they call Lieutenant Alvarado was left in charge of half of the Spaniards, plus what people in the *zócalo* say looks to be about four hundred Tlaxcalans."

Mama Amoxtli spit into the dust in the patio. "Tlaxcalans! Cowardly softspears! The Spaniards keep finding new ways to humiliate us."

"But we will still celebrate the festival of Toxcatl, no?" Cuicatl looked up from her weaving anxiously. "Remember, I am to be one of the god's maiden-brides."

"How could we forget?" Mama Amoxtli smiled at Papalopil.

"The festival will be next week, at least that is what they say in the market." Papalopil put down the armload of purple flowers she was carrying and began to divide them into bundles to decorate the altar. "The festival will go on and the Spaniards will be invited to watch the dances. There will still be the maiden-brides and the warrior who is the god. He will appear with you and the other three brides, playing the flute and blessing the dancers. But then he will disappear."

"Disappear?" asked Cuicatl.

"The Spaniards behave so outrageously at sacrifices that the most sacred part of the festival, the giving of the god's life, will be done in secret. People in the market say not even the Tlaxcalans will know." She grinned in delight at the trickery.

Mama Amoxtli shook her head. "I find no reason to be amused. The gods gave their lives so that we might live in this time of the fifth sun. In return, we give our lives, our hearts, and our blood to honor and nourish them. The Spaniards come from a barbaric land where they do not understand the concept of a sacred debt. They do not honor reciprocity the way we Mexica do. The Emperor obviously knows this and wisely chooses not to share too much information about our festival. It would only disturb the lieutenant and his pale goddess."

"Have you seen the statue of her?" asked Papalopil. When Mama Amoxtli shook her head, she continued. "I hear she looks just like the Spaniards but paler. She stands on curved horns held aloft by a child, and over her plain dress, she wears a long robe studded with painted stars!"

The women looked at each other in surprise. They knew the goddess Citlalicue created the stars. She even wore a skirt made of them.

"I wonder if that is a sign," said Cuicatl softly. "Perhaps the pale goddess will look after us."

"It could just as easily be an evil sign as a good one," said Papalopil. She brushed the leaves out of her skirt and took the flowers into the temple.

"Xochiquetzal looks after us," said Mama Amoxtli firmly, following Papalopil inside.

Cuicatl hurried after them. "I hear your nobleman has been sent to prison, Papalopil. They say he murdered his sister."

"Your nobleman?" asked Mama Amoxtli, raising an eyebrow as she turned to the Temple Dancer.

"Lord Atlatzin," Papalopil said nervously. "His sister was being given to Alvarado. I heard he had been arrested. I assume he killed her to spare her the shame. At least that is what they say in the marketplace."

"And just why is he your nobleman?" demanded Mama Amoxtli. "Cuicatl, why do you call him that?"

"She follows him in secret. Everyone knows it except for him," said Cuicatl. Papalopil shot her an angry look.

Mama Amoxtli turned and stared at her slave through narrowed eyes. Papalopil rushed to reassure her.

"I did follow him, but I no longer do. I stopped that some time ago," she said.

"And just why did you begin?" There was no warmth in Mama Amoxtli's voice.

"You told me to study the ways of men and I thought through watching him I could learn about noblemen. I thought that if I would be a successful *auianime*, I needed to understand those who would seek me out, especially those who could afford small gifts if I pleased them."

"And you thought Lord Atlatzin would seek you out?" Mama Amoxtli did not smile. "Foolish child! The man is chaste. And if he were not, there are plenty of *auianimes* who are far more beautiful than you who would fight for the chance to share his mat for a night."

"I just thought that I could learn by watching him," Papalopil said softly. "I need to learn to attract and please men with resources who could give me valuable gifts if I hope to ever buy my freedom," she defended herself without looking the elder priestess in the eye.

"And speaking secrets?" demanded the elder priestess.

"Who is speaking secrets?" Cuicatl asked curiously.

"That was a coincidence," Papalopil insisted. "I stopped following him then. One day, he just showed up at here the temple."

"What was a coincidence?" Cuicatl was intrigued now.

"Quiet, Cuicatl. This does not involve you," Mama Amoxtli dismissed the young priestess before turning back to the temple dancer. "Be careful, Papalopil. You have been extremely foolish. I know not if your head or your heart has led you to make these mistakes, but take care. You may aim high, way above your reach, but do not ever let your heart guide your aim. It is dangerous. At the very least, it will bring you pain."

"My heart is not involved," she said, and this time she turned and smiled tentatively at Mama Amoxtli. "I promise you, I have no intention of allowing love to confuse my life. I know my place and its limitations. I will not make those mistakes again."

Seemingly satisfied, the elder priestess sniffed went back to her work.

"What is all that about?" Cuicatl wanted to know.

"It was unkind of you to call him my nobleman. You can do your own hair for the festival," snapped Papalopil.

The morning before the festival, Mama Amoxtli joined the other women who were known for their ability to fast. They seated themselves on reed mats in the Patio of the Gods, before the Great Temple, and began to chew amaranth seeds. Alvarado's men walked among the women curiously, but they simply continued to chew the seeds into paste. Papalopil's job was to make sure enough fresh water was available, as the chewing was thirsty work. The women chewed, spit the seed pulp into baskets at their sides, rinsed out their mouths, and took another handful of seeds. When the sun passed over the temple and shadows began to grow on the other side, Papalopil gathered the individual women's baskets and dumped the contents into three large ones. The women gathered around them and, with their hands, mixed the paste with sacred blood from a previous sacrifice. Two priests brought them a frame made of wood and reeds. The women took handfuls of the mass and began to wrap it around the frame. Slowly it took the shape of a man's body. They worked through the night, and when the form was completely covered and smooth, they brushed the body with honey and pressed whole amaranth seeds against the darkened paste.

Before dawn, the women dressed the figure in the clothing of Huitzilopochtli. His loincloth was embroidered with skulls and hearts and ears and hands, all done in the most brilliant of blues. Around his neck was hung a collar of yellow parrot feathers, and on his head, a hummingbird crest glowed in the sun. A small golden arrow set with emeralds pierced his nose and mosaic turquoise snakes writhed in his earlobes. His bamboo shield was fringed with eagle feathers and coyote skin was wrapped in strips around one arm. The banner that flew from his staff was the purest of agave paper, dyed the color of fresh blood.

Papalopil, who had stayed by Mama Amoxtli's side, looked at the figure in awe. Even though she had seen it made and knew it was just seeds and sticks, it was still an imposing sight. At some time during the dance, the god himself would inhabit the form. She helped Mama Amoxtli to her feet and they watched as the priests propped the figure up so it stood next to the Palace, well inside the Serpent Wall.

A movement above her caught her eye, and Papalopil looked up to see the man called Alvarado leaning over the ledge on the Palace's second-floor balcony. She wasn't close enough to see his expression, but she assumed he was impressed by the women's artistry. How much more would he be impressed when the form became the god! she thought.

It seemed as though the streets of Tenochtitlan were coming alive with warriors. Serpentines of color began to coil their way through the Plaza of the Gods. Five huge drums were brought in and set on stands. Their wooden sides were carved into intricate designs and painted blue and red. The singers followed them with arms full of rattles and shakers. There was a handful of Jaguar and Eagle Warriors leading a few boys in their first battle feathers. Papalopil knew that warriors had been arriving in the city from all over the Empire. Their feathers and jewels would announce their ranks to the cheering crowd. They would be in full wardress, except for two things. The thin sheets of pounded silver that fit inside the padded cotton armor of the nobles had been left at home, along with all the warriors' weapons. The armor would weigh them down and all weapons were forbidden in the dance. The warriors came to sing and celebrate before their god, not to fight. It was the most glorious of days.

A sudden cry pierced her thoughts and she whirled around to see Mama Amoxtli on the ground. Papalopil dropped to her knees to help her rise, but the elder priestess whimpered in pain.

"I fear I have done serious damage," she said plaintively. "I cannot move my left leg."

"You are lying on it. That is why. Here, let me help you," said Papalopil, reaching to straighten the leg. But that only brought another cry of pain.

"Stop! Do not touch it. It must be broken to cause such pain!"

"Perhaps it is only sprained, Mama Amoxtli. Let me take you to the temple and get a healer for you."

"At my age I have seen enough broken bones to know my leg is broken, Child. Take me to the house, not to the temple. My medicines are there and I will need a tea for the pain." She lay back exhausted, and Papalopil saw she was trying to hide just how much pain she was in.

Spotting a young warrior from the crowd that was beginning to form in front of the figure, she asked him to carry the old woman back to the Street of Perfumed Nights. Once there, he laid her flat on a mat in her room adjoining the communal house, as she tried not to cry out. Papalopil quickly made tea with the herbs Mama Amoxtli indicated. As she drank, the priestess told her what to do next.

"This tea will dull the pain and make me sleep. When that happens, you must wrap my leg in the reed mat under the blanket I am lying on and tie it tight so the leg stays straight. Do not use the blanket. It is too soft and will not keep the leg straight. Take care not to make the wrapping too tight though, as the leg will swell. When it swells, make a tea of the shavings in the bag with the red tie in the chest under the altar. Those shavings also serve if I grow fevered. Better yet, make the tea before the leg swells, as I will need a lot of it. Then you must go to the festival."

"No, I need to be here with you," Papalopil responded.

"You are a Temple Dancer, you must dance," Mama Amoxtli said drowsily.

"I must take care of you first. Besides," she added, trying to distract the elder priestess, "Lord Atlatzin told me not to dance." Mama Amoxtli's face told her the tea was working and the woman had not heard what she said. It was a good thing, Papalopil realized with a start, as she had never told the elder priestess about running into him in the market.

While she wrapped her patient's leg as directed, she could hear the drums begin. The sound throbbed from the Plaza of the Gods, down the city's streets and drifting along the canals, calling people to the dance. Papalopil could feel the beat in her bones, and she swayed a bit with it as she made another pot of tea for pain. She heard voices raised in song, and song linked to song. As the leaves steeped, she lifted her arms and began to dance.

If she could not join the others in the Plaza, she could still dance her prayers, here, in front of the small altar in the communal house. In spite of what Lord Atlatzin had said, the gods loved the dancing. She loved the dancing. She came fully alive when she danced. Every touch was a blessing, every dance a prayer. She bent and turned and whirled as the deep voices of the drums quickened. Her feet moved in swift, small steps that seemed to dance almost on the edge of sound. Her thick hair came loose from its bindings and fell over her face like a dark waterfall. She slipped into the familiar trance as she moved with the rhythm for Huitzilopochtli. She danced her prayers for Mama Amoxtli, for her own freedom, for Lord Atlatzin. And she danced for his murdered sister.

So intense were her prayers that she failed to realize when the drumming stopped. It was Mama Amoxtli's voice that reached her.

"Something is wrong."

Papalopil whirled about and raced to the woman's side.

"Not my leg, Child. The drumming has stopped. Something must be very wrong." Papalopil listened, but heard only silence. The singing had stopped as well. "Run see what has happened," ordered Mama Amoxtli.

"I cannot leave you," insisted Papalopil.

"Just go and see and come right back. Run, quickly now!"

She leapt to obey. The nearby streets were empty, so she quickly reached the Gate of the Mirrored Snake that led into the great plaza. To her astonishment, the gate was closed and barred from the inside. This only happened in war! That was when she heard the screams. Raw and terrifying they rang out. She turned and raced down a side street, hoping to circle the plaza and enter through the Eagle Gate. But when she reached it, she found it closed and barred as well.

"They are killing us!" came the cries from inside. "Help! Mexica! Our captains have been murdered!" In shock, she heard the screams of the slaughter that was taking place inside. There was nothing she could do, no way she could help. Desperate, she turned and started running back to Mama Amoxtli. The streets were filling now. Those who had not been in the Plaza came running, some with spears and shields, others with whatever came to hand. Papalopil wove in and out of the growing crowd gathering by the Serpent Wall as she maneuvered her way back to the house.

Once there, she shared what she had seen and heard. Even from several streets away from the wall, they could hear the roar of grief and rage that shook the city.

"They have murdered our warriors! The heart of the Mexica is destroyed!" People beat their palms against their mouths, ululating their despair. The two women stayed there in the house on the Street of Perfumed Nights as darkness began to fall. There was nothing they could do but wait.

It was after midnight when Cuicatl crept in. She was near-hysterical and her gown was so covered with blood and feces and urine, that it was at first difficult to see that her injuries were not serious. Papalopil helped wash her, tensions between them forgotten, as the sobbing girl told them what had happened.

"The four of us maiden-brides stood there before the amaranth figure and the warrior to be sacrificed. The drums quickened and the dancers began to turn and whirl. It was a great and glorious dance and the moment came when the god would enter the figure. And then suddenly Alvarado and his soldiers were there, fully dressed for battle. Before anyone knew what was happening, they had their swords out and slashed off the drummers' arms!" She looked wildly around them as though seeing the butchering soldiers there in the small house.

"Then they fell on the dancers, stabbing them, spearing them, smashing their heads into pieces. The warrior who was to be sacrificed threw himself at Alvarado. But the butcher slashed him in the stomach. His bowels fell out to the ground. He tried to run, but they spilled as he ran and his feet got tangled in them. Another Spaniard cut him down.

"I could not move. They murdered everyone they could reach, without warning, without mercy," she sobbed. "Our warriors had no weapons, no shields. The Spaniards beheaded some, others had their heads split to pieces like ripe melons. I saw a young boy speared as he tried to climb the Serpent Wall and another tried to hold back a hemorrhage with stumps that had been his hands. The blood of our warriors flowed like water and formed pools on the flagstones. The Temple Dancers were split apart so that pieces of their bodies covered our fallen men.

"Some people tried to hide in the temples. But when the Spaniards had killed everything that moved in the plaza, they went into the temples and killed everyone they found there. Then they began to strip the bodies of their valuables, ear plugs, bracelets, chest plates."

"Xochiquetzal save us! Where were you?" asked Mama Amoxtli.

"I hid under the bodies and prayed," confessed Cuicatl. "I closed my eyes and pretended I was dead. I thought I would be killed next. The stink of the dead and dying made me start to gag, but I stuffed my dress into my mouth. I knew if I made a sound, they would spear the pile of bodies I was under. The goddess protected me and finally, when I thought I could not be still another moment, a miracle happened.

"From outside the Serpent Wall, the Mexica began to throw lances and spears. A barrage of missiles came over the great wall. Then I was afraid that they would hit me, that I would be killed by our own people where I hid. But I could not move. The Spaniards were still there. I lay there and watched as a blanket of yellow-feathered arrows flew over me. Finally, our people breached the wall and forced the murderers back into the guest palace. They fired off one of their thunder logs, so our people did not attack the palace itself.

"As soon as I knew I was safe, I came here. I did not know where else to go. Xochiquetzal's temple is full of dead bodies."

"You did the right thing," said Mama Amoxtli, ignoring her own pain to comfort the young priestess. She turned to tell Papalopil to make some soothing tea, and saw she was already doing so. "The families of our murdered warriors will come inside the wall and try to find their dead. They will carry the bodies home to wash and clothe them. But then they will be returned to the Plaza of the Gods. Such a massacre demands a public cremation.

"I am old and have lived through many wars but I have never heard of such a slaughter," she sighed heavily. "Even though I am not a warrior, I understand the ways of war. All the Mexica do. It is part of our lives. We know war has rules. There must be a formal declaration. There must be a truce for the holy days. But the Spaniards murdered unarmed warriors. They attacked on a holy day. They committed an act of butchery, slaughtering our finest warriors like domestic game for the table. This is a great sacrilege. The gods will not stand for it. The Spaniards may not know it, but a holy war has begun."

CHAPTER NINETEEN

The people of Tenochtitlan took back the heart of their city, all but the guest palace where the Spaniards had barricaded themselves. The Mexica forced open the gates in the Serpent Wall and reclaimed the Great Temple. They freed the few prisoners who had been jailed near the *zócalo* and students from the *telpochcalli* surrounded the guest palace so that no Spaniard might escape. Among the released prisoners was Atlatzin. There was no real order in the city. Moctezuma was a prisoner inside the guest palace. The Council members had been jailed there as well, along with some of the nobles who were suspected of being involved in the junta. Huitzilopochtli's priests were busy reinstating the statue of the god and ordering the Spaniards who had been captured to be sacrificed. Many of the war captains had been murdered in the dance and now no one was in charge. Atlatzin attended a meeting with the heads of the remaining noble families. Together, they decided to keep the markets closed, to starve out the enemy. Atlatzin personally supervised the blocking of the canal that took fresh water to the guest palace. Sooner or later, the Spaniards would have to try and make a break for it. The Mexica could wait.

There was disagreement about how to deal with Cortés when he returned. Since so many Mexica warriors had been murdered, it was decided not to attack him as he came back from the coast. The Tlaxcalans who traveled with him would outnumber the warriors the Mexica could gather in so short a time. It was decided to allow Cortés to return. They did not worry about the Tlaxcalans, as the Spaniard had never allowed but a few of them into the city. So they agreed to allow Cortés and his men to enter, and then prevent them from ever leaving Tenochtitlan alive.

Atlatzin watched from the shelter of a rooftop when Cortés returned to the silent city. Atlatzin knew that Tlaxcalan messengers had warned the Spaniard that the men he left behind in the capital had been driven back to the guest palace where they were surrounded by warriors. Still, Atlatzin had seen Cortés grow used to the awe and respect with which the Mexica had treated him. He suspected the Spaniard was surprised by the silence and emptiness that greeted him as he rode across the causeway into Tenochtitlan. Narváez and his soldiers, who had assuredly been bribed with promises of Mexica gold to follow Cortés rather than fight him, looked askance at the deserted capital. Atlatzin smiled grimly as he saw even their horses pranced nervously, their hooves clattering loudly on the flagstones.

No boats were on the lake and the chinampas floated free and unattended. Stones were piled next to the bridges that spanned the gaps in the causeway, and Cortés ordered a halt when he saw them. Atlatzin wondered if he recognized them as potential weapons. Cortés fired a round into the air and was answered by the boom of a thunder log that said his troops still held the guest palace. It was an uncanny echo floating across the lifeless lake.

Through the deserted streets the soldiers marched and past the empty markets. The only sound that greeted them was the frightened cry of an escaped turkey that crossed their path as it ran for safety. They entered the guest palace that had belonged to the Great Speaker's father and barred the gates behind them.

It was Tepin who managed to tell Atlatzin what was happening inside. Moctezuma had been isolated under Alvarado's command. He no longer had his own trusted servants to wait upon him, only Tepin, who looked so young he was seen as harmless when not ignored completely. The boy took the water jug that Atlatzin offered and drank greedily; small rivulets of cool liquid spilled over his bare chin and down his neck. With his thirst finally quenched, he wiped his mouth with the back of his arm and gave his report.

"The fruit that was not eaten immediately has rotted and the maize is almost gone. There are plenty of chilies, but the foreigners do not eat them, so they are beginning to complain of hunger. They dug a well after water from the canal stopped flowing, but now that there are new men and animals as well, water is rationed."

Atlatzin nodded with satisfaction. "I had the water diverted. They will have to make a move soon. Any other details about the conditions inside? No matter how trivial it seems to you, I want to know."

"Two of the new arrivals are ill. I hear they both are hot to the touch and one has raised sores, but that is all."

"How fares the *Tlatoani*?"

"He did something strange, my Lord. Cortés ordered him to reopen the markets and provide his troops with food and supplies, but the Emperor said he could not. He said the people would not listen to him any more. They could no longer love and obey him after what had happened. Cortés was very angry at that and said he had over a thousand men to feed. The Great Speaker said he had three times that number slain in cold blood by Alvarado. Then he said that either Prince Cacamatzin or

Prince Cuitlahuac could order the markets open and be obeyed. But Cortés said these were the men who planned the junta. Lord Moctezuma simply shrugged his shoulders and said they were the only men who could get the market open.

"So Cortés gave in and ordered Cuitlahuac to be brought from the dungeon. When the Prince arrived, he refused to pay obeisance to the Great Speaker and turned his back in insult."

"Of course," said Atlatzin, nodding slightly. "He knew it was Moctezuma who betrayed him."

"But then the Great Speaker said, 'Look at me, Cuitlahuac!'"

"Look at me?" asked Atlatzin in surprise.

"Look at me," insisted the boy. "The Great Speaker ordered the Prince to look at his face."

Of course. Cortés would not have understood the importance of those words. No Mexica could look directly at the face of the Great Speaker, the living god. But the Spaniard had never treated Moctezuma like a deity. He not only looked directly at the Great Speaker when he talked to him, he touched him without concern. No mere mortal could do that, at least not a Mexica. Only someone of equal rank might face the Emperor as a peer.

In commanding Cuitlahuac to look directly at him, Moctezuma had abdicated the turquoise throne in his favor. Prince Cuitlahuac must avert his eyes; Emperor Cuitlahuac would not. With that one look, Moctezuma had named his nephew his successor and heir. Cuitlahuac would have to be confirmed by the council, or at least what remained of the noble families, and then he would be declared a living god. But until then, he had the authority to act as Emperor. Moctezuma knew the Mexica would not act without an Emperor to lead them. Without Cortés' realizing it, Moctezuma arranged to send them one.

"Then Moctezuma said that he had given his word that the markets would be opened and Cuitlahuac would provide the Spaniards with supplies," Tepin continued. "His exact words were, 'This needs to be done immediately. Go now, and do what needs to be done.' Then the Prince dropped to the floor and made his obeisance and left.

"I must get back, Lord Atlatzin," concluded the boy. "It should be easier to sneak in and out now that food will be delivered, but I cannot be gone too long or it will be noticed."

Atlatzin praised the boy, who slipped back into the shadows. It would not be food that Cuitlahuac delivered to the Spaniards, but warriors. He went to the *calmecac*, knowing that the new Emperor would go there as soon as he left the guest palace. Atlatzin would use the information from Tepin to support Cuitlahuac's claim to rule. There would be no disagreement. The Mexica would have a legitimate ruler again.

In the very early hours of the morning, Cuitlahuac led warriors in the attack. Screaming Mexica stormed the barricades around the palace throughout the day. Although against all the rules of war, the attack continued after dark had fallen and all through the long night. Walls were breached and closed again as Mexica fell beneath Spanish steel. The night was lit with fire arrows that rained down upon the palace roof and flashes of the thunder log as it fired death at the warriors. Dawn came and still the battle raged. Wave after wave of warriors threw themselves at the walls their fathers had raised. Stones were launched from nearby roofs with an accuracy as deadly as the bullets that were returned. It seemed as though it would never stop.

In a desperate attempt to demoralize the Mexica, Cortés led a small band of soldiers on an unexpected mission. Fighting like a man possessed, he broke out of the palace, stormed the Serpent Wall, and recaptured Huitzilopochtli's temple. Steel swords met with obsidian-studded clubs in hand-to-hand combat, and bodies tumbled down the temple steps. Finally, the summit was captured and the last priest hurled from the high terrace. The wooden buildings on top of the pyramid were set on fire and

Cortés himself put the amaranth image of the god to flame. The statue of the Spaniards' goddess had disappeared from the altar. The brazier was again filled to overflowing with sacred fruit. The sight was too much for Cortés. With strength that seemed more than mortal, he lifted the huge bowl and flung it down the temple steps. Sacrificial hearts flew like missiles at the warriors and blood rained down on the stairs, the slickness slowing the advancing warriors only momentarily. But the sight of such blasphemy made the Mexicas' hate overflow, and they fought with a divine wrath that forced Cortés and his men down the steps they had profaned and back into the shelter of the guest palace.

Somehow, Tepin managed to slip outside and report to Atlatzin. Cortés had sent for Moctezuma but the Great Speaker refused to leave his room. The Spaniard's priest was sent to talk to him, to promise that Cortés and his men would leave the city forever if only Moctezuma would order the Mexica to withdraw.

"Then he began to speak about True God and how he was a god of peace and love. The Great Speaker got very angry." Tepin's unfocused eyes told Atlatzin he was beginning to recite exactly what he had heard.

"'Never speak to me again of this Christianity. If everything you say is true, it would mean I have betrayed my people and handed them over to nothing but a greedy conqueror. But this is not so. Our gods decided this battle should take place. It was they who announced the arrival of your ships. It was no ordinary arrival to be met with ordinary measures, but an event that would shatter the world. The universe is no longer in balance. I could no more stop all this than I could halt the great wheel in its turn.

"'The gods tell me this is only the beginning. The fabric of time will be torn and the great wheel will lose its rounded shape. Time itself will uncoil and lie straight like an arrow spent in vain. It began when you touched our soil, Priest. I thought I could prevent it, but it had already begun. The wheel cannot turn in reverse. The very moment you put your feet on our soil, we lost our land, and only the gods know if it will ever again belong to the Mexica.'" Tepin paused for breath before continuing. His eyes lost their glaze and he looked up at Atlatzin.

"The priest insisted that the Great Speaker could still save lives if he would just speak to the people. Lord Moctezuma looked very strange when he said that. But he just said he would speak from the balcony when the sun was high in the sky. Then he told me to prepare his best robe and jewels. I am to dress him in the morning."

Atlatzin stood next to Prince Cuitlahuac the next day when Moctezuma was taken to the top of the guest palace walls where he could be seen clearly. His loincloth was resplendent with embroidered suns and golden fringe. His most magnificent cape lay across his shoulders, deep green and ruby red. His crown was ablaze with turquoise stones and quetzal plumes. Jade hung from his nose and circled his arms in green bands all hung with feathers. His earplugs were the color of the midday sky, and his crystal lip plug, the finishing touch to his toilet, held the bright green feather of a kingfisher. He was gloriously adorned. There was a deadly hush when he was seen, and then the crowd drew nearer. Pipiltin stood with commoners, warriors with market vendors, priests with *auianimes*. They crowded in close together and moved forward to hear him speak. Moctezuma raised his hand in greeting. Atlatzin noted in particular what a strong, decisive gesture it seemed to be, like the Emperor he had looked up to as a youth.

"Lords of the Mexica!" cried the *Tlatoani*. "If you withdraw your troops and cease to fight, the foreigners say they will leave our land. Cortés has given me his word as a warrior. There is no need to continue this siege of the palace." Prince Cuitlahuac stared at him as though attempting to understand what he was doing, but Moctezuma relentlessly pushed on.

"Do this for me. Let this be the end. Put down your weapons and let the strangers leave us in peace. Let this be the end. Let this be the end," he repeated again.

There was an angry murmuring from the crowd beneath the palace walls and a voice rang out. "Coward! You betray us out of fear!"

"Whore!" screamed another.

Stones flew through the air. Moctezuma stood quite still, a small smile on his lips. His crown was knocked from his head and shattered turquoise fell around him. Two more stones found their target, and the Emperor of the Mexica fell to his knees. It was the signal for a hail of missiles, and the bleeding monarch was dragged into the palace by the retreating soldiers.

Atlatzin and Cuitlahuac were conferring at the *calmecac* when Tepin appeared unexpectedly.

"I have been sent away. The Emperor ordered me to leave him."

"What happened?" Cuitlahuac demanded.

"The soldiers took him inside after he was hit and bandaged his wounds. He was taken back down to the room where they had been holding him. But Lord Moctezuma tore the strips of cloth from his wounds and turned his face to the wall. When I tried to help him he pushed me away and ordered me to leave him forever. After that, he refused to eat. He refused to speak more. He just lay on a mat on the floor and faced the wall.

"I have failed you, Lord Atlatzin!" the boy threw himself to his knees and waited to be punished. But Atlatzin reached down and lifted him to his feet.

"No, Tepin. You have not failed. You are a brave and trustworthy warrior, a true child of the gods." Over the boy's head, Atlatzin met Cuitlahuac's eyes. They both knew that Moctezuma had decided to die.

"He encouraged us to attack him," said Cuitlahuac. "He kept asking us to end it."

Atlatzin nodded in agreement. "And since the stones did not kill him, he has decided to end it himself."

CHAPTER TWENTY

Atlatzin discovered the body in the canal. He pulled it from the water and saw the small metal knife protruding from its side. He wondered which of the pale soldiers had been coward enough to kill Moctezuma as he lay wounded by the stones that had been hurled at him. There was no glory in the Emperor's death. He did not die in battle, he could never join the sun. It was not even an honorable death. Atlatzin looked at the knife in his hands. It had tasted the purest of Mexica blood. With the gods' blessing, it would now drink deeply of Spanish. He wiped it off and slipped it into his belt.

That night a pyre was built in the *zócalo*. It was not as tall as the Great Temple pyramid behind it, but it was the finest that could be made under the terrible circumstances. Moctezuma's body was placed carefully at the top, and the small mountain of wood set to flame. His people may have felt he betrayed them, but Atlatzin and Cuitlahuac knew the emperor had sacrificed himself for them in the end. They watched respectfully as tendrils of fire crept upwards.

"He was no longer of use to them," the heir to the throne said softly. "But why would they let us know they murdered him? Why throw the body in the canal? Why not leave it to rot in the dungeon where we would never see it?"

"Perhaps the deed was not ordered," suggested Atlatzin. "Cortés may have been unaware of it. The coward who did the deed could have disposed of the body in order to protect himself."

The fire rose and licked at Moctezuma's fingers, and Cuitlahuac sighed. "He was not the only one to die ingloriously. I found Cacamatzin's body at sunset, as well as one of their soldiers. They both died of some strange sickness, their bodies covered with large putrid sores." He pulled his cape closer about him. In spite of the heat from the fire, Cuitlahuac was cold. "Why do you think my uncle acted as he did, Atlatzin? You knew him well. I will not believe he was a coward. Why did he welcome Cortés to this land and prevent us from killing him when it became clear he was neither Quetzalcoatl nor his messenger? I have never been able to understand this."

"Who can understand the workings of a man's mind, especially a man who became a god?" Unbidden, the memory of the crystal skull returned to Atlatzin. He remembered again its grinning face and he shook his head. "Moctezuma may have seen things we did not, my Lord. Who is to know in the long run if his vision was human or divine? He insisted it made little difference what he did, that it was like attempting to stop the great wheel of time. What was intended to be would be."

"We will defeat these intruders, Atlatzin. We did not ask for this war. We did not start it. But now that it has begun, the foreigners will never leave Tenochtitlan alive. I am to be the Great Speaker now and I will avenge my murdered warriors. Remove the bridges from the causeways and post lookouts along the canals. We will lure our enemies into leaving the safety of the palace, and then we will fall upon them like the eagle upon the snake."

Atlatzin smiled grimly at Cuitlahuac's words. The massacre would be avenged and the Spaniards would dance before Hummingbird's altar.

It was an old woman who gave the first alarm. She had gone for fresh water near the entrance to the Tlacopan causeway. As she straightened up from filling her jug, she saw something moving onto the causeway itself. It was difficult to see, for although there was a moon, rain fell steadily and blurred the shapes before her eyes. Then the hollow sound of animals' hooves thudded against the planking, and immediately, she knew the shapes were the loathsome Spaniards. She threw back her head and screamed. It was a scream filled with the hate and anger of a mother who has watched her sons slaughtered. Her cry was taken up and echoed through the streets of Tenochtitlan. Within moments the great snakeskin drum in the Great Temple began to throb.

The foreigners formed a wall of living flesh with the Tlaxcalans in the rear. Shoulder to shoulder they advanced upon the causeway. The alarm forced them to speed up their evacuation, and the portable bridge they carried jammed in the next breach of the causeway. Here the main thrust of the Mexica attack occurred. Hordes of warriors under Atlatzin's command swarmed toward them from a thousand canoes. Other canoes landed farther down the causeway to cut off the path to safety. The Spanish were surrounded on all sides and unable to use their terrible thunder log. The narrowness of the causeway prevented the Mexica from attacking in full force. From canoes, angry hands reached out and seized the legs of those who fought on the narrow road, pulling them into the water where they were clubbed to death. As they fell, gold tumbled from under their cloaks and into the dark water. The sight of Moctezuma's stolen treasure drove the Mexica to even greater passion. Soon women and children threw themselves into the meleé, smashing heads with stones and crushing the fingers of those drowning men who tried to climb back up the sides of the causeway. Arrows buzzed like angry wasps and the clash of obsidian and steel was loud as they met and moved apart to bite instead into soft flesh. The blood of two empires poured over the causeway and into the waters of the great lake. The screams of the dying once again filled the night.

The portable bridge was destroyed and the foreign army cut in two on either side of the gap. With the great horses in front, Cortés forced his way toward the shores of Tlacopan, swimming his men and animals through the other breaches. Those who could not swim to safety, those who were weighted down with Moctezuma's gold, filled the breaches with their bodies. Their companions climbed over their corpses. Only a few managed to reach the safety of Tlacopan. Over two-thirds of the enemy had been killed.

Dawn was gray and cold, and through the curtain of rain, Atlatzin could see the people of Tenochtitlan as they claimed the spoils of war. The bodies of the enemy were stripped naked and laid out in rows like white maguey shoots. The bodies of the horses were dragged out of the water and piled in a mound in the *zócalo* where the people could stare at them in wonder. The enemies' weapons and clothing fell to those who spied them first. Swords and knives, saddle pads and firesticks, shields and bars of gold were recovered and carried off to homes in every corner of the city.

Atlatzin watched as children dove for treasure as though it were a marvelous game. The children of commoners came away with as much gold as those of the nobility. They had all fought the enemy and deserved the reward, he thought. Some were joined in the water by adults, while still others searched among the fallen for friends and relatives. Atlatzin started as he recognized "his priestess" climbing out of the water. She had a wide gold bracelet in one hand and he could see turquoise stones tumbled in the folds of the wet skirt she had pulled tight around her thighs. He was glad she had not been killed in the massacre, glad that he told her not to dance.

She saw him then and stopped, as though she thought he might question her right to have gold. But Atlatzin simply smiled at her and moved on. From the red stains on her dress, he assumed she must have fought in the battle as well. Any gold was well earned.

Although he had not yet been officially crowned, Cuitlahuac called his new council together. Among those present were his young brother Cuauhtémoc and Atlatzin. The future Emperor paused before announcing the news that Atlatzin already knew. It was difficult after so glorious a victory to give them bad news.

"Upon the advice of my counselor Atlatzin, I ordered a regiment of warriors to follow Cortés and his remaining men and to destroy them before they could reach the safety of Tlaxcala. My runners tell me that we have failed. The war captain in charge of the expedition was killed in a battle at Otumba. His warriors, naturally, withdrew in respect."

Seeing the stunned looks of the men around him, Cuitlahuac drew himself up. "I have consulted with Hummingbird's High Priest to understand why the god would allow this to happen. It is now plain to me that we have been negligent in our duties.

"I know your intentions were good, Atlatzin, but I should never have heeded your advice and pursued the Spaniards. Once defeated and humiliated as they were, it was over. Cortés would never have attacked us again. We all know the rules of war." Cuitlahuac searched the faces of his men and was pleased to see them drop their eyes. "We are not animals. We fight because the gods command it, and we fight with skill and honor. But in the heat of the battle to rid Tenochtitlan of our enemy, we

forgot the rules given to us by Hummingbird. We lowered ourselves to the level of our enemy who knows no shame. We fought
at night. We killed more than we took as prisoners. We plun-
dered corpses and encouraged our women and children to do the
same. Huitzilopochtli has chosen to remind us with the defeat at
Otumba that the rules of war are sacred and we have holy obliga-
tions to fulfill."

"I do not think that our enemy knows the rules and respects
their sacred character, my Lord," said Atlatzin with bitterness.

Cuitlahuac shook his head sadly. "I think perhaps you are
right and they do not. But the god of war knows the rules, for
he created them. Never forget that it was he who led us to our
victory. He led us out of our home in far Atlan and through
the hundred years of wandering until he brought us to this spot
where we built Tenochtitlan. It was Hummingbird who drove out
Quetzalcoatl and set us over the tribes who ruled here. He will
guide and protect us as long as we obey him. We know Cortés
has some kind of magic we do not understand, for we have seen
it. He was able to use this magic against us only because we
failed to do full honor to Huitzilopochtli.

"I have decided that we will bring forward those who were
made prisoners in the battle of the causeway. We will honor their
bravery by bathing and clothing them and speeding them on their
way to Hummingbird's altar. When they have transcended time
and become divine, we will feed on the sacred flesh and take
communion with the god."

"I fear our prisoners will not appreciate the honor we bestow
upon them," Atlatzin commented dryly.

"It matters not. The gods of the Mexica will rejoice with us,
and we shall have done our sacred duty. A great battle is over
and we have won. Now it is time to turn our attention elsewhere.
Have the streets washed and the houses freshly painted. Order
the markets opened and the temples prepared for feasting. We

shall have a celebration fitting our victory, with a ball game and a competition of flower songs. We shall not mourn the dead but celebrate the living. Those who died did so gloriously."

"And the plunder taken by the commoners?" asked a member of the Council. "Shall you order it returned to the throne?"

"Not immediately," decided Cuitlahuac. "The people will be reluctant return it, and I will not send my warriors out to search the homes of those who fought our enemy. We will say nothing of the lost gold for now. We can deal with the issue later. It is not as though the commoners can wear it or spend beyond their rank. The gold will return to the throne eventually."

Atlatzin ground his teeth as he tried not to doubt the wisdom of Cuitlahuac's decision. It was as though the gods of war and peace fought inside him. Hummingbird led the Mexica into battle, but had strict rules about how and when they could fight. Feather Serpent abhorred the deaths war brought and forbade killing. Even though it had been proven Cortés was not his messenger, the god would have approved Cuitlahuac's decision not to spill more blood and destroy the retreating Spaniards. It made no sense.

As he watched the man who would shortly be the Great Speaker of the Mexica leave the room, Atlatzin decided that Cuitlahuac had to be right about Cortés. The Spaniard had been so humiliated he would disappear forever. If Cuitlahuac were wrong, everything the teachers and priests said of life and death would be wrong. There would be no way to understand the nature of the universe. Instead of divine order and balance, there would be only chaos.

Mama Amoxtli was not healing as quickly as expected, so Papalopil waited an entire month before recovering the gold bracelet and turquoise from where she had so carefully hidden them.

In the *zócalo*, people said that Cuitlahuac had been elected by the Council and formally installed as *Hueyi Tlatoani*. It was done with great ceremony and celebration, although less than there had been for Moctezuma. One of the first things that the new emperor did was to announce that those who had taken some of the stolen treasure and weapons from the escaping Spaniards would not be punished. Still, what the Emperor could order one day, he could take back the next, and Papalopil said as much to Mama Amoxtli.

"What will you do with all this?" asked the elder priestess, pointing at the small bundle that lay open in the temple dancer's lap.

"I will exchange it for cacao beans in the market before the Emperor changes his mind. He may demand return of the gold and stones, but anyone can have beans. I will use them to buy my freedom. This should be enough."

"And then?" The woman shifted painfully on her mat and Papalopil adjusted the pillows that helped prop her up.

Papalopil had thought this through. Once she was no longer a slave, her role at the Temple would be unclear. She had considered that the elder priestess might no longer need her. If that were true, where would she go? Would she be out in the street?

"I will stay here in the common house as long as you need me," she said quickly, hoping she had not said it so quickly it revealed how vulnerable she felt she would be. "I would like to learn more about the healing herbs you use. Not to be a real healer like you; I know that would take years. But you know so much about herbs. I have learned some from you, but I certainly could learn more. If I get enough beans, perhaps I could sell herbs in the market and support myself until I know enough to be a healer."

Mama Amoxtli sighed and restlessly pushed off the cotton blanket that covered her. "When you pay off your debt, keep your freedom a secret," she warned her. "If you stay here in the common house, you will have to act like the other temple dancers who live here or it will cause problems and draw the attention of the priests. You do not want to do that. They would turn you out on the streets. But if you stay here, I will teach you all I can about healing. You will have to learn quickly, though. I suspect my journey to Mictlan will begin soon."

Papalopil, focused on the task that lay before her in the market, almost missed the last part of what Mama Amoxtli said. Instead of responding, she decided quickly that it was the old woman's pain speaking, not her head, so she simply nodded, tucked her bundle carefully in the folds of her skirt, and set off for the *zócalo*. Soon she would be a free woman.

CHAPTER TWENTY-ONE

Little by little, Tenochtitlan came back to life. The market had opened immediately after the Spanish had been routed, and every week more vendors arrived in the city to sell their wares, displaying them on mats and in stalls decorated with colored paper banners. As if to erase the great loss of life that had occurred in the massacre, women put on their brightest *huipiles* and maidens flirted with the young men who had survived. The remaining warriors wore their most magnificent feathers in public and paraded proudly through the *zócalo*. The area surrounding the ball court was packed with excited spectators, and there were new heads on the skull racks. Some of them had hair the color of maize, a color never displayed on the rack before. All again seemed right in the world, and the high priest, ignoring the flies that circled around him like greedy sycophants, strutted proudly.

If the markets did not offer the same abundance as before or the gambling at the *tlachtli* was for stakes so low they once would have been spurned, no one objected. The people reminded themselves that the Spaniards were gone. They had been humiliated and driven out, and they would creep away in shame, never daring to return. When he heard people say this, Atlatzin shook his head with doubt.

But he was pleased that Cuitlahuac was popular with the people. The young man even married one of Moctezuma's daughters in order to prevent any possible dispute to his claim to the throne. The new emperor wore a splendid feathered cape and hung the sacred turquoise from his nose. Nevertheless Atlatzin knew the rose screen hid no Enemies of the House, no secret partners in the Flower Wars, during the games and sacrifices. When he and other members of the *pipiltin* bowed to pay homage and then stood, looking at Cuitlahuac full in the face, they all knew what was not being said. The Council had chosen him to be their leader and would follow him. But the Great Speaker would never again be considered divine. Never again would it be unthinkable to question his word. If he failed to serve the Mexica, the Mexica, in turn, would refuse to serve him. The world had changed since the massacre in front of Huitzilopochtli's temple.

Cuitlahuac took it upon himself to mend the torn mantle of the Mexica Empire. In order to begin, he called on all the city-states and provinces to join in alliance against the Spanish, so that they would be forced to return to their own lands across the sea. They would regain the land they had lost. Atlatzin was with the Council when they heard the response to this proposal.

"Only our allies on the lake have even bothered to respond!" said Cuitlahuac angrily. "This is an insult! Less than a year ago, this would have been unthinkable! The provinces would never have dared to refuse such an alliance, much less ignore a direct call from the Great Speaker."

The members of the Council shifted uncomfortably on their mats and looked at each other in concern. Although no one said the word rebellion, every one of them knew one when they saw one, and they also knew they were not strong enough to reconquer the Empire if such a rebellion spread. Too many of their young warriors had been killed. Apparently, the provinces knew it as well.

"We could offer to suspend the payment of tribute and taxes due by any tribe that joined our alliance," suggested the High Priest. The Council agreed that this was a good approach.

Still the provinces did not respond. Most of them did not even bother to resume the payment of their regular taxes either.

"Will they rise against us?" Cuitlahuac demanded worriedly of his advisors.

"They wait to see what Cortés will do, my Lord," said Atlatzin. "They believe if they take no side, they cannot lose."

"What do they expect the Spaniard to do? He has been humiliated and chased from the city like a wounded coyote."

Atlatzin shook his head stubbornly. "I believe Cortés is simply resting and will regroup his forces. Just because he lost at Tenochtitlan does not mean he will not attack Texcoco, Tlacopan, or even Chalco. We too were defeated in the early days of our history as a people. We did not crawl away in shame. No, we returned to fight again and to win."

Cuitlahuac looked confused, and Atlatzin remembered that history had been rewritten when the scrolls were altered. Was the defeat he had learned of as a child erased from the scrolls? He would have to check in the *calmecac*. Moctezuma would have understood. If nothing else, the deceased ruler would have known that the winner always writes the history that is taught to the children.

"I think perhaps Atlatzin sees Spaniards in the mists that creep over the lakes at night," Cuitlahuac finally said, forcing an awkward laugh from members of the council. "Our concern is only to finish crushing them and then to reestablish the flow of tribute to Tenochtitlan."

"My Lord, the Spaniards are not men like us," insisted the

nobleman. "They do not think the way we do. At least send an emissary to Tlaxcala. My spies say Cortés is headed that way. If we can convince the Tlaxcalans to join us in an alliance, there can never be any danger from the foreigners. I know the Tlaxcalans have been our enemies and may not agree, my Lord, but we must try something. Before Cortés can build new ships and escape, let us join together to drive them back into the waters to drown. That way he will never return."

Cuitlahuac allowed himself to be persuaded, but no one on the Council was surprised when his offer was rejected. Even Atlatzin had known it was a gamble. The two mighty tribes had been enemies for too long. Why should things change now? They did not see Cortés as a threat and would never trust the Mexica.

But it was still frustrating, and when he heard the news, Atlatzin swore in exasperation. Why did neither the Tlaxcalans nor the Mexica see what was happening? Why were they blind to the danger? The old ways had been destroyed. New alliances had to be made. Tribal jealousies and feuds were like summer rain in the face of the terrible storm that threatened. He, Atlatzin knew. The skull had shown him the horror that lurked ahead. The memory of battle for survival fought in crystal colors returned to haunt him. The figure in the hummingbird cape flashed before his mind's eye and he pushed the visions away. Whatever else those visions foretold, he knew with absolute certainty that the Spaniards would return.

With this weighing on him, he decided to return to the temple of Xochiquetzal. It had been some time since he had spoken secrets and perhaps seeing his priestess would ease his mind.

He almost expected the old woman, the elder priestess, to be guarding the entrance when he arrived, but she was nowhere to be seen. He half-smiled as he recalled how big the tiny woman had seemed the last time he was there. He caught sight of a young woman sweeping the floor and called her over.

"Where is your elder priestess? I expected her to be here to greet me," he said pleasantly.

"If you mean Mama Amoxtli, I am sorry to tell you that she has passed on." Cuitcatl leaned the broom against the wall and smoothed back her hair. "I am in charge until another senior priestess can be found."

"Passed on? To another temple?"

"No, my Lord, to Mictlan. She took a fall and never recovered. She died several months ago."

"I am sorry to hear it." Atlatzin, his eyes adjusted to the darkness inside the temple, looked around. "Where is the other young priestess that I have seen here? I think her name is Papalopil."

Cuitcatl laughed. "Papalopil is no priestess, my Lord. She is a slave, a slave and an *auianime.*"

He shook his head. "No, you are mistaken. This Papalopil is a priestess."

"Forgive me, my Lord, but I knew her well. She is a slave, or she was a slave. I hear she bought her freedom after the foreigners were driven out. I have not seen her since."

A slave! She had lied! Betrayed him! Made a fool of him! Furious, he whirled around so quickly his cape whipped out and snapped at Cuitcatl's leg. She let out a yelp, but he was too angry to speak, much less to acknowledge her.

At first, no one was alarmed when Cuitlahuac fell ill. Atlatzin had noticed the Great Speaker seemed listless, but thought it was due to the Tlaxcalan rejection of his offer. But then the Emperor developed a mild fever and a rash. The fever soon burned high and the rash became hard bumps and then sores that spread until they covered his entire body. Within a few short days, Cuitlahuac was dead. His younger brother Cuauhtémoc was next in line to be the Great Speaker. He too married one of Moctezuma's daughters. This time, Atlatzin noted that the coronation was even smaller and the gifts could be counted with ease. Cuitlahuac was not the only one to fall to this terrible new disease. It appeared to be creeping through the city like a hungry animal, striking poor and rich alike. There were rumors that it struck with such swiftness that there were those who fell to their knees and were dead within hours. The disease started in the center of the city and spread in all directions. No one was immune and the physicians and magicians were helpless. Nothing could be done about this fearful plague they were beginning to call the Red Death. Some survived; most died.

As he left the new Emperor and passed through the *zócalo* on his way home, Atlatzin puzzled over what had been suggested in Council. There were those among Cuauhtémoc's advisors who believed that Cortés was responsible for the Red Death. These advisors still believed Cortés had special magic; whether he was from Quetzalcoatl or Emperor Carlos was unimportant. A god who could send such a horrible disease was a god to be greatly feared indeed! Others argued that the disease was a curse from Chalchiuhtotolin, the terrible underworld god of disease called Jade Turkey. Atlatzin dismissed this idea that the disease came from any magic of Cortés, but worried how much the Great Speaker would be influenced by this thinking. For now, Cuauhtémoc reacted by ordering fresh sacrifices to Jade Turkey.

So much had happened in the past few days that the Council, including Atlatzin, had been pressed to stay several nights in the royal palace so that Cuauhtémoc could confer with them at any moment. It was tiring, and Atlatzin was relieved to be able to return and spend the night at home. He wiped the sweat from his neck and paused by one of the hollow bridges that carried fresh water through the city. The man whose job it was to draw wa-

ter saw the symbols of the *pipiltin* in Atlatzin's dress, and leapt
to the top of the construction to scoop up water to offer him.
Atlatzin drank greedily, grateful for the privileges of rank.

On the other side of the market, he paused again. For some reason, he felt strangely weak. He forced himself to push on through
the crowd, but his eyes were beginning to blur. He leaned against
a stall and fought to steady himself.

It was the fever. He grimaced and felt the back of his neck.
The sweat that a few minutes ago had held his hair damp against
his skin had disappeared. His skin was dry and hot. He tried to
look about for help, but his eyes blurred and he could not focus.
He feared that if he fell there in the street, no one would rush to
his side with help despite his rank. The shoppers in the market
would run in terror from the Red Death. Atlatzin reached out
desperately and grabbed a handful of cloth.

"I am Lord Atlatzin, the Emperor's counselor. Take me home
and I will see you are rewarded." He stared blankly at the face
turned toward him. It was a vaguely familiar blur, but he was
suddenly too exhausted to even try to focus.

Papalopil looked with concern at the tall nobleman who had
hold of her *rebozo*. It was obvious something was wrong. His
face was flushed and his eyes did not seem to focus well.

"Take me to my home in the nobles' quarters!" The demand
came out in a loud whisper and decided her. Apart from everything else, she owed a debt to this man who had warned her not
to dance, whose warning had saved her from the massacre in
front of the Great Temple. She nodded quickly and he slipped
his arm around her shoulders. They made a strange sight as they
followed the winding streets into the wealthy section of the city.
Atlatzin was too ill to notice that she was able to find his home
without his guidance.

No servants came to greet them when they reached the door
of his house. The young woman pushed it open with her foot and

helped Atlatzin into the innermost rooms, where the hearth was cold and gray. As he sank gratefully onto a mat, he murmured something about servants and his mother. She watched him for a moment and then went to find the servants.

No one answered her call. She noted the fire in the kitchen had been allowed to go out, although wood was stacked up and waiting against the wall. An opening led to a large patio lined with brightly painted pots spilling over with plants. Several held red and green chilies in various stages of ripeness. In one corner was a very large wicker birdcage crafted to resemble Moctezuma's palace. Small birds darted about within, their colors catching and reflecting back the hot sun like the jewel sellers in the *zócalo* trying to make a sale. Inside, Papalopil marveled at the bright frescos painted on the walls and the rich hangings and gilded screens that separated room from room. She had never seen anything so splendid.

She was dawdling and knew it. Mama Amoxtli would have scolded her. There had to be a servant around someplace. She thought of her priestess with sorrow when she saw honey next to the thick *atolli* in the kitchen. The corn drink had gone bad. She decided it must be several days old. Mama Amoxtli would never have permitted food to stand around to rot. She would have ordered the drink thrown out and the kitchen scrubbed from top to bottom. Papalopil poured the *atolli* into a slop jar as she thought about the old woman. She had learned so much from the elder priestess. Her broken leg never healed and had pained her for months before she died. Even though Papalopil had paid off her debt, she had stayed on in the common house and had arranged for Mama Amoxtli's cremation. She even paid for it. The old woman had been good to her, even up to the end. And afterwards, she still stayed on, keeping her freedom a secret as had been suggested. After all, where else could she go? No one said anything. Too much was going on and, although people seemed to pretend that everything was fine, Papalopil had a sense that things were beginning to fall into disarray.

Atolli would never go bad around Mama Amoxtli, she thought with a sad smile. It never lasted long enough to spoil. She wrinkled her nose and sighed heavily as she realized that the odor of rot was not just from the drink. There must be rotten meat in a storeroom. The sight of a stairway to the second floor of the house distracted her. She had never been in a house with a second floor. Such luxuries were reserved for the nobility. She gave in to temptation and started up the tiled steps.

Papalopil was so fascinated by her surroundings that she was totally unprepared to find the body of an old woman on a sleeping mat. The body was covered with dried pustules. It was impossible to tell how long the woman had been dead, but from the stink coming from the mat, Papalopil assumed it had been at least a day or two.

She stepped back in horror. It was the Red Death. It had to be. One of the dancers had come home with fever and a rash a few days before. Those were the same symptoms in Atlatzin now. There was no question. Unconsciously, she wiped her hands on her skirt. Little wonder the servants had disappeared! She was a fool for having exposed herself. She whirled and ran in terror for the front door.

She ran to the temple, hoping that somehow Xochiquetzal would protect her in that sacred place. But the smell of death was there before her. She did not even look inside. She knew there would be at least one body on the stone floor before the goddess' altar. She crossed the *zócalo* and headed up the Street of Perfumed Nights, avoiding even eye contact with the few people she saw. In the common house, two of the temple dancers lay in fever dreams on their mats. When she looked closer, she realized only one lay in dreams. The girl who had come home ill several days earlier was already dead.

"I must be getting used to the stink," she muttered to herself as she hurriedly gathered her few belongings. She opened the small chest under the communal altar and gathered all the sacks of herbs that she had learned to use and piled them into her *rebozo*. She turned as a young woman stumbled through the door crying.

"People are dying everywhere! In the *zócalo*, in the market! I am burning up! Water!" She collapsed on an empty mat and Papalopil filled a water jug and set it down next to her, careful not to make physical contact. Never in all the stories Mama Amoxtli had told her was there a story of illness striking so many at once. And she had never heard of a sickness that looked like this. It was a new sickness and it looked like everyone was going to die.

Papalopil could not stay there. It was the only home she could remember, but she could not just stay there and wait to die with the others. She would go crazy sitting and waiting. She tied her *rebozo* over one shoulder and left.

But in the *zócalo*, she stopped and looked around her. The market was quieter than she remembered it that morning. There were fewer shoppers, and even the vendors seemed to be packing up early. It suddenly struck her that the vendors and shoppers had someplace to go to, while she had nowhere. She sank down on a step and tried to think calmly. If everyone were dying, or even most people, she would probably die as well.

At least I will die a free woman and not a slave, she thought grimly and then she laughed and tossed the dark hair that she had let grow since buying her freedom. She was free now, and she could go anywhere. She just had to decide where that was. If the goddess could not protect her own priestesses inside a sacred temple, then there really was no place that was safe. It did not matter where she was. If he wanted to, if it were her fate, Jade Turkey would find her. Ever practical, Papalopil decided that since there was nothing she could do to avoid death, the only question before her was where she chose to meet it.

There was really only one place.

She found Atlatzin on the mat where she had left him. He was worse and beginning to develop a rash on his face. After staring at that handsome face for a moment, she went for water. Taking a soft cotton cloth, she gave him a sponge bath, trying to cool him down and the lower the fever as Mama Amoxtli had taught her. The water was like hard-driven sleet against his hot skin. He cursed the pain and her, but was by now too ill to prevent her ministrations. He was so weak that, when he vomited, she had to turn his head for him so he did not choke on his own spew. When she was done cleaning him, she made tea with a few of the leaves she had brought with her. She did not know if it would help him, but decided it could not possibly hurt.

There was a little food in the storeroom. She would not die hungry. The laws against theft were severe and it never would have occurred to her to steal from the nobleman's house. She may have been an *auianime*, but Papalopil was honorable. The man had saved her life once. She would tend him as best she could as he lay dying. They might as well both be as comfortable as possible as they awaited the inevitable. She looked down at the soiled dress she was wearing. A large stain from vomit seemed to stare back at her. There was probably a little in her hair as well. She would have to wash and tie it back. There had to be something in the old woman's room that she could use. Wearing a clean dress and having something to eat wouldn't be stealing, she said to herself. She intended to pay in services for her comfort while she waited for Jade Turkey. But first she had to do something about the smell of death in the house.

While Atlatzin was lost in fevered sleep, she went back upstairs and managed to wrap the old woman's body in the mat it lay on, much as she had done with Mama Amoxtli's leg. Tearing her own faded *rebozo* into strips, she tied the mat securely around the corpse. Getting the body down the stairs was difficult; the head thumped loudly on each step, and she was afraid it would split open and leave a putrid mess. But the mat must have cushioned the head and held the body together. Papalopil pulled and pushed the awkward bundle until it lay in the street. She had thought it would be collected and burned. That is the way things were customarily handled. But it was not the only body in the street. The city officials must be busy with so much illness, she decided as she reentered the house. Well, it was their problem now. Then she burned a few leaves upstairs and in the room where Atlatzin lay. The clean scent of sage helped only a little.

She checked to make sure that the nobleman's condition was unchanged and then went into the patio to see if she could operate the steam bath by herself. Fortunately, the fire was already laid against the stone wall of the small circular hut. All she had to do was light it and wait inside until the stones were hot enough to pour water on them. A jug of water was waiting inside, as though the missing servants had prepared the bath for Atlatzin's return before they fled. She smiled with satisfaction, lit the fire, stripped off her ruined agave dress and fed it to the flames. She would be wearing embroidered cotton when Jade Turkey came to claim her.

The rash turned into hard bumps like pellets under Atlatzin's skin. The fever that she thought was disappearing came back even stronger as the bumps became pustules. She struggled to get tea down Atlatzin's throat; food was out of the question. Sometimes she sat and stared at him. She had removed the tattered feathers from his hair and the clothing he had soiled in his fever. She could tell he disliked the sponging, but it was also clear that it helped, if only just a small bit, so she continued doing it. Sometimes she sang, snatches of phrases she thought might have been from her childhood. Other times she sang hymns to Xochi-quetzal, songs the *auianime* sang. Time seemed to pass so slowly.

She dressed in his mother's clothes: embroidered cotton *huipiles* and fringed skirts, and she took special pleasure in wearing anything red she could find. Sometimes she sat in the interior patio and wove feathers into the braids that kept her hair out of her face or tried on bracelets and earrings of carved stone while he tossed fitfully on his mat. After admiring herself in the forbidden jewelry, she put them away carefully. No matter what she did, she always stayed within hearing distance of Atlatzin. He no longer had the strength to turn over without help.

She was thankful the storerooms still held some supplies. When forced to venture out for fresh water, she was horrified at the change in the city. The plague was born on the wind and, whenever it passed, the streets were beginning to be clogged with the dead and dying. The markets were long since closed and the stink of decay was heavy in Tenochtitlan. There was no longer any order, no attempt to maintain sanitary conditions. Baskets of night soil stood by doorways. Clouds of flies hovered over the human waste that had lain there for days. She looked quickly at the place where she had left the body days earlier, and sent a quick prayer of thanks to whichever deity had allowed it to be collected. There were other bodies in the streets. There was no one left to cremate the dead, no one to tend the dying.

The pustules on Atlatzin's body began to break open, making sponging down his skin a difficult task. She tried anyway. Her patient could only lie there and moan. She held his head in her lap as she forced broth down his parched throat. He finally was able to keep it down. She continued to bathe him several times a day, as one sore seemed to run into another and finally begin to crust over.

There was a night when Papalopil lay down on a mat beside Atlatzin. Underneath the cotton blanket, the young women resigned herself. She had the fever at last. She gave herself over to the illness, ready to face the Red Death. But Jade Turkey merely played with her. A slight rash appeared on her face and hands; one sore broke out, then another. That was all.

She was up and around when Atlatzin's fever broke the first time. She sat by him as wave after wave of sweat soaked the fresh blankets and mantles she kept over him. It never occurred to her to wonder why the disease had touched her so lightly when others had been felled. That was simply the way things were. There was no point in puzzling over things that could not be understood. She had long ago learned to accept and make the best of any given situation.

Atlatzin woke from a fever dream one morning to hear the rhythmic slapping of a woman's hands flattening dough into tortillas. It was a reassuring sound, and for a time he lay there peacefully. But the sight of Papalopil in his mother's clothing brought him more fully awake.

"I should kill you." The voice was soft with weakness, but there was no doubt about the anger in it.

Still, Papalopil was unsure whether the man was still in a fever dream, so she flashed one of her best smiles and put down the water jug she carried. "Welcome back to the living, my Lord. I was afraid you were half way to Mictlan."

"I should kill you for betraying me," he said.

"Well, I think you will have to get much better first," she said calmly. "You lack the strength to kill me right now." Nevertheless, she took a small step backwards.

"You betrayed me," he repeated.

"I never told a single person anything about what you said and I never said I was a priestess. You assumed I was. I never told you so." Atlatzin closed his eyes and she wondered what he remembered. She could hardly nurse him if he were bent on killing her. He really was too weak to do her any harm just then, but it certainly complicated things.

"Perhaps the fever has burned your memory. You took ill in the *zócalo*. I was there and you asked me to bring you home. Actually, you did not ask, you demanded it," she added almost as an aside. "You have had the Red Death. It is a new plague of some kind. The gods must favor you; you are still alive, and I think you are getting better." She poured water into a cup and carefully bent over to place it in his hands. His fingers failed to close tightly around it, so she patiently guided the drinking vessel to his lips.

"My mother?" He drank thirstily and looked up when she did not immediately answer.

She shrugged and turned away. "There was an old woman in one of the rooms when I brought you home. She was dead of the sickness."

"Dead?" The word was flat, unbelieving. For a moment Papalopil was impatient. What difference did one death make when the whole world seemed to be dying?

"Close to a quarter of the city is dead, my Lord. Everyone has been ill. They are only now beginning to burn the bodies," she said simply. She decided to spare him the news for now just how his mother's body had been taken outside and left.

Atlatzin lay back weakly, too exhausted to maintain his anger. She could tell that what she was saying was too much for him to grasp at once. She left the room as he slipped again into the darkness. The fever returned. He had no idea how much time had passed when smell of food brought him back to his senses. She had returned, and he was strangely glad to see her.

"Here is some honey water and a tortilla. Later I will make a bean tortilla for you if you can keep it down. There are some beans and chilies left in the house but no meat and the markets are closed. I put honey on the tortillas for now."

Atlatzin tried to eat the flat maize pancake, but at the second bite, he began to vomit. He curled up on his side and lay there retching, too weak to sit up. Papalopil quickly put down the drink she was holding for him and raised his head away from the spew. When he was done, she gently wiped his face with the edge of his mother's skirt and held the cup for him to wash the bitter taste from his mouth. Finally, he lay back on the mat and watched her from under his lashes. Something teased at the corner of his mind, something just beyond his ability to reach. He gave up the effort and focused instead on her face. She truly did have beautiful eyes.

Aware of his gaze, she looked down and played absently with the multicolored ribbons in her braids. She had to admit that he had reason to be angry. But with the world falling apart around them, it did seem a bit silly. Besides, he was really ill and she was saving his life.

"Have you eaten?" he whispered. She nodded quickly and tried not to smile.

Had she eaten? They had been there for days. Of course she had eaten. But then, he could have no idea how long it had been. He interrupted her thoughts.

"Why did you bring me home?"

"You asked me to, my Lord."

"Yes, but you knew how angry I would be when I found out you were an imposter. Why did you help me in spite of that?" She could still hear anger in his voice, but she thought she detected a softening.

"I think it not quite fair to say I was an imposter," she insisted.

"What were you then?"

"I was a temple dancer, and a slave," she said with reluctance, "but I am no longer. You mistook me for a priestess. You were in a hurry and insisted on speaking secrets."

"And you allowed it."

"Who was I to refuse you? You were Lord Atlatzin, leader of the Jaguar Warriors, Counselor to *Huey Tlatoani* himself! I was just a slave."

"You should have told me." The hard edge was gone; what remained was exhaustion.

"Yes," she admitted, "I should have." There was silence then, as though neither of them knew how to proceed. She played with the red fringe on blouse she wore until finally Atlatzin spoke.

"Are so many people truly dead? And the Great Speaker?"

"There are bodies everywhere," she said rising. "I know nothing of the Emperor."

"I must have news." Atlatzin tried to sit up and failed miserably. He lay back on his mat and studied the young woman who had nursed him. "You favor my mother's clothes," he said finally.

She had the grace to blush. "I did not think it would hurt her for me to wear them. There was nothing but cotton and my dress was soiled from tending you. I did not steal the clothes, my Lord. I only borrowed them. I will put them back."

"Keep them. They do my mother no good now." He sighed wearily. "Stay here until I am better," he said, as though she were a common house servant.

She looked at him with a touch of amusement. Where else would she stay? He acted as though the *pipiltin* could still demand obedience and expect everyone to obey. Did he not realize that the world had been turned upside down? Of course not. How could he? Even though she had told him, he could not possibly understand the devastation the Red Death had brought upon the city. If she had not seen the streets with her own eyes, she would not have believed it herself, not of mighty Tenochtitlan. Instead of explaining, she simply nodded and covered him again with the blanket, before getting a wet rag to clean up the vomit on the floor.

"I will stay. Sleep now. You need your strength."

CHAPTER TWENTY-TWO

Papalopil had never spent time on her own. As she had been sold so young, she had been raised always surrounded by other dancers or priestesses. After Mama Amoxtli died, she still spent her days in the midst of other women. The silence that engulfed her since she left the Street of Perfumed Nights was at first welcomed, but it began to weigh on her, reminding her of the death that crept through the city. She wandered from room to room until she stumbled on a basket of cotton bolls. Someone had begun to de-seed them for spinning. With relief, she took the basket into the room where Atlatzin lay. The spindle and whorls were smaller and more delicate than she was used to and carved of bone, but the familiar feeling of the fiber between her fingers and the rhythmic movement of seeding and spinning were soothing.

She found herself talking to Atlatzin as she spun, especially in the mornings, when his mind was fairly clear. But late in the afternoon, his fever would return again. She took to sleeping on a mat in the room where he lay, as sometimes he thrashed around at night and then was wet with sweat when the fever broke before dawn. She could tell his muscles ached, especially his back, from the way he twisted and moaned when he slept. He never said as much, of course.

Even when his fever was down, she couldn't tell if he always heard what she was saying. Sometimes his eyes were open but did not seem to focus. Other times they were closed, but he would make soft noises when she cooled him down with a wet cloth and she knew he was conscious. In the days that followed, she began to think perhaps Atlatzin looked forward to seeing her when he woke. Sometimes, when the weather was nice, she would help him out into the patio where he could sit in the warm sun and listen to the birds sing in their cage. It was pleasant there and seemed to sooth him some. He found there were times she almost reminded him of Quetzali, and he found himself telling her about his sister. Papalopil did not seem surprised at how Quetzali had met her death.

Instead the temple dancer nodded knowingly and said simply, "We all do what we must. She was lucky you were there."

For her part, Papalopil tried to amuse him by telling him funny stories about Tlaloc's priests and stories the *auianime* told each other when there were no men about. It pleased her to be able to make Atlatzin smile. She even shared with him how she would dance well, but never too well, and so had avoided the obsidian club.

"How did you know to do that?" he asked one morning when they were sitting in the patio.

"It was not hard to figure out. I watched the very best dancer be honored. She lived a long life and was old when she was kissed by the god. The second best dancer received the god's kiss in a few turns of the wheel, as did the one after that. The poor dancers lasted only a very short time, sometimes less than a season. Those of us in the middle were usually ignored, unless a particular priest took an interest. They are supposed to be celibate, you know, but sometimes one of them failed in his vows."

"Shameful," commented Atlatzin, picking up a piece of oak he had started to carve into a dart for his spear thrower before he fell ill.

"We had to study the ways of men," she continued. "I was taught that men care about sacrifice and flower wars and for other men to admire them. Priests tell them what the gods want and men believe it and go out and fight for honor and a beautiful death. Women just do what has to be done to survive. We always have.

"So as a temple dancer and as an *auianime*, I learned a lot about men. But I never understood about celibacy." She put down her spinning and searched his face. "Why do men choose celibacy?" she asked.

"It is required of the lesser priests." He raised an eyebrow as though explaining the obvious to a child.

"But not of you," she responded quickly. "Why did you choose it?"

He looked away then. Even his mother had never asked him why. She had complained about his choice, but never asked him why he made it. "It is a long and personal story," he said finally.

"Well, we have all the time we need for you to tell it, and as far as personal, goes, I think you cannot get much more personal than I have, cleaning up after you and washing down your body when the fever rises." Feeling that she might have overstepped, she bent over the seeded cotton bolls and pretended to clean them.

But he was not offended. "Quetzalcoatl was celibate." When she did not respond, he continued. "I was dedicated to him and studied to be his priest."

"But you are a warrior!" She was clearly surprised.

"My brother was supposed to be the warrior in the family. When he died, my father took me out of the temple and dedicated me to Huitzilopochtli. He told me I had to make up for Chimali, my brother. I had to be the perfect warrior for my family."

"Did he die in battle?"

"No. The healer said it was his stomach. We were practicing our *tlachtli* shots here in front of the house when he suddenly doubled over in pain. He died the next day. My father died before the year was completed. Mother said he had lost the will to live."

"What sadness." Papalopil did not know what else to say.

"I made the vow the day he died—father, I mean, the day my father died." Atlatzin let the wood fall to the ground. "I think I need to rest now," he said.

Papalopil helped him inside to lie down. She still did not understand about celibacy, but she knew Atlatzin's vow was more complicated that she had thought.

A few mornings later, it was his turn.

"Why did you become a prostitute?"

"I was never a prostitute, Lord Atlatzin," she insisted defensively. "I was a trained *auianime*. I did not walk along the canals looking to sell my body. I blessed the young men going into battle and then helped bring their spirits back home from the war."

"You blessed them with your body?"

"Of course."

"And they paid you?"

"Sometimes they gave me small gifts. Sometimes the gifts went to the temple."

"I am not sure I see the difference," he commented, dismissing the distinction between the two.

"I think perhaps that is because you are celibate. There are things you cannot be expected to understand." She smiled sweetly and he almost felt sorry he had asked, almost. She lay down her spinning and got up to clean out the elaborate birdcage against the patio wall.

"We only have about a week's worth of seeds left for the birds. I am not sure where to get more with the markets closed."

But Atlatzin wanted to know more about her and would not be deterred.

"Why did you become an *auianime* then? Did the temple order it?"

"No. Mama Amoxtli, the temple's elder priestess, suggested it to me. She knew I wanted to buy my freedom and said I could keep anything the warriors gave me personally for my service." Papalopil gently blew the empty seed husks off the feeding cups, exposing the fresh seeds beneath. She turned and smiled at Atlatzin. "It was not the worst work in the world, my Lord.

"Oh, I admit I was afraid the first time. But I knew what to expect. I probably knew more than the young warrior I was blessing. And I knew I was doing the goddess' work. In its own way, it was an honor, especially for a slave."

"How did you become a slave?" Atlatzin was relieved to change the subject, however slightly.

"Mama Amoxtli said that my father sold me to pay some debts. That is all I know. I was only a toddler, under five turns of the wheel. But I had been dedicated to the temple right after I was born. Mama Amoxtli saw the mark on my thigh and bought me because of it."

"What of your real mother?"

Papalopil finished giving the birds fresh water and sat down next to him.

"I cannot remember her face," she said softly. "I used to lie on my mat at night and pray that she would come for me, that it had all been a terrible mistake. That she loved me and never would have allowed me to be sold. I would lie there in the dark and try to force myself to see her. But I never did." She shook her head in tiny, tight moves.

"I think she may have worn white tuberoses in her hair. Whenever I smell their perfume, I think of her. But perhaps I just imagine it." When Papalopil finished, his eyes were fixed on her face, and he slowly reached out and took her hand. He did not say a word, but it was more compassion than she had received in a very long time. She was not quite sure how to react to it and, after a moment, pulled her hand away.

Atlatzin had never spent time with a woman other than his sister and mother. Papalopil's forthrightness was both refreshing and a little shocking. It surprised him when he realized that he was no longer angry with her. Instead, he actually felt comfortable when he knew she was near. He was slowly recovering his strength. He decided to bathe himself, although he had to ask her to lay the wood for the fire. Afterwards, he was worn out from the steam and she teased him gently as she dried him off. The sores covering his face and body were hardening into scabs and she had to be careful not to knock them off with the towel. She was especially careful around his face, suspecting that he would be shocked if he saw just how scarred it was beginning to look.

"I need to get to the Palace," he had said earlier in the day.

"People will take one look at you and run screaming," she had responded, only half teasing.

But after his bath, he said, "I need to send word to the Emperor that I am healing. He needs to know I am alive."

She agreed to carry a message the next time she went for water.

The news she brought from the palace was not reassuring. Cuauhtémoc had been touched lightly by the illness but most of his advisors had succumbed. The *pipiltin*, already drastically reduced in Alvarado's massacre and later in routing the Spanish, had been struck down along with the commoners. No one had any idea how many of them had survived. Many escaped to the countryside, but word was coming in that they took the illness with them, and now deaths were mounting outside the city. Tenochtitlan was barely beginning to function again. Those who had survived the worst of the Red Death talked about gathering and cremating the bodies that had been left in the streets, although they were not actually doing it yet and the night soil was still not being collected. The markets had not opened and no one seemed to know when they would, especially as food was not coming in from the countryside.

"We have enough food in the house for a few days if we are careful," she told Atlatzin with concern.

Before the food ran out, the Emperor sent a message to Atlatzin, ordering him to move to the rooms reserved for the nobility in the palace. His place was with the Emperor, and if he were healing but still too weak to travel back and forth every day to the palace, he needed to move there. Atlatzin told Papalopil that Cuauhtémoc was sending servants as an escort, for the streets were not safe for the nobility. Hunger and disease were leading people to behaviors once unthinkable. The news that Atlatzin would be moving to the palace caught Papalopil by surprise.

"And what will happen to me?" she asked anxiously. If Atlatzin moved to the palace, it would be over for her. She would never see him again, and once the food in the house ran out, she would starve. How could she survive in a world shaken so violently by Jade Turkey? The only skills she had been trained in would be of little use.

He looked at her and she could see the surprise on his face. Had he not considered that? Was he so accustomed to the privileges of his class and sex that he had dismissed her now that he was well? Or had he just assumed she would go with him?

"You may be a lord, but I am not your slave, Atlatzin. I am not anyone's slave, not now. Nor am I one of your servants, fortunately for you. They all ran away when the Red Death entered this house." Papalopil stared at him challengingly. Only the hand that twisted the fringe of *huipil* she wore betrayed her anxiety. "I could have left you there in the market, you know. Someone might have helped you, but I suspect you would have fallen there

in the street. It was not my duty to tend you all these days. I gave
you water and kept you from starving when you could not feed
yourself. I cleaned you when you soiled yourself and wiped the
pus from your sores. Now that your storeroom is empty, you will
move to the palace and cast me back into the streets? Is this how
you intend to repay me? Where do you think I will go? I gave you
back your life, Atlatzin. Does that mean nothing to you?" She
suddenly noticed he was staring at her fingers twisting in the red
fringe, and she buried her hands under her *huipil* as she fought
the prickles of panic that threatened her.

His voice, when he found it, was gruff. It matched the clumsi-
ness of his words. "You will come with me to the palace," was
all he said.

"You are inviting me or ordering me?" she asked, reassured
now that her immediate future was decided, but irritated all the
same that he did not seem to appreciate her position. "I have
been a respectable *auianime*, Atlatzin, not a servant. When I took
care of you it was my choice, not my obligation. How can I go
with you to the palace? What will I be there with you? Your
slave? Your servant?"

He seemed to have heard the spark of anger in her words, as
he quickly shook his head. "I will not repay my debt by making
you my servant."

"Will I be your concubine then?" she said testily. She faced
him like a warrior and thought she saw the flicker of a smile on
his face. They both knew what her fate on the streets would be
if she did not go with him. If he did not take responsibility for
her, she would die. His brief smile infuriated her. "I deserve your
protection, my Lord," intoning the title with a note of sarcasm,
"but I will not beg for it."

"Not my concubine." He dismissed the suggestion with a
wave of his hand. "I am foresworn. But I owe you a debt. I will
simply say you are from my mother's family."

"But I am not noble-born! I have only your mother's clothing and it is forbidden for me to wear cotton."

"If you are a relative, you can wear whatever you want." He scratched at a scab impatiently.

"What if I am seen by a warrior with whom I have..." she broke off.

He refused to think about that. "Dress and behave like a noblewoman and that is how you will be seen. If you come with me, your days as an *auianime* are over. Here," he said, sliding a jade bracelet from his arm and holding it out to her, "since only the *pipiltin* can wear jade, put this on. Believe me, you will be accepted as my cousin. People have far too much to deal with now to worry about one woman. No man will question you," he tried to reassure her.

"The other women might," she replied.

He dismissed the idea impatiently. "Gather just what you need for a few days. Once things settle down at the palace, we'll send someone to get anything we missed. We may be at the palace a long time."

In spite of her misgivings, she went upstairs to gather a few things and decided she could dissemble when needed. She would wear her hair like noblewomen did and avoid the trappings of her past. She would make herself so helpful that no one would think to question her. She would be like a snake shedding its old skin, emerging new and glistening in the sun. The thought made her smile.

Atlatzin's skin, on the other hand, was becoming scarred and pitted as the scabs from the plague fell off. Neither his jewels nor his feathers would ever make him the symbol of the perfect warrior again. But he was alive and, unlike many of the survivors, his sight was undamaged. To Papalopil, he had never seemed more handsome.

Just before the escort arrived, she went out to the patio. She poured the remaining birdseed on a dish and placed it near the wicker cage before opening the cage's little door and carefully tying it to the side.

"There you are, my beauties. I am not about to leave you locked in to starve. Now you are even freer than I am!" But the birds, huddled in a corner of the ornate wicker palace, simply stared at her.

CHAPTER TWENTY-THREE

Atlatzin and Papalopil were assigned a single room in the palace, as were the other counselors and their families who were disease free. They spread their sleeping mats there along with the few belongings they had brought with them, but spent little time in the room. They were far too busy with their own respective tasks. As so many people had died, the strict divisions between nobles and commoners were blurred. Women of royal blood helped in the palace kitchens and Mexica warriors helped fill work parties. Atlatzin was pleased to see that Papalopil settled in easily. When she was not in the kitchens, she could be found helping the healers that served in the palace. No one challenged her presence. If the women she worked with questioned her, she did not mention it to Atlatzin.

For his part, he joined the Emperor's Council in pouring over the maps and scrolls that trickled in from all parts of what had once been the Mexica Empire. Beyond the city, the plague struck again and again, until the red marks on the maps that showed its path seemed to run into each other, soaking the land in blood. Finally, the red stains began to shrink, and Atlatzin knew the plague was weakening. It had been two months since it claimed its first victim and the deaths now numbered in the tens of thousands. According to the scrolls, the whole country had suffered, but Tenochtitlan had been struck worst of all. Even though Cuauhtémoc had ordered work parties to clean the streets of rotting bodies, the air in the city still stank of decay. The temples were once again busy with sacrifices. No one on the Council would mention it directly, but it was obvious that a god who could send such a devastating sickness was an awesome god indeed. The priests said it was Jade Turkey, but some wondered if it were not the Christian god instead.

Atlatzin's spies brought word that Tlaxcala had welcomed Cortés and allowed him to recuperate inside its walls after he had been defeated in Tenochtitlan. After a few short weeks of rest, the Spaniard had led his troops, swollen with Tlaxcalan allies, to the Mexica town of Tepeaca on the crossroads to the coast and the south. The Mexica garrison fell, and the way to the coast was opened once more. Within days, new giant ships had appeared and supplies flowed freely from the coast up to Cortés, back in Tlaxcala.

Late one night, Cuauhtémoc summoned the Council to an emergency meeting. Atlatzin entered the Emperor's audience room to see an exhausted King of Texcoco, his cape and feathers tattered and stained. The story he told drove away any thought of sleep.

"Tell them what you told me," ordered the Emperor.

"I have been betrayed. You have been betrayed," the king amended quickly. "Cortés and his Spaniards appeared outside my city with ten thousand Tlaxcalan warriors. I ordered my men to take defensive positions when I was seized by my own guards! My city fell without a single spear thrown! One of my nobles planned the whole thing. He must have bribed the palace guards and my war chiefs. Cortés marched right into my Texcoco with no opposition and my usurper greeted him affectionately."

Atlatzin was shocked. If the lake city had fallen, it meant that Cortés was returning to Tenochtitlan for sure. He was on the far side of the lakes, but it was clear the man had no intention of leaving the Mexica victorious. As he moved closer to hear every word, the counselors exchanged frightened looks. By the look of the deposed king, Atlatzin suspected they had not yet heard the worst.

"The traitor not only demanded to be dedicated to the pale Jesus, but he made himself King of Texcoco!" the dethroned monarch spit out angrily. "There was nothing I could do. I learned later that night that, when his mother heard what her son had done, she told him he was out of his mind. The traitor promptly set fire to the palace where his mother was installed! His own mother! The poor woman had no choice but to accept the water dedication to the new god or be burned alive!"

"How did you escape?" asked Cuauhtémoc quietly to calm the man.

"One of the guards was so appalled that a man would threaten to burn his own mother to death that he let me go and gave me clothing to disguise myself. I hid until I could steal a canoe and then came straight here. I paddled all night." Overcome with his humiliation, the man sank to his knees. The Emperor signaled to a servant, who helped the former king to a room where he could rest.

"The Triple Alliance has been destroyed." Cuauhtémoc said the words slowly, as though the taste of them thickened his tongue. "It can mean only one thing. Our enemy defies logic. Against all the rules, Cortés has returned. He will attack Tenochtitlan. You were right, Atlatzin, and my brother was wrong. We should have destroyed Cortés when we had the chance. Now it will be a fight to the death. This time there will be no driving him from our lands. I want every one of those Spaniards dead."

"He may mean to take the lake towns one by one and then attack us," cautioned Atlatzin.

"Then we will prepare to meet him in Iztapalapa and Tlacopan. Build up the garrisons in Coyocan, Tenayuca and Chalco."

"The Red Death still stalks in Chalco, my Lord," said one of the advisors. The Emperor shuddered at the words. He would not send his warriors into a city where the plague still reigned.

Atlatzin sent Jaguar Warriors to the causeway town of Iztapalapa. Where once the people had welcomed Cortés with songs and flowers, they met him now with weapons. After many hours of fighting, the enemy was driven south. It was a victory, but a brief one.

Eight nobleman from Chalco arrived in Tenochtitlan. Cortés had descended upon the southern lake city like a hawk on a hare. Atlatzin listened as they told the Emperor that the ruler of the Chalco lay dying of the plague when the arrival of Cortés was announced. The king was one of those who believed the new god was responsible for the plague. He ordered his nobles to welcome the conqueror. It was clear, he had whispered to them, that a god who could send the Red Death could also take the weakened city with ease. There was no point in resistance. Before he died, he wanted to see his heir installed and his legacy secured. He was convinced the pale god would not send the illness to one newly converted and bound to him. The disease only touched a few of the Spaniards, why should it take a convert? The lords told Cuauhtémoc and his counselors how they were forced to watch as the king's son swore fealty to the Emperor Carlos and received the water dedication to the pale Jesus. Cortés had ordered the lords' release and sent them on to Cuauhtémoc with a message. If the Mexica Emperor would accept the sovereignty of Spain and give up his gods, Cortés promised to spare his life. If not, he was a dead man.

"He dares to threaten me?" At hearing these words, Cuauhtémoc shook with fury. "Send word to Chalco that any Spaniard captured will be forwarded to Tenochtitlan for sacrifice!"

A spy brought strange news to Atlatzin. A procession of fifteen thousand porters had marched from Chalco to Texcoco, carrying bundles of wood covered with large pieces of cloth. Along the way, they had been met with celebration. Drums, trumpets and colorful banners announced their arrival along with shouts of welcome. There was something else even more disturbing. Cortés had ordered the digging of a wide canal. It led from the freshwater lake into the city itself. Atlatzin knew the city had no need of more aqueducts. If Cortés were expecting a siege, it might be understandable. But with Chalco fallen, the Mexica no longer controlled the northeast, so the purpose of the canal was a mystery. As he sat in the room assigned to his family, Atlatzin tried to think like Cortés but found it impossible.

He was seated and pouring over the message from his spy and grinding his teeth when Papalopil came into the room. She shook her dark head when she saw the unrolled scroll in his hands.

"Bad news?" she asked softly.

"News. I cannot tell for sure how bad it is. The people of Texcoco have welcomed Cortés, but then I knew they would. Once the king was betrayed and the city handed over to the Spaniards, the people had no choice. I did not expect them to do so with such pleasure, however. They must have resented us and the taxes they had to pay us even more than I realized."

"What do these mean?" she asked, bending over him and pointing to drawings on the scroll.

"Porters are carrying wood of different sizes, it looks like hundreds of pieces, and thick rolls of cloth from Chalco to Texcoco. I cannot understand what it means. Texcoco is on the far side of the lake to the north of us. Chalco to the southeast. What can he have in his head? Does he think he can build a giant bridge across the lakes with all that wood? Texcoco lies at the widest part of the lakes."

Papalopil tried to smile in reassurance, but he could see his words had worried her. She slipped around behind Atlatzin and began to massage his neck and shoulders. She did not like to see him disturbed, but he was so used now to her presence, that he continued to speak his thoughts aloud, not expecting a response.

"Since he has Chalco in his grip, Cortés has free access to the whole eastern coast of the five lakes. That city must be retaken, and retaken quickly."

She continued to knead his muscles in silence, and he found himself beginning to relax under her skilled hands.

"We cannot afford to permit Chalco's treason. It means the south end of the lake is in enemy hands as well as the lakes to the north. With Texcoco fallen, only the western bank is totally under our control. Cortés must be planning some kind of surrounding action. It is strange though that he has made no move to take the causeways after his defeat at Iztapalapa. It would be the next logical move. I would do it. But he is not logical. The man does not think like a Mexica."

Lulled by the strength in Papalopil's hands, Atlatzin sighed heavily and stretched out on the mat. His thoughts began to wander as her fingers worked the muscles in his back and along the ridges of his spine. He closed his eyes and tried to picture a map of the great lakes with the causeways and towns. A languid warmth was stealing through him and the image of the lakes was long in coming. He sighed again. The small hands loosened the muscles in his feet, crept up the sinews of his legs and worked at the hardness of his thighs. They squeezed the muscles of his buttocks and rubbed them in deepening circles. Atlatzin lay there as the warmth grew. The image of the lakes was forgotten, Chalco and Cortés as well. A soft animal sound escaped his throat. As though in response, her hand slipped between his thighs and the warmth leapt into flame.

"No!" he said loudly. He grabbed her wrist and wrenched her hand away from his flesh.

"I can help you, Atlatzin. Allow me to comfort you."

He started to thrust her away angrily when he saw the look in her eyes. The woman was really frightened. She needed comforting, but she only knew how to give comfort, not receive it. He released her wrist and stood up.

"I am sworn to celibacy, Papalopil. You know that. Do not tempt me this way." There was no longer any anger in his voice.

"You say you are foresworn, but you never told me why," she protested, rubbing her wrist.

"I did tell you. I swore to be a perfect warrior for my family, for the Mexica," he corrected himself quickly.

"And the perfect warrior can never know a woman?"

"Quetzalcoatl was celibate."

"Quetzalcoatl shared Xochiquetzal's mat! Afterwards they slept in each others' arms! That is one of the first things I learned from Mama Amoxtli!"

"Yes, he broke his vow. But then he had to go into exile because of it. It weakened him," insisted Atlatzin.

"I never heard that love weakened him." She wrapped her arms around her knees, hugging them to her chest.

"Is that not why the *auianime* sleep with warriors, to weaken them so they can return to their families after battle?"

"No, of course not. We sleep with them before to bless them, to make them stronger and even more beloved of the goddess. To protect them. Afterward, we do it to bring their spirits back home from war, to remind them of life and love and pleasure. We take the death from before their eyes. We take away the war, not the warrior.

"Besides," she continued, "Quetzalcoatl was no warrior."

"Huitzilopochtli is. I was dedicated to both Feathered Serpent and Hummingbird." He stood and quickly redraped the clothing around his waist and thighs as though to hide the fact that his body desired what his words refused.

"And will your gods protect us now, Atlatzin? Will your vow save us? Save the Mexica as our allies turn enemy?" She shook her head and the darkness of her hair fell around her face as her voice dropped. "If Cortés returns, will we survive?"

"The gods will protect Tenochtitlan! They must! I have been taught this all my life. We live decent lives, we offer sacred fruit, we follow the Emperor's laws. And the gods protect us. I have heard this about them all my life. I must believe! What else is there to believe in?" He crossed abruptly to the embroidery hanging over the doorway, but stopped when she called out.

"But do you believe it, Atlatzin?" she insisted. "You said you must believe, not that you do."

Instead of answering her question, he said, "I cannot lie with you, Papalopil. The gods test me."

"You test yourself, Atlatzin," she responded.

He stood there with his back to her and could not find the strength to turn around and face her. He had questioned the gods for almost two years now, and the doubts haunted him every day. Who knew the truths that had been painted out of the scrolls? Who could guess at the prophecies that had been changed? He had fought in the flower wars and sacrificed blood in Hummingbird's honor. He had always believed in these gods as he had believed in Moctezuma. But the Emperor had betrayed them, and Huitzilopochtli, protector of the Mexica, had allowed Our Lady to invade his temple. The god had stood by as city-states fell from Cholula to Chalco. Cortés himself spoke of strange a new god, a jealous one who denied the existence of the others. Red Death was borne on the wind, while kings broke alliances and sons threatened to burn their mothers alive.

All the braziers of hearts had not stopped Cortés from returning from defeat. And now fifteen thousand men had carried pieces of wood to Texcoco. Where was the meaning in any of this? What was there left to believe?

"Atlatzin, you do not answer." He heard the pleading words close behind him, but he leaned against the door frame and would not turn around. He had never actually given voice to his doubts. He could not do so now.

CHAPTER TWENTY-FOUR

Atlatzin was training young warriors in the northern part of the city when word came to him of Cortés' new magic. He rushed to the edge of the island city and saw across the lake to the east the great white wings that had been painted on the scrolls so long ago. Around him people shared their fears in loud whispers. They had all heard of the Spaniards' floating mountains. Now it seemed that these mountains had flown across the land to the great lake, like giant birds of prey.

Atlatzin knew it was no magic. The meaning of the messages he had received months ago was suddenly clear. The pieces of wood and cloth carried through the mountains to Texcoco and the huge canal leading from the lake into the city itself now made sense. Obviously Cortés had not only built new ships but had launched them from inside the city itself in secret. The nobleman watched the wing-like sails grow larger against the horizon and wondered why Cortés thought his ships were such powerful weapons. How could they stand up to the mobility of Mexica war canoes? One thing was certain. If they could be seen at such a distance, they were larger than many canoes or *chinampas* tied together. No wonder the first messenger to see them had thought they were floating mountains.

Before he had the opportunity to see the ships closer, Atlatzin received an order to return to the palace immediately. He found it in an uproar. In an attempt to retake Chalco, Cuauhtémoc had dispatched a force of twenty thousand warriors to claim the city and, with it, control of the Mexica breadbasket. But the ancient Enemies of the House had joined the Spanish in alliance at Chalco, and for the first time, a major battle was fought between equal numbers. Cortés had trained the enemy forces in a new kind of warfare, one that broke all the sacred rules. The Mexica were defeated. Cuauhtémoc was disgraced in the eyes of the lake world. Truly, the days of the Mexica Empire were over.

Atlatzin was with the Emperor and his remaining counselors when more bad news arrived. Cortés had divided his land forces into three, marching one group into Iztapalapa south of the city, and another into Coyoacan, which lay across the narrow part of the lake to the southwest. The remaining went west to Tlacopan. Their first act was to destroy the aqueduct at nearby Chapultepec and leave Tenochtitlan without fresh water. Thirteen of the great ships were sighted off Iztapalapa. Cuauhtémoc quickly dispatched war canoes by the hundreds to fight the battle on water as well as on land. The ships waited until the canoes were almost upon them, and then came about and turned their firesticks and thunder logs on them. The canoes were quickly outflanked and out maneuvered. Blood flowed and canoes overturned as the struggling warriors were swept from the lake. The Mexica garrisons were defeated in the south, and the great lake was cut in two, much like a fish caught between the pinchers of a giant crab.

"It was Quetzalcoatl," insisted the High Priest in counsel. "As Lord of the Wind, he whipped the waves that fought our canoes, while his breath filled the great cloth wings that moved the Spanish ships and led them to defeat us."

'Whatever the cause, we have now lost the three main causeway towns and our supply of fresh water. Tenochtitlan must prepare itself for siege," warned Atlatzin.

Cuauhtémoc agreed. "The rainy season has begun. Every possible jar and watertight container must be placed on rooftops all over the city. Put guards on the few fresh water wells we have. We may get a little hungry, but enough canoes can run the barricades at night to keep us fed and fighting. We will continue to draw Cortés into the capital by pretending to retreat until his forces can be cut off from behind. We will give any prisoners we capture to Hummingbird and use their weapons against them."

"Only the swords, my Lord," urged the High Priest. "The firesticks are evil magic and must be destroyed."

"No!" The word was wrung from Atlatzin.

"No one knows how to make them work and the people are afraid of their magic," the High Priest responded. Much to Atlatzin's dismay, the Emperor agreed.

"Cortés may hold command of the lake, but his ships are limited to our eastern shore because the causeways block access to the other lakes. He cannot destroy the city. Our warriors will hide their canoes in the reeds as his huge ships sail past. Enough provisions will be smuggled to the island. We will survive. Cortés may order his foot soldiers to advance along the causeways, but if they fill in the gaps we make during the day, we will reopen them in the darkness of the night. Little by little, we will capture the enemy soldiers as they try to advance. When all the Spaniards have been killed in battle or had their hearts offered to Hummingbird, their allies will melt away."

Atlatzin could not tell if Cuauhtémoc really believed what he was saying. But then, what else could the Emperor do? What options were left? He said as much to Papalopil when he went to their room to try to catch a few hours of sleep.

"How long do you think the siege will last?" she asked as she braided her hair for sleep.

"Only the gods know," he said. He thought he heard her snort and turned to look at her.

She did not meet his eyes. "We will fight as long as we have to. We have no choice. The Spaniards destroy everything they touch. They have no sense of honor, no sense of what is right or wrong. They are fanatics, beyond reason. But they are brave warriors," he grudgingly admitted. "It is the one thing I can say for them."

"If it were not for them and their horrible disease, you never would have noticed me," her voice came softly from her mat.

"I noticed you."

"When I saved your life," she said a little louder, and he could tell she was paying attention now.

"Before, I think. I did not remember you until I fell ill. Oh, I remembered speaking secrets well enough. But I think I remember you from before. It was your eyes that reminded me. Was it at the *tlachtli* game before the Spaniards came? I think it was. I think you smelled of deer musk and I remember the scent stayed with me until the next day. Then I may have seen you when you helped clean the temple for their goddess, when you were supposed to be in your mother's village. At least I thought it was you. You were coming down the steps carrying water that splashed around your thighs and ..." He broke off and paused before continuing. "And sometimes I thought I had a glimpse of you on the street or in the *zócalo*, but when I looked more closely, you were not there." He leaned over and upturned the small bundle of burning pine sticks that lit the room, putting them out against the flagstone floor. He lay back saying, "I noticed you, Papalopil. I noticed you."

She said nothing. He stared up into the darkness and wondered if she were smiling. It had felt good to say what he had. It was as close as he dared allow himself to be with her.

The siege went as the Emperor had foretold at first. Gaps in the causeways were filled and opened again. Canoes slid between reed curtains and smuggled food into Tenochtitlan from the mainland. Others held warriors who attacked from both sides as the Spanish attempted to advance along the causeways. Handfuls of Mexica fighters were cut down with Spanish steel and some Spanish soldiers did a death dance for Huitzilopochtli. Neither side was able to advance and hold its ground. It looked to Atlatzin as though the siege might last forever, although he knew it could not.

He learned that the towns remaining loyal to the Mexica had been surrounded by Cortés' troops. The towns were unable to send warriors to attack the Spaniards from the rear. The Red Death that had so weakened Tenochtitlan still prowled for victims on the land surrounding the five lakes. The healthy men who had been blockade runners struggled to find food for themselves and their families as enemy war canoes began to patrol the lakes. Some of the lake towns sent assistance to Cortés. Their warriors helped to swell the enemy troops to over one hundred thousand men. Finally, Atlatzin learned that the Spaniards were cutting a wide passageway through a causeway that would give the great ships access to all the lakes. In Tenochtitlan, there were those who began to urge negotiated surrender.

"Those who suggest surrender are traitors!" declared Cuauhtémoc. "I want them arrested and executed! Our ancestors built this empire and we know how conquerors behave. I cannot permit the Mexica to become a vassal tribe. We are not cowards. I will not allow us to bow our heads like naughty children." He looked around at the remaining members of his council.

Atlatzin met his eyes and nodded in assent. The *Tlatoani* was right. It was better to die fighting than to be subjected to the kind of humiliation they could expect.

"And I want a public execution for the traitors. Let it be a lesson for those who even think about surrender." The Emperor signaled an end to the audience.

But within a few days, Atlatzin had worse news to deliver.

"Cortés has taken a new tactic, my Lord. Instead of the lightning raids we have been facing, he now is attempting a slow advance up the causeways. His troops systematically destroy everything they come upon, houses, temples, walls, everything. He is using the rubble from the neighborhoods he has razed to fill the canals where we've removed the bridges. And we can't open the gaps back up at night because his men are now sleeping with their horses and weapons on the causeways themselves. We can't attack him from the rear now and he holds every piece of ground his cursed foot steps on."

"It is like a plague of locusts devouring Tenochtitlan, my Lord," said the High Priest.

The animals in the royal zoo had long since been eaten and the beans and corn in the royal storehouses were gone when Atlatzin told Papalopil what they could expect.

"The city is falling stone by stone, step by step. I do not think we will survive this."

Papalopil put down the *huipil* she was mending and looked at him. "I know, Atlatzin. The women having been talking about it in the palace kitchens. The beans are gone. We have been eating soup made of insects and water plants, and those are getting scarce now. And it is dangerous to go to the lake to hunt them. The enemy is everywhere."

He watched her small hands darn the small tear in the fabric. A shaft of sunlight fell on her and spilled over the red fabric in her lap. It reflected back up onto her face, giving it a golden glow. She was so calm. He thought again how like a warrior she was in her own way.

"The Spaniards are moving up the causeway from the south. Cuauhtémoc will have to leave the palace and retreat to the northern part of the city soon."

She bent her head down over her sewing and said nothing.

"I will be moving with him." He paused, struggling for words. "You should stay here, or better, see if you can leave the city. That way you will be safe."

She put down her mending and looked at him for several uncomfortable moments before asking, "Are you leaving me now?"

"I no longer have anything to offer you, Papalopil. I cannot protect you. I will be fighting wherever and whenever the *Tlatoani* orders me to. I cannot even promise you food. If you stay here, you might be able to escape or at least survive when this part of the city falls.

"What I am saying is that you need to leave me. I am the head of the Jaguar Warriors. I will fight to the end, because it is who I am. I have no choice. But you need not retreat with us. You have your freedom. You can do what you want."

"I always thought that having my freedom would be enough. Mama Amoxtli warned me that it was not," she said almost to herself. Then she looked at him challengingly. "Yes, I have my freedom and can do what I want. And what do you want, Atlatzin?"

"Truthfully? I want you to come with me. I cannot order it and I will not assume it. But that is what I want."

"Then it is what I want as well," she said simply and bent her head again to her mending.

From the rooftop in the northern part of the city where he stood, Atlatzin could see the smoke rise. He shaded his eyes with his hand and located the exact source of the black column that climbed slowly toward the sun. Huitzilopochtli's temple was in flames. It was as Moctezuma's magician had foreseen. Atlatzin swore beneath his breath before crossing the roof and descending to the room where the council was meeting.

"Cortés has sent word he wants to meet with me," said Cuauhtémoc.

Atlatzin studied the young man who had once been Prince of Iztapalapa. He had aged greatly during his few months as Emperor. There were lines on his face, grown thin with hunger, and there was even a new touch of gray in his hair. He was obviously exhausted but he managed to set an example for all of them to follow. He was a fine warrior, the nobleman decided. His ancestors would be proud of him when he went to join the sun.

"Atlatzin, are your thoughts with us?" demanded the young ruler.

"Forgive me, my Lord." Atlatzin straightened his soiled cape and made himself as presentable as possible. He could not admit that his thoughts had been on death. "The Great Temple is aflame. The smoke can be seen from the roof."

Cuauhtémoc frowned and sucked his lowered lip angrily. "The only way Cortés can take Tenochtitlan is to destroy it. That is what he does, street by street, house by house! The city may be burned to ashes, but it will never be captured. Our people will fight to the death.

"His has sent word that he knows of the hunger that walks among us. He has announced terms for our surrender because he believes we cannot hold out. He wants to meet with me to discuss terms of surrender."

"It is not safe for you to meet with him, *Tlatoani*," put in Atlatzin quickly. "The man has proven himself dishonorable. He will violate the flag of negotiation and not hesitate to take you prisoner as he did your uncle." The other advisors murmured their agreement. Cortés had shown them often enough that he had no respect for the rules of war.

"If he truly knows the extent of our plight, we will be unable to withstand him." Cuauhtémoc stood and stared vacantly at the wall. "We must find a way to trick him and throw him off his guard. Let us outfit an envoy to meet with him. Perhaps we can outwit him and turn the meeting to our advantage."

"Let the envoy take a bag of food with him, my Lord. Somewhere in this part of the city we should be able to find some maize cakes or at least a few handfuls of gain to make them," the High Priest suggested. "In the middle of negotiations, the envoy must leisurely lay out his food and begin to eat. He might even offer Cortés food. That should confuse the infidels!" The men smiled at each other for the first time in days.

Atlatzin snorted. What a stupid idea! Cortés had them surrounded and was squeezing the life out of them. Pretending they had food might gain them a day or two, nothing more. But the emperor seemed to think it was a good idea.

"I have received word that Toluca is preparing to rise against the invaders," he said. "It is possible that our sacrifices have finally been noted. We will follow the High Priest's suggestion. Atlatzin, can we hold on until Toluca comes to our aid? We still might win this miserable war."

"If Toluca hurries, my Lord," the nobleman.

As Atlatzin left the room to look for Papalopil, he felt that perhaps there was a small chance after all. If Toluca attacked from the rear, Cortés would be vulnerable and unprepared. The lake towns would abandon him at the first sight of the warriors from the far west. They would know it signaled the return of the Empire. He wondered if the Emperor would order new sacrifices to Hummingbird. They really could not spare a single warrior.

Papalopil was with the other woman in the communal kitchen. The sight of her small frame bent over the fire brought him a sudden moment of pleasure. Hunger and hardship were taking their toll on her as well, making her large eyes stand out even more against her face. She was thinner then when he had first seen her. The simple tunic she wore was too big now and she had to tie a cord around her skirt to keep it from slipping down. He smiled as she paused to pin a lock of hair out of her eyes and then bent back over a large pot. Only Papalopil had ever been able to coax laughter from him during the long siege. Only Papalopil made sure he stole moments of sleep when he was exhausted from fighting. Only she took care to see that he ate when there was food to be scavenged.

She looked up from her task and her face lit up when she saw Atlatzin. She gestured at the pot she was stirring. Even the *pipilt-in* now faced the terrible hunger, and Papalopil was among those who foraged for food in the streets. Today, apparently, she had skimmed insect eggs from the lake and had even managed to find a small handful of dried corn for the pot. He tasted the hot broth eagerly. If Toluca hurried east, all this would be just a memory.

CHAPTER TWENTY-FIVE

Two messengers, both arriving the same day from different directions to Cuauhtémoc's camp in the north of the city, crushed Atlatzin's hopes and informed the Emperor that the end had come. One man arriving from the west told the Emperor's Council about the battle of Toluca. Upon hearing that a massive army was assembling on the plain outside the valley city, Cortés had attacked. Sixty thousand men caught the warriors of Toluca unprepared. Cortés' victory was overwhelming. No more help could be expected.

The other messenger came from the east coast. More Spanish ships had arrived on the coast from across the water, bringing with them cargos of firesticks and black powder.

"There is no possibility of fighting our way out," Atlatzin informed the Council grimly. "We are being attacked from both the land and the lake. We have been pushed into one small section of the city, and we cannot hold it but a day or two more. Our supply of arrows is almost gone and we have not the means to make more. We are even short of stones to throw from rooftops."

"The time has come to decide," announced Cuauhtémoc

formally. "Thousands of us are dead from hunger; those of us who remain are starving, reduced to drinking lake water polluted with human waste, eating maggots and chewing on leather. The Red Death took the flower of our warriors, those Alvarado did not murder." He stopped and moistened his lips with water, grimacing at the bracken taste. He sighed heavily before continuing. "Treachery and years of resentment have stolen our allies. We have no weapons, no food, no water. All that is left is a question." He paused and looked at the tired men around him. "Shall we surrender or shall we die in the attack that will come tomorrow?"

"Wait, my Lord. Perhaps the gods will save us yet." The High Priest stepped forward and pulled his black robes about him, throwing back his head importantly. "When we were forced to abandon the Great Temple, I did not come away with empty hands. The god has not deserted us, though it is true he tests us sorely. I have brought with me a secret weapon, the means to win this war. A thousand cycles ago the god gave his High Priest a weapon that was to be used only when all else had failed. You know of its existence in legend. But none of you have ever seen it. Those of you who have questioned the god's power, see what I hold. For I have here that sacred war arm that Huitzilopochtli himself carried. With this weapon, the god sprang full grown from his mother's womb!"

Atlatzin narrowed his eyes suspiciously. The war arm of Huitzilopochtli was a thing of legend. No one had seen it since the beginning of the first sun when creation began. How could it have survived the destruction of the four previous suns? How was it that the High Priest had kept it so hidden that not even the *Tlatoani*s knew about it? He stepped closer to get a good look as the priest uncovered the sacred relic. It was longer than a man's arm and curved like a snake moving across sand. Its gilded scales and emerald eyes flashed in the light from the setting sun that spilled in through the window. As it was held aloft, fragments of stones and shells inside the carving fell from baffle to baffle, sounding for all the world like ocean waves crashing on the shore. The mere sight of the weapon was enough to intimidate a few of the Council. Even Atlatzin, for all his doubts, was impressed. The snake seemed to be looking directly at him and appeared both beautiful and deadly at the same time.

"I also brought with me the sacred war dress of the god." The High Priest announced, nodding with satisfaction at the spectacle he had created. "We must choose among us a warrior who will wear the god's feathers and carry Huitzilopochtli's arm into battle at the head of our forces. It has been promised that the Hummingbird himself will enter the body of one so arrayed. The sight of such awesome power will terrorize our enemies and they will be rendered harmless."

"They will still have weapons and food. And the messenger said their reinforcements have landed. This is madness!" cried Atlatzin with disgust. The war arm had surprised him, but this was no way to fight a battle.

"It is Hummingbird's promise," the High Priest said firmly.

"Then it is only fitting that I be the warrior to carry the War arm," Cuauhtémoc said calmly. "As *Tlatoani*, the responsibility is mine."

"As *Tlatoani*, you must be protected at all times," Atlatzin frowned in disagreement. "If anything happens to you, we will surrender immediately. You must remain to the rear of our forces in case escape is necessary. You have no heir, my Lord."

"The god has promised to protect us," the High Priest protested again.

"Gods have made promises before. I intend no disrespect toward Hummingbird, but I insist on the Emperor's safety." Atlatzin was pleased to see the other counselors nod in agreement.

"Then who will carry the sacred arm?" asked the Emperor.

"Atlatzin," suggested the priest quickly. "Let him learn the power of the god's promise. Our counselor has always prided himself on being the perfect warrior and example for our young men. I can think of no one more suited for the task."

"I will go proudly if ordered, of course." He should have known this was the way it would go! An image started to form, colored dots slowly floating together in his mind like tiny feathers caught in a whirlpool. He could not quite grasp it, and the Emperor was staring at him.

"Still, I am not as pure as you think, priest. I have had doubts. I have them right now." Atlatzin shook his head and the image disappeared. Instead, all his doubts come to the fore. "There have been times I have questioned the god. I have questioned his thirst for blood and our willingness to quench it. It always seemed excessive to me, an excuse for something I never understood. Perhaps it is due to my early dedication to Feathered Serpent, but I have questioned the daily sacrifices we all make, why the sacred fruit was never enough. I even question this promise you tell us about now." He stole a quick look at the Emperor, who was staring at him in disbelief.

"This story is not one I have heard before. Oh, I knew that the god was born with his war arm, but not that he would return to save the Mexica if a warrior carried it into battle. Did the god speak to you personally, Priest? Did Huitzilopochtli promise you this or was it a priest who told you this story as a boy? Perhaps only one of your purity deserves to carry the god's arm. I do not know that I am pure enough for Hummingbird to enter my body."

The priest smiled and Atlatzin knew his fate was sealed. "You are not the first man to question the gods, Atlatzin. You will not be the last. You questioned silently but you never faltered in your duty. It matters little if the belief is in your heart or not. The god does not need your belief or faith; he does not need your purity. He needs your blood. That blood you have given him in daily sacrifices. You are the one to carry the war arm. And if the promise was made to me by a man and not by a god, what difference does it make? If there is a miracle tomorrow, we will live. If not, we will die."

"It is settled then," Cuauhtémoc announced with relief. "Atlatzin will appear before the Spaniards and their allies at dawn. When they see the god himself at the head of our forces, the battle will be won. If the god does not manifest, we die fighting."

He was forced to acquiesce. As he took the sacred snake weapon and the bundle of woven feathers, he looked at the faces of the Emperor and the High Priest. He could not tell if they believed in the god's promise or not. In silence, he proceeded to the room where he slept. He had no faith this desperate attempt would save them, but the priest had said faith was not necessary. He wondered if there were any chance the god would really enter his flesh. Atlatzin sat there in the dark and thought about the sacred sacrifice. He had been taught from childhood that the god and the victim became one in death. That was the reason for eating a token of the victim's flesh; it was communion with the god. But he had never heard of the god entering the body of a man who was to live, not in the scrolls, not in the legends.

Unbidden, the vision from the crystal skull returned: the feathered cape that shimmered with the fire of emeralds, the god's huge obsidian eyes, his own face staring at him. The god did not enter him in his vision. He wore the god's cape, but all the jewels and feathers in the world did not make him a god. He was just a man. It could only mean that the god in his vision was a man! Was that what the crystal skull was telling him? Hummingbird was not the awesome power born of the Lady of the Serpent Skirt. He did not lead the Mexica. He could not because he was not real. Huitzilopochtli was a story told to frighten children, to control parents and give the priests power. It was a lie told for generations – a lie that had claimed thousands and thousands of lives, of beating hearts torn from breasts, of wars fought and cities conquered. It was clear to Atlatzin then that he was to be a sacrifice, the very last human sacrifice to Hummingbird, and the god did not even exist.

He felt suddenly cold and started to lie down on his mat to wait for the dawn. A sound on the adjoining patio draw his attention and he went to the door.

There is the light of the dying moon, danced Papalopil. She was naked and her long hair whipped around her as she whirled and turned, her small feet beating a rhythm on the stone pavers. She sang a wordless tune as she moved, throwing notes up to the moon that bathed her skin and down to the ground as she swooped and swerved, kicked and tapped. It was a prayer she danced, whether it was a prayer for the Mexica, for him, or for herself was unimportant. The sight was so beautiful, his chest tightened and he had to turn away. He felt a stab of guilt that he was intruding, so he quietly returned and lay down on his mat. Tonight, of all nights, she deserved to pray in private.

Eventually, she came inside. Atlatzin froze as she lowered herself and lay next to him on the mat. She made no move to touch him; she simply lay there in silence. After a moment, he forced his muscles to relax. They lay there in the darkness side-by-side, each aware that the other was awake. His nostrils were filled with the scent of her body. Her hair smelled of the white night-blooming flowers and he wondered that she was able to keep herself so clean in spite of the siege. Even though they did not touch, he could feel the heat from her skin. It seemed to reach out and warm his own cold flesh. He could hear her rhythmic breathing and his chest felt tight again. He took a deep breath but it failed to help.

The image of the goddess tempting Quetzalcoatl with her beautiful vulva came to him. Whether or not the gods were true, desire was. He pictured Papalopil, her cheeks dusted with yellow, dancing with the warriors, offering them her sweet-smelling body. An emerald set in obsidian, a rose surrounded by sacred fruit, life in the midst of death. With a soft groan, he reached out for her.

She responded with a fierceness that took his breath away. With wet kisses she devoured his mouth, his eyes, his neck, while at the same time her skilled hands undid his loincloth. The shredded foreskin throbbed as she guided him into her. He bit his lip deeply and knew the night would be one of pain as well as pleasure. Still clinging to him, Papalopil rolled them over until she was above him. Slowly she sat up, astride his body. Her hair brushed across his face and body until, with a long shudder, she threw the dark mass over her shoulder. He could just make out her body outlined against the night, the slimness of her waist, the small, high breasts. She began to move above him and he cried out as her hand gently massaged the sack between his legs. She moved faster, totally in control. He arched his back as a fine sweat soaked his body, and grabbed her hips tightly. She increased her movements, guiding him as he slipped in and out of her wet warmth. He felt a force gathering within him, something coiling, ready to strike. Suddenly, he seemed to explode in a spasm of white light. It took him some time before he realized the searing flash had been inside his head.

He lay there trembling as she blew softly on him and dried his sweat with her hair. She curled into the curve of his arm and pressed her full length against his side. She lay there quietly, as though waiting.

He understood now why the legend said that Quetzalcoatl had succumbed to the goddess. Every touch had felt like a blessing. It was glorious and terrible all at the same time. No warrior should be asked to die without knowing this. What a travesty to die if one's senses had never lived. For a long time he stared into

the blackness of the night, his thoughts turned toward the morning that was fast approaching. Then he reached out again for the
woman at his side.

CHAPTER TWENTY-SIX

She expected to help him dress. It was the only thing left that she could do for him. But the High Priest came to their room just before dawn. She followed behind as they led him to the Emperor. She sprang to help as priests tied back his long hair and painted his scarred face white, but was waved away. She stood there helpless as they slipped the thin sheets of beaten silver inside padding and then wrapped the armor around his body. She knotted her trembling hands in the fringe of her shawl and held them in tight fists, when they reached for the close-fitting clothing of the warrior bird. She would not show her fear. She would be brave for him.

The Emperor himself tied on the breastpiece of tightly woven hummingbird feathers that covered Atlatzin's neck down to his chest in the bluest of turquoise; the feathers that rippled down to his knees were iridescent green. The cape thrown over his shoulders held the feathers of a thousand more birds, gleaming green and purple, catching and throwing back the light as Atlatzin moved. His dark hair was hidden by the headdress of the god, an awesome thing with huge jeweled eyes. She watched as he was blessed by the High Priest and then bowed before the Emperor, bringing earth to his lips for the last time. He took the huge Serpent Arm in both hands. Atlatzin turned and gave Papalopil a long look.

In that moment, he wished he had told her how beautiful she was. She had come to mean more to him in the months they had been together than he had ever thought possible. He noticed her hands twisting so tightly in the red fringe that the skin was deathly pale. It almost broke his heart. It was too late to tell her how he felt. And so he simply caressed her face with his eyes.

She caught her breath and was able to muster a small smile of encouragement. He no longer believed. His actions the night before had told her that. But she was convinced that, if they were to live, Atlatzin would save them. If they were to die, his would be the most glorious death of all. And then she would die, for she would not, could not live without him.

"It is time. The god begins to ascend his high throne in the sky," announced the High Priest with ceremony. Atlatzin nodded and strode from the room.

Papalopil raced for the rooftop where she could watch. Other women were there before her. Each knew her fate would be sealed in the next few moments. Breathlessly, they watched the troops assemble in the street below. From where she stood, Papalopil could make out where the enemy was amassed, several blocks away. As the sun began to warm the gray streets, the Mexica followed behind their warrior god. They advanced through the silent streets until Cortés was in sight. The feathered figure, a splash of emerald and amethyst now in the rising sun, lifted the Serpent's Arm high above its head, where it glittered in the air. From her vantage point on the roof, Papalopil heard a war cry and knew it was Atlatzin.

A firestick exploded and then another. Her love fell in a pool of crushed feathers and blood.

No! It could not end like this! She tore down the stairs and tried to run out into the street, but was forced to wait until the first wave of Spaniards passed over him. Then she ran to where he lay, calling out silently to her goddess as she dodged straggling fighters and people trying to escape. Around her was madness.

Xochiquetzal, make him live! I know you blessed him! I felt you flow through me last night! Please, Goddess, please! Please. Make him live!

Bending low over his body, she could feel the flutter of his breath on her cheek and knew he was alive. Around her people ran screaming. A Tlaxcalan warrior ran past and, with a slash of his knife, cut down a child before he himself fell, Mexica dagger in his neck. The sounds of steel on stone grew closer and Papalopil knew she had to get Atlatzin away from there. Grasping the unconscious man firmly under the arms, she managed to drag his body to a nearby building and through its open gates. Once inside, the great stone serpents told her she was in Quetzalcoatl's round temple. Her eyes searched the dim interior, seeking a place where Atlatzin could be hidden. In the far back, between one of the carved snakes and the wall was a space big enough to hold a man, and with the last of her strength, she dragged him behind the stone coils. Sitting down to catch her breath, Papalopil pulled off the headdress and tried to examine his wounds in the poor light. There was a cut on his forehead; he must have hit it on the stone pavers when he fell, but the layers of feathers had cushioned the blow. It had probably knocked him out, but did not look too serious. Head wounds bled freely. Mama Amoxtli had taught her that. With the hem of her skirt, she tried to wipe away the blood on his thigh. The gash was long and shallow. The metal ball had opened the fleshy part of the leg, but the wound was superficial. Atlatzin was lucky. One slash of sword made of the Spanish metal would have cut off his leg.

A small fire burned in front of the main altar. She would need light, and so she crossed to one of the resin torches. A bundle of dark green cloth lay before the huge basalt statue of the serpent god, and as she drew closer, she realized it was the body of a man. His thin arms were thrown wide in a gesture of supplication, supplication or despair, she decided. She noticed a knife gripped tightly in his hand. It looked like the priest had slit his own throat. With a gesture of contempt, she pried the fingers loose from the dagger.

Old fool, she thought angrily, has there not been enough killing this day? She cleaned the knife as much as she could with the priest's robe and realized she would need the cloth. She pulled it off the body and took the torch back to where Atlatzin lay. With patient determination, she cut strips from the hem of the robe. From a small pouch hanging at her side, she took out her remaining medicine bags. Most were empty. They had eaten the leaves that were safe to ingest when the hunger grew severe. Now she only had a few left, but she had kept the empty bags, intending to refill them if she ever got the chance.

She carefully took three pieces of bark from one of the few bags that was not empty. With the heel of the priest's dagger she ground the bark into powder and sprinkled it on the gash in Atlatzin's thigh. She bound the leg with strips she tore from the robe before turning to his head. Her fingers gently probed the bone around the wound. It was swollen, but she did not feel broken pieces. There was no water to clean the wounds, so she sprinkled a bit more powdered bark on the spot and glanced fearfully toward the front of the temple, as she wound more green strips around his head. It was not the way she was taught to heal, but it was the best she could manage at the moment. She put out the torch and curled herself against the stone coils. Back and forth she rocked in the darkness, trying to ignore screams from the street. She was waiting for something, but had no idea what it was.

Hours later, Atlatzin regained consciousness. Without water, all she could do was to moisten his lips with her tongue. Although he was in pain, she was relieved to find there was no sign of fever. In low whispers, she explained where they were and what had passed. He pulled himself up to a sitting position and questioned her about the battle. She had little to tell him that he did not know. As they sat whispering in the darkness, they gradually became aware that a deep silence was falling over the city. There were no longer any shouts, no death cries, no sound of running feet. The conch shells were hushed and the drums no longer throbbed. The silence was thick and heavy. They looked at each other in fear. Papalopil finally tore her eyes away and stood up.

"I will see," was all she said. She slipped out between the serpent's fangs at the entrance and was lost in the street.

It was well after dawn when she returned. At first Atlatzin thought it was an old woman who entered the temple. She was stooped over and the tattered *huipil* that hid her hair was the color of the mud rubbed into her face. He realized that it was Papalopil as she drew closer, but the look on her face kept him from questioning her disguise.

"Cuauhtémoc has been captured," she said softly as she lowered herself next to him. "He tried to flee by canoe but they caught him and forced him to kneel before Cortés. They say he begged for death, but was denied. The canals run red with blood. The streets are filled with bodies and the houses are on fire. It is over, Atlatzin. We have surrendered.

"The Tlaxcalans are looting both the living and the dead. They tear the gold from our ears and the jade from the arms of the *pipiltin*. No one is safe. The soldiers take hot irons and brand our warriors on the cheeks, as though our defeat were not shame enough. Spaniards seize the young women. Those who run are chased to earth by their huge dogs and dragged away by the hair.

The men prefer the younger ones, but the old women don't always escape. I took care to make myself filthy and look diseased. They are monsters!" Her breath caught in a sob but she forced herself to continue recounting the horror she had seen.

"The soldiers stop us on the streets and search the most secret parts of our bodies demanding gold. They hunger for its gleam as Huitzilopochtli hungers for blood. Rumor says they dive along the causeway to Tlacopan to recover the gold drowned during their route from the city a year ago.

"People are trying to escape by canoe. Those they search with special attention. Tonight they say they will begin to allow some of us to cross the northern causeway to Tenayuca. We must try to join them when night falls, Atlatzin. No one will stay in the city. There is nothing left to stay for. Everything has been destroyed. What little is left is better burned. Even our conquerors complain about the stink of blood and death in the city."

Atlatzin unclenched his jaw and shook his head. Pain shot through him and he regretted it immediately. "You must leave, Papalopil. I will only slow you down. Even if I can walk, they may know my face. I cannot protect you. I am no longer the leader of the Jaguar Warriors; I am not even much of a warrior now. Leave without me and be free. Save yourself."

She sat down suddenly and stared at him in disbelief. "You may not be the leader of the Jaguar Warriors, but you are the bravest man I have ever known! You knew the god's cape and war arm would not save you, and still you went out and faced the enemy alone! You refused to abandon us, even though you lost your faith in the god. You went out and stood there for the Emperor, for all our warriors, for all the Mexica, believing you would die!" She wanted to shake him; she was so frustrated that he did not understand.

"Be free? Free and without you? Without meaning? I will not! I will not leave you and save myself! Never! You and I have not survived this horror, this butchery so far to leave each other now! Can you not see? It is a miracle we are together – I, a slave and an *auianime*? You a member of the *pipiltin* and counselor to the *Tlatoani*? In the midst of this devastation, this violation of everything we have believed in, you and I have found each other. It is our fate to be together. The world has been shattered, but you and I are together! I will not leave you! Not now, not tonight, not ever! And we should never speak of this again!"

Atlatzin reached out and took her hand. They sat there for several moments while the truth of what she had said hung in the air. Finally, he took her hand, raised it to his lips, and gently kissed her palm. "You are right and I am yours," he said softly, and they both knew it was true.

"Xipil is dead," he said after some time.

"Xipil?"

"The priest of Quetzalcoatl. I studied with him as a child. He is dead by the altar."

"Yes, I saw his body. Many of us are dead, Atlatzin." She tried to speak gently, but her weariness betrayed her. "Does one more matter so gravely?"

"He believed in the god's return, He thought it would be an age of enlightenment."

She shrugged and drew her cenzotl closer about her. "He died by his own hand, Atlatzin."

"You would not understand. He must have believed himself betrayed. There is a time when hopelessness is the sharpest bade of all." He suddenly grabbed her shoulders so tightly she winced. "This is the earthquake they warned us about. The world has been shaken to its core and destroyed. It is over."

"What is over is the war," she tried to calm him. "The world as we know it may be over, but the world has not ended. The Spaniards have toppled the Empire. They will make a new one.

You and I have survived! We can leave tonight and escape all this. Together!"

He smiled then and let go of her shoulders, but it was a smile of such weariness that it did not reassure her. Nor did his words that followed.

"If I leave here, there is something I must take with me, a burden Xipil placed on me. It will make it dangerous, even more dangerous for you to be with me. I did not ask for this burden, Papalopil! I swore to Xipil I would pay the price, but I did not know what it would be!"

She reached out swiftly and laid her fingers on his lips. She had no idea what he meant, but the intensity in his voice alarmed her and she did not want the enemy to find them huddled there in the temple.

"I may not understand but I will help. Atlatzin, whatever it is. Danger does not frighten me as much as losing you would."

His smile was genuine then. He released his grip and pressed one of her hands against his chest. "Then we will do this together. There is something of great value we must take with us when we escape, something that belongs to our people. The enemy must not see it or they will steal it, as they have everything else we had. It belongs to the Mexica. I cannot leave Tenochtitlan without it, I cannot!"

"Perhaps, if it is very small, I could wind it in my hair now that it is long," she suggested. "We need to be careful. They search woman as well as men. But if it can be well hidden and the causeway is crowded with refugees..."

"It is the size of a *tlachtli* ball," he said flatly.

"No. We could never smuggle anything so large out of the city, Atlatzin. You do not realize what you ask. It is impossible."

"We have no choice."

Papalopil looked at his scarred face and knew he would not give in. If they could not escape with whatever it was, they would die in the burning city. He could not make it without her, and she would not consider leaving him.

"Then we must figure out a way to hide it. Tell me where to find this treasure." The sheer audacity of their intended act struck her and she could not prevent a small laugh. The sound echoed hollowly against the stone snakes.

That night, Papalopil and Atlatzin joined those who were fleeing the ravished city. They were stopped at the entrance to the causeway. The wounded warrior was given a cursory searching for weapons as he leaned heavily in the arm of his woman. The Spaniard wrinkled his nose in disgust as he moved upwind of the woman. He eyed her soiled skirt and saw she was pregnant. A sudden suspicion seized him and her loud groan of pain confirmed it. The woman was in labor. The soldier decided to hurry the couple along, lest the woman squat down and give birth right there in the middle of the causeway. It would hold up the line for hours and make him miss his share of the gold some refugees were trying to smuggle out of the city.

"*Vayase!* Move!" he shouted the order. Although the Mexica couple did not speak Spanish, they seemed to understand. They trudged painfully past and he turned his attention to those in line who came after them.

Papalopil watched Atlatzin's face as he dragged himself along. The wound in his thigh would heal faster than the one in his spirit. But both would heal eventually. The world they knew had been crushed. Nothing had any meaning now except what they felt for each other. They would both have to learn new ways to survive.

But survive they would, she vowed. They had not escaped the Red Death and the devastation of the city only to give up now. She had not soiled herself and passed the god's jewel under the enemy's very eyes in order to die like an animal in the hills.

Somehow, she would find food and shelter for them both. In the time that Atlatzin's leg took to heal, his spirit would begin to mend as well. Until then, she would find a way to provide for them, for she could not imagine being without him.

The Mexica warrior was unaware of her thoughts; his mind kept returning to the scenes of blood and death, His eyes dropped to the swelling of Papalopil's skirt. Underneath the remains of Xipil's dark robe was the bundle they had taken from Quetzalcoatl's secret vault. He grimaced in pain from wounds that were both physical and mental. He did not understand the magic in the crystal skull, and the vision he had from within its faceted depths still was strange to him. He did not know if the jewel did indeed belong to a god, or if the gods even existed beyond the stories men told. But the crystal skull had shown him the truth and it must be protected. Like Papalopil, he thought. She too had told the truth. It was their fate to be together. They had each other, and that was much more than most had.

Behind them, a woman began to lament:

> *Dark is the night without stars.*
> *Arrows are broken, lances shattered.*
> *Bodies are scattered like petals,*
> *the canals run red.*
> *Tenochtitlan has fallen.*
> *We are left without our homes,*
> *our children,*
> *our gods.*

Atlatzin stumbled and Papalopil slipped her arm about his waist to help bear his weight. Together they continued down the causeway and their figures disappeared into the thick blackness of the long night.

Author's Note

Like all historical novelists, I have brought my own interpretation to agreed-upon events that took place in the past. We always bring our own life experiences with us when we set out to tell a story. Nevertheless, I have tried to be as accurate as possible in regards to the life, customs, and history of the people who today are called Aztec.

There are two exceptions to this. The first is the crystal skull. I saw a skull of rock crystal in the Museum of Mankind in London many years ago. The piece was labeled as "Probably Aztec" and the date given for it was 1300-1500 AD. However, there was also a note that said one line of the carving suggested a jeweler's wheel may have been used, which would date it after the Spanish Conquest, not before. I chose to disregard that line. In addition, I used my imagination, not my life experiences, for what was seen in the crystal. I have never seen visions in a crystal of any shape, but some people seem to.

The second thing I have no historical evidence for is the custom of "speaking secrets." That was a literary device inspired by the ways in which people in many cultures speak to the gods. That means I made it up because it moved the story along, but it was based on something that is intrinsically human and not completely impossible. There is a black "mirror" in the British Museum that is ascribed to an Aztec god. And after all, what we know of the times comes primarily from the writings of Spanish priests and friars, as the Aztec's written language was a pictographic one. It is not unlikely that certain religious customs of the Aztecs were missed or misinterpreted by those who wrote them down. The Spaniards too brought their own life experiences with them when they set out to write history.

The Fifth Sun is the first book in what I hope to be a series called The Crystal and the Cross, a series that will explore the diverse peoples and the rich history of a land that extended from north of the Isthmus of Panama almost up to Canada.